A VICIOUS MACHINATION

BEATRICE HYDE-CLARE MYSTERIES
BOOK XII

LYNN MESSINA

potatoworks press • greenwich village

Cover design by Jane Dixon-Smith

ISBN: (ebook): 978-1-942218-91-3
ISBN (Paperback): 978-1-942218-92-0
ISBN (Hardcover): 978-1-942218-93-7
ISBN (Jacketed Hardcover): 978-1-942218-94-4

Title Production by The Book Whisperer

Published 2024 by Potatoworks Press

*To the remarkable team at the Book Whisperer, without whom I would be scrambling all the time (as opposed to just *some* of the time). Thank you for everything you do.*

Chapter One

Opening the *London Daily Gazette* to the first spread, Beatrice, Duchess of Kesgrave, perused the text in the farthest-right column and noted that it contained a lengthy account of Mrs. Fawcett's recent tumble on the grand staircase of the Drury Lane theater. A trifling event, for the matron's knee had barely grazed the step in front of her before she reassumed her usual grace, it nevertheless warranted a five-paragraph exegesis that detailed the varying levels of audible gasps from nearby members of the beau monde and provided a comprehensive description of the lobby's elegant rotunda.

After devoting several dozen words to the opulence of the arched ceiling and verd-antique Corinthian columns, the author concluded his report with a subtle insinuation that drew the reader's attention to how close Lady Bentham had been standing to her rival when the poor woman undertook her fall. The proximity was curious, was it not, for Mrs. Fawcett had navigated those stairs without incident at least a dozen times since the new building had opened its doors four years ago, in 1812, and yet somehow, she managed to misjudge the height of the step in a mortifying display of clumsiness.

As relations between the two reigning society hostesses had been chilly even before her ladyship's husband arranged for Mrs. Fawcett's spouse to rot in Newgate for a murder he did not commit, it was not high fantasy to imagine the former had given her rival a gentle push.

Ultimately, it was impossible to know what exactly transpired on Tuesday night at the premiere presentation of *Timon of Athens,* and the benefit of the doubt should be paid to Lady Bentham. In the absence of proof, the most generous understanding must always prevail.

Mr. Twaddle-Thum insisted upon it!

Regardless, the Leaky Fawcett, as the inveterate gossip had long ago dubbed the matron for her unflagging ability to bring her victims to tears, suffered no ill effects from the ordeal and went on to enjoy Mr. Proctor's tour de force performance.

As Bea raised her eyes from the newspaper, the duke smiled faintly and said, "No, do not tell me. Let me guess. The Swansea Swan's doomed effort to gain entry to Almack's whilst sporting a pink cravat."

"Incorrect," she said, firmly rejecting his supposition, which, to be fair, was a reasonable attempt, for Mr. Crider's dismissal had caused quite the stir, with several of his most ardent admirers gasping in dismay as he was turned away for daring to display his audacious sense of style. "Mrs. Fawcett's spill on the steps of Drury Lane."

Kesgrave furrowed his brow in surprise. "That minor slip?"

"It is described here as a tumble," she replied with a gesture to the page.

"And that makes how many days now?" he asked as he

examined the assortment of kippers before selecting a pair and sliding the dish toward Bea.

The answer was thirteen.

It had been thirteen days since she and the duke had called on Viscount Barlow and Mr. St. Ives in the company of Penelope Taylor, and Mr. Twaddle-Thum had yet to write a single word about it. Her Outrageousness spent an entire afternoon driving around London in the company of her husband's former mistress, and England's most scurrilous gossip, the mocking wretch who had composed an ode to the grains of sugar atop the Duchess of Kesgrave's beloved rout cakes simply to eke out one more embarrassing anecdote about his favorite subject, had yet to give this shocking development an iota of attention.

Bea could not imagine supplying the prattler with more enticing fodder—unless it was the sight of the always impeccable Duke of Kesgrave carelessly strolling the streets of Mayfair with vomit dripping lugubriously from the lapels of his evening finery, an event that had actually transpired eleven days prior and had also failed to spark a reaction from Twaddle.

If one started the count from June fifth, which was the date Kesgrave called on Miss Lark at her Bethel Street address, the interval without derisive commentary increased to a staggering fourteen days. It grew another two if one used Her Outrageousness's last appearance in the newspaper as a marker. Twaddle had made no references to either her or the duke since describing their visit to Fortescue's Asylum for Pauper Children on the third of June.

Obviously, there could be only one explanation for the protracted silence.

Citing these figures, Bea asked the duke if he was ready to concede the validity of her thesis. "You must admit that his making an entire meal out of a slight misstep is proof that

Twaddle has decided against using our exploits as material for his columns. The notion that he is unaware of our recent inquiry is ludicrous when Hannah Humphrey's shop window is filled with caricatures of our investigation, including several drawings of my hiding under Miss Lloyd's bed in the company of Mrs. Taylor. To make no comment even in his sly not-a-comment way is a specific choice he is making."

Kesgrave, spooning eggs onto his plate, agreed that Twaddle's lack of interest was undeniable and swore he did not question it. "I merely took issue with your certainty that Miss Lark is to thank for the change of heart," he explained, returning the platter to the table directly next to Bea's plate in a pointed reminder that she required a more substantial breakfast than toast and butter.

"And that is another thing," she said, looping her finger through the handle of the teacup as she glanced toward the doorway of the room through which Joseph had just passed to fetch apricot marmalade from the kitchens. "Not a single allusion about the cherub! He must have some inkling by now. Dr. George has visited us twice in two weeks, and my family know. The only way Aunt Vera has not spent the better part of the past fortnight lamenting the poor darling inheriting either my plain features or intractable curiosity to Mrs. Ralston is if she has lost the ability to speak, which we know she has not, as she aired those concerns last Saturday. Given Twaddle's tendency to ferret out obscure details and his fondness for ornate prose, he should have published five hundred words by now on my apprehension of Miss Lloyd's killer, feigning breathless excitement at the horrifying prospect of a breeding female dashing madly down a staircase in pitch blackness and flinging herself through the air."

"Flinging, Bea?" Kesgrave asked smoothly.

Devil it!

Her animosity toward the gossip had led her to make a

needless blunder. The bounding leap from the descending staircase she had taken to capture the villain had been reckless and foolish, endangering not only herself but also the tiny life she carried. Her excuse was simply that she had been too caught up in the chase to consider the ramifications of her actions. The fact that the cherub was still so small as to be physically undetectable may have also contributed to the poor decision.

It was one she would not make again.

Despite her delicate condition, the duke had been reassuringly sanguine about her activities, presumably because he knew he could rely on her good sense.

She would not prove him wrong.

Accepting the rebuke, Bea allowed that she had been slightly overzealous in her determination to apprehend the killer but insisted she had exaggerated her part as an example of Mr. Twaddle-Thum's florid style. "As you will recall, the staircase was not entirely dark. The outline of the steps could be seen in the light from the transom."

Unsurprisingly, his expression did not soften at this reminder, as he appeared not to share her memory of the events. "The outline was faint at best and only at the bottom, where the light reached. The rest of the time you were blind, Bea, and I would appreciate it if you refrained from revising history, at least not so soon. You should have the decency to wait a few months before trying to convince me black is white and vice versa."

Instantly contrite, she swore that was not her intention. Rather, she hoped only to keep the matter in perspective. "It was heedless and stupid, but the physician was here two days ago and said I am in excellent health, which you know. And you must not worry it will happen again because I have learned my lesson. Look, I am eating these kippers," she said, spearing a fillet with her fork even though her stomach recoiled at the prospect of the smoky fish. Since she had learned of the cherub, her preference had tended more toward sweet than salty. Still, she added a third kipper to her plate and pointed out how much fish oil she would get from the serving. "Dr. George will be so pleased. He also prescribed pork jelly, did he not? Let us ask Joseph to serve a plate of that as well so I can fully demonstrate my remorse."

It was a ploy, of course, for she had no intention of ingesting the greasy delicacy, whose gloppiness caused her to gag at the best of times as Kesgrave very well knew. She assumed that was why he agreed to the suggestion and immediately tugged the cord to summon the footman.

As Joseph ran to the kitchens to comply with the request, Bea realized how far off the topic they had strayed and wrenched it back by repeating her original proposition: They owed Mr. Twaddle-Thum's benevolent indifference to Miss Lark. "It is clear to me now that she exerted her influence as the journalist Robert Lark to convince her colleague at the *London Daily Gazette* to cease tormenting us with his attention as a thank you for helping her thwart a massacre in St. Dunstan's Field."

Having resisted this interpretation for almost a sennight, the duke now allowed that her explanation seemed likely, for her point regarding Mrs. Taylor was well taken: The inveterate gossip would never be able to withstand the provocation of Her Outrageousness consorting with the disreputable courtesan without cause. Previously, he had argued that Twaddle simply had too much evidence to sift through to produce a comprehensive report swiftly, a theory, he conceded, that seemed increasingly without merit.

Gratified by this admission, Bea managed to swallow a kipper without flinching, although she found it beneficial to immediately follow the bite with a sip of tea to offset its flavor. "I wonder if you might want to send Miss Lark a note thanking her for her efforts on our behalf," she offered mildly, casually, as if the idea had only just occurred to her.

It was a pose, of course.

She had been contemplating how to raise the issue of further contact with his sister from the moment she had learned of her existence, and after careful consideration, had decided that suggesting a missive expressing gratitude for a kind turn was a benign proposal. Having met Verity Lark in the most unlikely of circumstances—as she was dashing to Whitehall to compel an interview with the home secretary himself to try to stop a horrible tragedy from unfolding—Kesgrave had been impressed with her ingenuity and charmed by her resourcefulness.

Despite holding this positive opinion, the duke remained unwilling to cultivate the connection, and if he refused to reconsider his position, then Bea would honor it. She would not go barreling behind his back to satisfy her own curiosity.

But nor would she cede the territory without making an effort to change his mind. Intimidated by the great disparity in their upbringings, the duke could not imagine the chasm between them being filled with anything other than stilted sentences and painful silences, and Bea accepted the validity of his perspective. He was a grown man with an unusually open mind for a peer of his rank and breeding, and if he was resistant to something, then it was no doubt with good cause. Regardless, she believed the potential relationship was worth any number of awkward conversations and was reasonably confident Kesgrave would ultimately arrive at the same conclusion.

With a helpful nudge, perhaps.

Responding to her suggestion now, Kesgrave insisted that sending such a note would be an intolerable breach of courtesy. "One should not foist the need for further gratitude on someone who is already grateful. If you feel differently, then you must send Miss Lark a message yourself."

Assuredly, it was a taunt.

Although she had never said a word about her desire to meet his half sister, he had to know how very ardently she desired it. Even so, she demurred placidly, replying that she felt no particular urgency to contact Miss Lark. "I merely thought you might make the effort since you had met her, and she has clearly performed the service as a favor to you. I have no desire to insert myself into the situation."

Amused, Kesgrave murmured, "Do you not, brat?"

Bea blinked her brown eyes innocently as Joseph returned with the pork jelly, which had been transferred to a silver platter to make it appear less revolting.

"Ah, yes, just what the doctor ordered," Kesgrave said with approval as he accepted the dish from the footman and placed it in front of Bea. "Thank you, Joseph."

The servant beamed as Beatrice tepidly echoed the duke's gratitude. Then he refreshed her teacup, adjusted the position of the butter so that it was next to the basket of toast, and swept from the room with a gratified air, leaving his mistress to contemplate the best way to avoid the gelatin. It seemed as though she had two options: flat out refuse to consume it or pretend to eat it by taking infinitesimally small bites.

Surely, Kesgrave had better things to do with his morning than spend half of it watching her consume pork jelly at a snail's pace. His steward was probably waiting in his office at that very minute for the duke to arrive to discuss their removal to Haverill Hall in a few weeks. The season would draw to a close by the end of July, and the household would retire to the country. Although the preparations had only just begun, there was an air of excitement about the staff, who appeared to adore the large ancestral estate and looked forward to returning to its vast grounds.

Bea, alas, did not share their enthusiasm. Despite being mistress of Kesgrave House for almost three months, she still felt dwarfed by its grandeur and winced every time Marlow or Mrs. Wallace sought her advice about a room she did not know existed, a circumstance that happened with alarming regularity. Indeed, she sometimes feared they were making up rooms just to tease her and then they would lead her down one endless hall or another until there she was—in the Royal Suite.

The prospect of occupying a residence filled to the rafters with hitherto unknown Royal Suites petrified her.

And the servants!

A manor of that size required so many servants to see to its care and upkeep that Kesgrave had provided her with a chart listing all their names and positions. Crediting the duke with the best of intentions, she nevertheless thought it displayed an egregious lack of judgment to believe that presenting her with an ostensibly endless array of rows and columns would ease her anxiety.

Inevitably, the table had the opposite effect, underscoring the vastness of the staff that oversaw the immense property. Properly horrified, she had placed the offending chart in the bottom drawer of her escritoire, where it joined an increasingly large stack of unopened letters from Aunt Vera and Lady Abercrombie, who were also eager to discuss the removal to the country.

Contemplating the value of eluding things that unnerved her, she entertained a third way to evade the repellent jelly: knocking the plate to the floor in a clumsy accident. That would render the dish inedible, but poor Joseph would be left to scrub greasy globules out of the Axminster, which did not seem fair.

Before Bea could settle on an approach, the door opened again and the Dowager Duchess of Kesgrave entered. As was her custom, she clutched an ebony walking stick in her right hand, but her movements were unusually assured and independent as she strode into the room.

It had been a fortnight since Kesgrave had confronted his grandmother with the existence of Verity Lark and discovered that she was generally indifferent to the plight of the abandoned child. The dowager could not fathom what interest the duke could have in his mother's by-blow and seemed annoyed even to be forced to discuss the issue.

The attitude she had displayed during the encounter had led to the first rupture* between grandmother and grandson, and although Kesgrave had sent a polite note apologizing for losing his temper, the rift had yet to be mended. The letter's icy condescension was partly responsible, for the duke graciously allowed that the limits of her generosity were defined by the morality of her generation, and it was wrong of him to expect a woman of her years to have a modern understanding of decency. But the dowager's refusal to acknowledge the estrangement was also to blame. Accepting her grandson's condemnation without bristling, she acted as though nothing untoward had occurred and made no attempt to offer mitigating factors that might soften Kesgrave's stance. Blithely, she had discussed Kean's latest performance and Miss Petworth's new bonnet, and Bea had wondered as she listened to these determined trivialities if it was simply beyond the septuagenarian's ability to broach the deeply personal matter.

Disheartened by the situation, Bea had made several oblique references to Miss Lark in an attempt to introduce

* To see the rupture from the dowager's point of view, check out the prologue of A Lark's Conceit.

the subject, but the dowager was no more willing to discuss it with her and responded with unwavering courtesy. For weeks, the other woman's conversation had been bland and desultory, a development that saddened Bea, whose affection for the dowager was deep and abiding. Learning that the duke had decided to shackle himself to a drab nobody rather than one of the Incomparables who swarmed the gracious drawing rooms of Mayfair, Kesgrave's grandmother could have rebuffed her dismissively.

Nobody would have blamed her.

Instead, she had received Bea warmly.

Kesgrave, rising to his feet to welcome his grandmother, congratulated her on her excellent timing. "Bea is about to explain why she cannot possibly eat pork jelly at this juncture, and I am sure it will be as elaborate as it is entertaining. Do sit down and allow me to pour you tea."

Although the duke pulled out a chair and offered his arm as assistance, the dowager insisted it was not necessary. "I do not intend to stay long. I am here only to explain that the supplementary income I paid to Fortescue's Asylum for Pauper Children to ensure the care and welfare of the child known as Mary Price was pocketed by a venal headmistress who resented the girl's fortune and treated her with excessive cruelty," she said as she pulled a slip of paper from her reticule and laid it on the table. "Here is an account of the investigation that my solicitor conducted, which contains all the information you might require about the circumstance. Do please pay no mind to his angry asides. The incompetence of his predecessor infuriates Spivey. If you require more information, you may apply directly to him. Now I bid you good day."

Astonished, Bea stared at the folded sheet for several seconds as the dowager turned to leave and Kesgrave asked her again to sit down. Stiffly, she declined on account of another appointment, which caused the duke to swear at her with exasperation and order her to stop being a stubborn mule.

"I cannot conceive why you mentioned none of this when we spoke of Miss Lark two weeks ago, but now you have and we will discuss it," he snapped impatiently. "Do take a seat. I can see your knee is paining you and there is no reason to be pigheaded about it. You will have some tea, and if you ask very nicely, I am sure Bea will share her pork jelly."

Bea paused in opening the letter to push the plate across the table. "It is yours. You do not even have to ask."

Although the dowager looked as though she wanted to argue, she nodded curtly and lowered herself into the chair, her cautious movements seeming to confirm Kesgrave's observation regarding the condition of her joint. "I shall have one cup of tea and remain to answer any questions you may have in regard to Spivey's document."

Irritated by her continued obstinacy, Kesgrave told her to stop being childish and explain why she had deliberately withheld the information. "Why would you encourage me to think the worst?"

"I did not encourage anything. You were already inclined to believe it, and I did not have the wherewithal at the time to formulate a convincing defense. Your questions were so astounding and unexpected, I did not know how to respond. You took my confusion as equivocation, and by the time I had gathered my thoughts, you had made your opinion known. As something had gone awry with the payments, I decided it was better to discover the truth rather than offer a halfhearted justification that may or may not have been believed. As you can see, Spivey has detailed every step of his inquiry. He even located the headmistress and put the question to her directly. She was unrepentant in her thievery and only bitter that she had not been able to convince my representative to set up a larger annuity so that she could pilfer more money from the child."

Although Kesgrave objected to this characterization of their exchange—Bea could see it in the way he tightened his jaw—he made no attempt to counter it. Instead, he apologized for calling on her when he was already distressed by the situation. "I should have allowed my temper to cool and visited in the morning with Bea."

The dowager, who knew all the on-dits even if she refrained from airing them, smiled brightly and observed that the sensible decision would have proved fatal for Mrs. Taylor. "If you had not been there to receive her, then she would be in Newgate even as we speak. Or at least that is my understanding. It is difficult to know exactly how events unfolded without Mr. Twaddle-Thum providing a thorough account. I find it curious that he has not mentioned the investigation, as it has so many of the salacious elements he relishes. Given the timing, I suppose it has something to do with your meeting Miss Lark. They work at the newspaper together, do they not? Perhaps there is a prohibition against writing about one's colleague's illegitimate half brother's wife. It does seem a bit uncharitable."

Bea's expression brightened with glee and, turning sharply toward the dowager, she said with alacrity, "That is precisely my theory! Only minutes before you arrived, I was urging Kesgrave to send Miss Lark a missive thanking her for using her influence with Twaddle."

The dowager lent her support to the project, adding that courtesy demanded nothing less, but she could not help lamenting the notorious prattler's sudden descent into decency. "The attention is vulgar and uncomfortable, to be sure, but his reports are so entertaining and the best way to follow Her Outrageousness's exploits."

Amused by the hint of regret in the older woman's voice,

Bea replied she was happy to give the dowager a description of her recent activities, starting with her initial introduction to Mrs. Taylor in the entry hall at Kesgrave House and continuing through their interviews of the courtesan's various former suitors. "I can also tell you about the thrilling pursuit of the villain and the revival of the Barrington Feint, which Nuneaton brought out of retirement to aid in the capture."

Despite these tantalizing tidbits, the dowager remained disappointed by the unscrupulous gossip's high-minded turn, for she enjoyed his light touch and spirited descriptions—as well as his finely honed sense of relevancy, of course. "He always includes just the right level of detail to keep the reader's interest but not overwhelm her with puffery. Successfully relating a murder investigation is a different skill from successfully conducting one. I am sure you understand, my dear."

Although Bea took issue with this critique, for it was indeed easier to tell a story when one fabricated aspects to heighten its dramatic effect, she refrained from commenting. Instead, she tilted her head down to examine the document on the table. Any effort to defend her accomplishments against the encroaching tattle would make her appear ridiculous.

Noting the amount her grace had settled on Lorraine Price's daughter, she murmured, "You were very generous. I am amazed at the headmistress's cheek in complaining."

The dowager demurred, insisting it was the least she could do. "And I really do mean the very least. It was not as though I, a complete stranger, could wrench her from the orphanage where she had been placed by her mother and give her to a couple on one of my estates. That would have been an act of intolerable presumption, and frankly I did not want to deal with the commotion it would cause or La Reina's smug amusement at the notion that I had fallen prey to treacly sentimentality. It seemed easier to pay a large sum and forget about it, which is precisely what I did."

Pausing, she wrapped her hands around the teacup, as if drawing strength from its heat, then raised it to her lips. After taking a deep sip, she sighed and returned the delicate porcelain to its saucer. "That is why Damien's questions were so confusing to me. I had put her entirely from my mind. And even when he reminded me of the episode, I was convinced I had handled the awful thing in the best way possible. I genuinely believed that until Spivey discovered that the headmistress had used my generosity as a reason to be especially cruel to the child. I have been told that the beastly woman would have been cruel to her either way, for it was in her nature to treat all her charges with brutality, but that information does little to salve my conscience. I tried to alleviate my guilt by compensating Miss Lark financially, but she refused to consider it."

Bea looked up sharply. "You sent Miss Lark money?"

"Heavens, no!" the dowager exclaimed. "I would never be so gauche as to offer the child payment via a messenger as though she were the fishmonger. I called on her myself with instructions for how she could draw the funds directly from my bank, but as I said, she would hear nothing of it. I was told that I must learn to live with my remorse, which, you may be assured, I found to be quite unwelcome advice. That is why I visited Fortescue's yesterday and gave the money to the head matron, whom Spivey swears is worthy of my trust. I was subjected to a twenty-minute dissertation on the leakiness of the roofs but otherwise found her unremarkable."

Kesgrave, endorsing the solicitor's findings, said Mrs. Caffrey had impressed him with competency and steadiness. "Your donation will be put to good use, you may depend on it."

Naturally, Bea shared this opinion, for she had likewise

noted the matron's prudence, but she was far more intrigued by the other portion of the dowager's statement. Leaning forward, she said, "You have met Miss Lark, then?"

Her grace smiled faintly as she replied that she had met the girl on Monday. "It was a most unusual call*. None of it proceeded as I expected."

It was, Bea thought, almost the exact same description Kesgrave had used of his own meeting with the woman, a fact that the duke himself noted. "Miss Lark herself is unusual."

"As you had so intimated during our conversation on the topic when you called to ask me about her," his grandmother confirmed. "But the word *unusual* does not begin to describe it. When I arrived, she was stepping out of her home in a wool reticule and mob cap, with an unruly basset hound on a lead and a pronounced limp."

"I think we can safely assume that was another one of her disguises," Bea said, aware of Miss Lark's propensity to adopt characters and personae. "What was she dressed as?"

The dowager regarded her pensively for several seconds before flitting a censorious look at Kesgrave. "As my grandson explained little about the child before he began hurling accusations of indifference at me, I was not familiar enough with Miss Lark's habits to know she had donned a disguise. I was confused by the limp, for I felt certain Kesgrave would have mentioned it as further proof of my cruel disregard for the child, and assumed it was a recent acquisition. Therefore, I believed she was genuinely under attack when a coachman assaulted her from behind. He had toppled her to the ground before I was able to hit him with my cane."

Stunned, Bea felt her jaw drop open and she began to rise to her feet as if to dart across the room to her visitor to ... to ... what, she wondered.

---

* To see the call from Verity Lark's perspective, check out A Lark's Conceit.

Inspect her for damage?

Clearly, the dowager had come through the scrape without injury. Her posture was as straight as ever, and her stride upon entering the room had borne the slight hesitance that was known to anyone familiar with her gait. Her joints, which frequently bedeviled her, appeared to be no worse for wear, which was astonishing. Although the dowager duchess was not excessively frail, she was still a woman well beyond seventy with various aches and pains and it was difficult to imagine her mustering enough force to incapacitate a full-grown male villain.

Only, *was* he a villain?

Her grace had mentioned something about Miss Lark not actually being under attack. If that was the case, then what peculiar scene had the dowager witnessed?

Kesgrave, seeming to have an innate understanding, asked if it had been a trap of some sort with Miss Lark as the lure. "For she displayed no signs of an infirmity when I met her and she does not strike me as the type of female to wear a wool coat in the middle of June. Furthermore, setting herself up as a decoy is in keeping with her other efforts."

"As you failed to enlighten me about her other efforts before taking a pet at my supposed heartlessness, I cannot speak to them," the dowager said tartly in yet another reference to her grandson's immoderate judgment. "But in this case your speculation is correct, and there were several men on hand to apprehend the ruffian as soon as he attacked Miss Lark, including the Comte de Morny."

Bea stared in amazement. "The French ambassador?"

Although the dowager tightened her lips in an attempt not to grin, her delight was still readily apparent. She kept her tone mild when she replied, "Yes, the French ambassador to the Court of St. James. You may be assured I was as surprised as you."

"Are you saying the assailant was the man from the embassy who killed his own secretary in a plot to undermine the peace between England and France?" Bea asked, for reports of the scandal had been in all the papers the past few days. Although the details were vague and varied depending on which reporter wrote the story, the comte's heroism had been consistent across accounts. Discovering perfidy within his own ranks, Morny had swiftly devised a scheme to capture the scoundrel in the act of betraying his country. "You found yourself in the middle of that calamity? How fascinating. And what was Miss Lark's connection to it?"

The dowager swore she had no idea how the girl had gotten herself involved. "However, given that one of Sidmouth's lackeys from the Home Office was there as well as that scamp Lord Colson, I can only assume she frequently finds herself embroiled in one contretemps or another."

Well, well, Bea thought, struck by the presence of the Marquess of Ware's ne'er-do-well second son, who had figured prominently in Kesgrave's adventure with Miss Lark as well. Tasked with investigating a reformist organization by the Home Office, he had been waylaid by some of its members who suspected him of double dealing. That Sidmouth had entrusted Lord Colson with an operation critical to the country's safety was a bewildering turn because his lordship was by all accounts a wastrel and a thief—and "by all," Bea meant Mr. Twaddle-Thum's numerous reports of his degeneracy and dissipation. The gossip had chronicled Lord Colson's downfall with the sort of relish generally reserved for impertinent duchesses, most recently issuing a scathing refutation of a widely circulating claim that credited the infamous scapegrace with acts of heroism during the war.

Snidely, Twaddle mocked the notion of the Coal Son—so called to heighten the contrast with his brother, the Earl of Goldhawk, flatteringly dubbed the Gold Son—as a brave spy whose covert machinations helped England win the war and placed the valor where he insisted it actually belonged: on the broad shoulders of Mark Kingsley, lately an under-secretary in the Home Office.

To be sure, the report was nonsense.

Kingsley was a pompous feather-wit whose mistaken confidence in his own abilities had led directly to the catastrophe Kesgrave had helped Miss Lark to avert. The former government official could never have held his lavish ego in check long enough to complete one crucial mission for the Alien Office, let alone several, and the notion that Twaddle had not uncovered the full extent of his incompetence was risible. Within forty-eight hours of the Earl of Bentham's attack on Her Outrageousness, the notorious prattler had ascertained the exact number of diamonds adorning the magnifying glass she had used to repel the deadly assault and how much Kesgrave had paid for it.

Twaddle, knowing every detail of Kingsley's ineptitude, had made the particular choice to hale the bumbling functionary as a hero because it benefited him in some way.

How precisely, Bea had not paused to wonder when she read the article two days ago. After noting that it was yet another column that did not pertain to her, she scoffed lightly at the absurdity of Kingsley being a heroic anything, let alone a heroic spy, and returned the newspaper to the table.

Consider the question now, however, in light of Lord Colson's appearance in a second episode involving Miss Lark, she found herself contemplating an extraordinary answer: The gossip had his own safety to gain. He pointed the attention toward an unlikely agent because he himself was the spy.

Lord Colson Hardwicke was Mr. Twaddle-Thum.

Instinctively, she rejected the theory because it simply felt too outlandish, and yet it had several things to recommend it. A seasoned operative would be adept at discovering covert information and convincing people to share their secrets. With his years of experience, he would know precisely when to apply pressure or issue a bribe or resort to cajolery.

And his position in society—that granted him entrée to the beau monde and its most glittering affairs. He did not have to slink stealthily into London drawing rooms to report on the events as they unfolded but simply stride in with assurance.

Furthermore, he had a connection to the *London Daily Gazette.*

The significance of that link could not be overstated.

Although the exact nature of Miss Lark's relationship with Lord Colson was unknown, the fact that he figured so prominently in her escapades signified it was an association of longstanding.

Twaddle had been publishing his slanderous reports for years.

Doubtlessly, then, he would abide by her request to cease writing about Her Outrageousness.

Knowing what she did about Miss Lark's pride and sense of honor, Bea imagined the woman was mortified by her friend's reports poking fun at her brother's wife.

As Bea pondered the plausibility of these conclusions, Kesgrave asked if by "lackey," his grandmother meant Daniel Grint, and a shrewd look entered her eye as she wondered how he could know that. Rather than provide a detailed account of his interaction with the under-secretary, he announced that he had to run off to keep a prior commitment.

"I agreed to look at horseflesh with Hartlepool, who has his eye on one of Stratten's fillies," he explained as he rose from the chair. "We're riding out to his estate in Watford this morning. I should be back by five if you would like to return for dinner with me and Bea. I can tell you all about my encounter with Grint then."

The invitation pleased the dowager, who accepted with enthusiasm—an indication that her relationship with her grandson had returned to solid footing.

Kesgrave nodded with approval before pressing an affectionate kiss to Bea's forehead as he bid her goodbye. In return, she offered her best wishes to Hartlepool in a mostly sincere gesture. Although she harbored no great fondness for the lord, whom she found top-lofty and priggish, recent events had somewhat softened her opinion. It was hard to dislike any man who had twisted himself so egregiously in a tangle of bedclothes that he could not free himself from the snarl in time to aid in the apprehension of a murderer. It was simply too bumbling an image to sustain resentment.

She also advised the duke to reconsider sending a missive to Miss Lark. Brightly, she noted that a little positive affirmation would not go amiss. "We do not want her to change her mind and allow Twaddle to return to his pernicious ways."

The duke refused to believe Miss Lark could be that fickle. "But if you are determined to worry about it, then I urge you again to send her a letter yourself. As you are the primary beneficiary of her intervention, it would make more sense if the message came from you."

Firm in her resolve, Bea declined the offer, insisting it was not her place as a stranger to Miss Lark to initiate contact over a service that had been performed on someone else's behalf.

"Fustian!" the dowager said, scoffing at the needless display of humility. "Everything Damien said is on the mark. You are the primary target of Twaddle's attention, and as such you do have more cause to be grateful for Miss Lark's interference. And while you are a stranger to the child, I am not. Allow me to arrange an introduction. I have no plans for the morning, Damien will be in the country looking at horseflesh, and you are currently without a corpse to inspect," she said confidently, then drew her brows contemplatively. "As least, that is what I assume is the case. It is so hard to know these things without that infernal gossip filing his reports. Are you sure we wish to *thank* Miss Lark? I wonder if it would be more helpful to ask her to reverse course."

Kesgrave laughed and confirmed that the residents of Berkeley Square were enjoying a rare respite from the onslaught of murders that had befallen them since the former Miss Hyde-Clare had arrived in London for the season. "Tomorrow marks two full weeks without a cadaver," he said before endorsing his grandmother's proposal. "I think it is a fine solution provided Bea does not have something else arranged for the day."

She did not, no, which he knew very well, for they had been discussing the very topic when Joseph entered the room to deliver the *London Daily Gazette.* She had owned herself thrilled at the prospect of passing an entire day reading quietly in the library, as Mrs. Palmer had been forced to cancel their excursion to Regent's Park due to a head cold. She had already selected her book—Nicholas Culpeper's informative tome on herbal remedies—and settled on a mid-morning snack with Mrs. Wallace.

Naturally, she would happily cast aside these comforts for the opportunity to satisfy her curiosity about Miss Lark. It was precisely the thing for which she had been angling for weeks. Even so, she wanted to be respectful of the duke's wishes, and she looked at him now in an attempt to discern his true feelings. By every measure, he seemed unbothered by the prospect.

Indeed, if anything, he appeared amused by her efforts to restrain her enthusiasm.

He was probably grateful to be spared further discussion

of the matter, Bea decided. No doubt he thought she would lose interest in the woman after the one meeting.

Well, no, the Duke of Kesgrave possessed no illusions about his wife's character and knew just how relentless she could be. Whatever Bea learned today from Miss Lark would be used in support of her objective of furthering a relationship between the siblings.

And that was only the first step.

According to a remark Kesgrave had recently made in passing, there was also a grandfather rattling around London.

She had high hopes of meeting him as well—eventually.

Oh, yes, Bea was content to play a long game, and after accepting the dowager's kind offer, she reminded the duke that they were joining Flora and Holcroft at the theater at nine.

"I am in no danger of forgetting," he said confidently, pressing a kiss against his grandmother's cheek before striding to the door. As he crossed the threshold, he advised Bea against taking leaps off any staircases, which caused the dowager to gasp and pester her for an explanation while Joseph refilled her teacup and removed the plate of pork jelly from the table.

Chapter Two

Although the dowager duchess firmly believed Mr. Twaddle-Thum was the more reliable source of information regarding Beatrice's exploits—witness, for example, the girl's continued insistence that she had never examined the decapitated head of Monsieur Réjane despite all evidence to the contrary—she considered her granddaughter-in-law to be an adequate substitute in a pinch and allowed her to regale her with the tale of her latest investigation.

Nevertheless, she begged Bea to cease talking when she arrived at the part of the narrative where the murderer accosted the duke with a bucketful of vomit. "No, please, do not describe the stench that emanated from Damien's clothes," she said, pressing a hand to ease the disquieting roil in her own stomach. "It is altogether disgusting and not at all entertaining for your audience. Twaddle, I am convinced, would not make the mistake of including it."

"Well, you asked why Kesgrave and I were spied strolling home from the Kempton ball rather than taking the carriage," Bea replied somewhat defensively. "The stench is the reason. I could not stand to be in an enclosed space with him smelling as he did, especially in my condition."

The dowager murmured sympathetically and asked how she was faring. "Your color looks good, and Damien does not appear unduly worried. I understand preparations have begun for your removal to Haverill Hall. You shall like it there. The park is spectacular."

Bea did not doubt it.

Presumably, every inch of the estate was spectacular.

Alas, picturing Cambridgeshire's natural splendor did little to calm her trepidation and she resolutely turned her attention to the more pressing matter of Verity Lark. Given the dowager's eagerness to call on her again so quickly, she concluded the woman had impressed her, which Bea considered significant. The dowager was a discerning judge of character and not easily overwhelmed. Kesgrave was likewise discriminating in his tastes, and his half sister had moved him to baffled expletives. As a consequence, Bea found herself unduly anxious about the imminent meeting.

Did she fear she would make a lackluster impression?

Possibly, yes, for that was the most common type of impression she had made during her unimpressive six seasons. She knew it did not apply to the current situation—Miss Lark was not a hostess of Almack's expecting sparkling banter—and yet she felt the familiar frisson of alarm that her tongue would get tangled at precisely the wrong moment.

The wrong moment, Bea thought scornfully.

As if there were ever a *right* moment to stare dumbly.

"Ah, here we are," the dowager said with a bright smile as the carriage drew to a stop on a leafy street. "Before we go in, I just wanted to remind you not to mention my donation to Fortescue's to Miss Lark. I do not want her to think I am trying to alleviate my guilt with money. That is precisely what I *am* doing, but I am certain she would not approve."

Bea, readily agreeing, wondered if the dowager was a little apprehensive about the forthcoming encounter herself, for why else worry about something so unlikely to occur. The subject of the Dowager Duchess of Kesgrave's charitable contributions was not typical drawing room fodder.

"But it did make me feel better," her grace added with an almost prickly edge to her voice. "Mrs. Caffrey at the asylum was so very grateful, which was lovely because one does wish to be appreciated, even if it is just for one's fat purse. She offered to give me a tour of the building so I could witness firsthand the good work my generosity would support, but I had to decline. Seeing all those parentless little waifs would make me sad again, and I could discern no value in that."

The carriage door swung open, revealing the groom, who held out his hand to help the dowager descend. As Bea climbed down, she examined number twenty-six. Three stories tall, it was a tidy residence, well cared for, with a stone facade and a pair of white pillars at the entryway. To the left of the freshly painted front door was a small ficus tree, its manicured elegance standing in stark contrast to an overgrown arborvitae a few residences to the right.

All in all, it looked like a comfortable home.

Miss Lark, despite the drawbacks of her upbringing, had done well for herself.

"I took the tour," Bea said as the groom soothed the horses. "When Kesgrave and I visited during the Dugmore investigation, Mrs. Caffrey insisted on taking us around the asylum, primarily so she could show us the wretched state of the roofs and induce a donation. All the same, I was impressed by what I saw. The children appeared content in their lessons. It was difficult for me to believe, having feared orphanages all my life."

"Of course you were expecting the kind of brutality Miss Lark endured at the hands of Miss Wraithe, for that is far more frequently the case," the dowager said with a sympathetic frown. "From what I understand, the Wraithe, which is how Miss Lark and her companion, Miss Drayton, refer to the former headmistress, a woman named Agnes Wraithe, was a veritable ghoul. And I suppose that is another subject from which to steer clear. Miss Lark is quite sensitive about it."

Soberly, Bea promised to keep the discussion to her gratitude over Twaddle and the weather. "Unless you think mention of the rain might also bother her."

Drawing her features into a thoughtful moue, the dowager pointed out that it *had* been an excessively wet spring. "I suspect it has made all of us a little irritable."

Accepting the rebuke without protest, Bea said, "Twaddle and only Twaddle. Noted!"

Even without the dowager's prohibitions, she had decided against mention of Lord Colson. The exchange would be fraught enough without her speculating as to the identity of the rapacious gossip.

Obviously, that was a conversation more suited to their second meeting.

"The drawing room is pleasant," her grace offered as she grasped the knocker and thumped it against the door. "You may comment on the elegance of the curtains."

"Excellent," Bea said with satisfaction. "Some of my best conversation is about drapery. It is one of the advantages of being raised by Vera Hyde-Clare."

"Undoubtedly, the only advantage," the dowager murmured softly as the door opened to reveal a housemaid with dark brown hair and a grim expression that grew darker the moment she recognized the caller.

"Your grace!" she shrieked, stiffening her shoulders and grasping the edge of the door with fingers that were suddenly white.

If the dowager found this reception remarkable, she did not reveal it as she affirmed her identity and asked if Miss Lark was accepting callers.

Tightening her grip, the servant said no, not at all. Then she blanched and apologized if her reply sounded rude. "I meant to say, Miss Lark is not at home to visitors at this time. Please come again at a later date," she explained, before muttering in almost a whisper, "A much, much, *much* later date."

And then she grinned, her mouth twisting into an unnaturally bright curve.

Obviously, something was wrong.

Bea darted a look at the dowager to see if she also thought the maid's behavior was bizarre and observed only impatience. Before her grace could air the snappish retort that rose to her lips, a voice called from within the house, "Is it news? Praise the lord, please tell me it is news."

The abnormally happy smile widened even more as the maid said with an eagerness ill-suited to the situation that it was in fact the best news. "Look, the Dowager Duchess of Kesgrave is here again, and now she has a friend with her. Our humble home is so fortunate to be graced by their august presence at this particular time. I scarcely know what to do with myself I am so delighted to see them."

Crushing disappointment swept across the other woman's face before she, too, adopted a pose of excessive cheerfulness. She was significantly older than the maid, her figure plump and matronly, and her blue eyes were a gentle shade. "We are blessed indeed! And I am certain Miss Lark will feel the same way when she returns. She will be so disappointed to have missed you. Oh, well, then, goodbye, your grace. Thank you for calling," she said, slipping past the maid in an attempt to close the door.

The dowager, wielding her walking stick with impressive

speed, blocked the motion and said with a mildness at odds with the ferocity of the action, "If your mistress is not at home, then please present us to Miss Drayton. Something havey-cavey is going on, and I trust her to tell me the truth, for she does not mince her words."

Bea, who knew well the septuagenarian's various physical complaints, stared in wonder at the dexterity of her movements and could easily conceive of her conking Miss Lark's assailant on the head. Whatever indignities her team of hated physicians routinely subjected her to, they appeared to yield excellent results.

Startled by the request, the housemaid darted a look at her associate before explaining that Miss Drayton was also away from the house. "There is nobody here but me and Cook, and we have to go. Cook has ... has ... muffins in the oven, and we cannot let them burn. Miss Lark will get upset."

As the dowager tightened her lips in annoyance, Bea pointed out the time.

Hesitantly, the maid agreed that, yes, it was eleven o'clock.

"Muffins are generally considered to be a breakfast food best served warm from the oven," Bea said with a thoughtful tilt of her head as she contemplated the irregularity of the situation. To be sure, the dowager was correct: Something peculiar was afoot. "Eleven o'clock is an unusual hour to make them, especially when the prospective diner is not at home to enjoy them. Either Miss Lark *is* at home or the muffins are a fabrication. Which explanation is accurate?"

The maid stared dumbly as Cook said she was making pastries for nuncheon, not muffins, then chastised the other woman for mixing up the two, which, apparently, she did all the time. "The poor girl doesn't know a dinner roll from Yorkshire pudding!"

"It is true," the maid affirmed with a nervous chuckle. "I

am a complete clunch when it comes to anything involving flour. I would eat a biscuit and call it a bun. It's so embarrassing!"

"Yes, so embarrassing," Cook echoed, tittering uneasily.

It was a terrible performance, and Bea could not imagine anyone but a small child being persuaded by it. Nevertheless, she was a stranger and had no right to press for answers she deemed acceptable. Miss Lark's privacy was worth more than the Duchess of Kesgrave's curiosity, especially since the purpose of her visit was to express gratitude for a service rendered. It would be a fine display of appreciation to interrogate the absent woman's staff and demand information to which she had no right.

The dowager, however, did not share her scruples and tartly dismissed the explanation as poppycock. "This business grows more higgledy-piggledy by the minute, and I will not be fobbed off with facile nonsense. Now, I do not know Miss Lark well, but in our brief acquaintance I have learned that she is apt to involve herself in ambitious schemes, and if that is what has happened now, you may trust us with the truth. Neither the Duchess of Kesgrave nor I is prone to idle gossip, and we may be able to help if the situation is dire, as I suspect."

Inhaling sharply, the maid exclaimed, "Her Outrageousness!" then immediately clapped her hand over her mouth as if she had uttered an invective.

Even as Bea tensed at the recognition, the dowager nodded avidly and said, "That is correct! Her Outrageousness. If you have read anything about her exploits, then you know her skills are unmatched. There is no mystery she cannot solve, and I am sure if you tell her what the problem is, she will provide you with a solution posthaste."

No, she would not.

Whatever proficiency at solving mysteries Bea possessed,

it was painstaking and slow, requiring the acquisition of a great deal of information before a conclusion could be drawn. In a typical investigation, she conducted a dozen interviews and searched various rooms for evidence.

Identifying murderers was not a parlor trick.

She did not make small glass figurines vanish into the air with a wave of her hand.

Rather than outright deny the dowager's claim, Bea sidestepped it by confirming her eagerness to help. "Understandably, you are reluctant to accept my assistance, for you do not know me, and you must be allowed to consider all your options in private. Here, let me give you my card and you may send a message or call on Kesgrave House when you decide how you would like to proceed."

Cook, accepting the calling card, said they would keep her generous offer in mind just as the maid exclaimed, "Miss Lark is in Newgate!"

Appalled, Cook squealed, "Lucy!"

"She is in Newgate!" Lucy repeated defiantly. "I do not see the point in pretending otherwise! She has been carted off to that horrid place, and it is perfectly wretched and we do not know what to do other than wait for news. But there has been no news. We are both beside ourselves, and there are no pastries or muffins in the oven. We have barely eaten in two days because we are so sick with nerves. It's awful."

Although the cook glared at Lucy balefully for her honest admission, she said nothing to contradict it. Instead, she let out a hefty sigh and pulled the door open wider. "You may as well come in. Let's not make it worse by providing the neighbors with gossip."

Agreeing that it was best to avoid a public display, Bea followed the servants into the house, where they stood self-consciously in the hallway, as neither the cook nor the maid had the daring to invite guests into the parlor.

Even with the situation being so very dire, the staff knew their place.

Regarding the extent of the catastrophe, the dowager had her doubts and suggested it was another one of Miss Lark's larks. "It is for the Home Office, isn't it, or some other governmental department? They sent her to Newgate to investigate a crime or some such. It cannot be a genuine thing that has happened," she said, her grip on her walking stick tightening as she shifted her weight from one leg to the other.

"It is genuine," Lucy insisted, tears welling in her eyes. "It is as serious as anything. They say she killed a person. Miss Lark, who wouldn't hurt a fly."

The dowager also found this prospect dubious, noting that Miss Lark seemed too sensible not to hurt a fly if the insect in question was causing harm to her or someone else. "Perhaps that is the situation here as well, and she was forced to act in defense of herself or another. She is probably in Newgate only as a matter of form, and she will be released as soon as the magistrate is apprised of all the details. Lord Colson or Mr. Grint will see to it. You have nothing to worry about."

Despite the confidence with which this heartening speech was delivered, Lucy began to weep and Cook explained that Lord Colson's efforts on the mistress's behalf had so far come to naught. "I do not know about Mr. Grint, but Miss Drayton calls him a useless slug and said that the Home Office will not allow itself to become embroiled in the minor dramas of the kingdom. She said we can expect no help from that quarter."

"Pishposh!" the dowager declared impatiently. "Of course you can. If necessary, I shall see to it personally. Sidmouth has dined at my house too many times not to consider my wishes."

Although the cook did not appear at all relieved by this

promise, she knew what was required of her and promptly dropped into a grateful courtesy. Lucy performed as expected as well, eking out a thank you even as her sobs intensified.

Graciously, the dowager duchess swore it was the least she could do.

And it was true, Bea thought. Noblesse oblige demanded nothing from the peeress except the accrual of credit for treating others with kindness and decency.

No wonder the servants were not reassured by her grand pronouncement. Having a bottom-up view of the world, they understood well how it worked and knew Verity Lark was simply not significant enough to excite the home secretary's sympathy.

She would not even warrant his attention.

The connection to Kesgrave, if it was made known, would do little to counter Sidmouth's indifference. If anything, he would assume he was sparing the duke the embarrassment of an inappropriate relation by allowing the injustice to proceed.

But *was* it an injustice? Bea wondered.

Knowing nothing about the charge, it was impossible to tell.

That said, she was inclined to believe in Miss Lark's innocence, if for no other reason than the woman Kesgrave and the dowager described was too clever and resourceful to allow herself to be caught killing anyone. If she was disposed toward murder, she would do it quietly and discreetly, adopting one of the dozen personae in her repertoire.

Even so, Bea could make no determination based on a sense she had.

She needed evidence.

First, however, she had to find out what happened.

Contemplating the awkwardness of inviting herself to tea when the mistress was not only abroad but also confined to a prison cell, Bea dared to suggest they adjourn to the kitchens to discuss the matter more comfortably. "So that I may ask you a few questions about Miss Lark's situation."

It was impossible to say who was more horrified by the proposal—the dowager or the staff—but Bea blithely ignored their reactions as she began to stride down the corridor.

After a moment of hesitation, the maid seemed to recall herself, and she darted to the front to lead the way. Bea slowed her gait, allowing her grace to catch up, and offered her arm for support as they descended the steps.

Testily, it was batted away. "I am old and infirm, but I am not old and *infirm*."

Pretending to perceive the distinction, Bea murmured, "Yes, of course."

At the bottom of the staircase, they turned to the left and proceeded down a narrow corridor to the kitchens, which were both cluttered and clean. Pots, pans, and cooking implements covered the various surfaces, but all had been recently scrubbed. Lucy hastily grabbed a trivet, a cleaver, and toasting tongs to make a space at the center table.

"Here, your grace, please sit down," she said with a nervous laugh as she looked across the room to the hearth, where Cook was heating up the fire to boil water for tea. "I am sorry it is not more comfortable."

The dowager assured her it was adequate.

Bea seconded this observation, and after a brief pause to allow the maid to settle in the chair across from her, asked how Miss Lark had wound up in Newgate for murder.

"That's the thing, you grace, we don't know!" Lucy replied on a pitiable whine.

"But we do actually," Cook said calmly. "They say she shot someone—a woman in Brompton Grove called Agnes Wraithe. They say she walked into her home with a pistol and shot her in the back of the head while she was sitting quietly. And that is how I know it is a mistake: Miss Lark would never shoot someone from behind. I don't believe she would shoot anyone, at least not without good cause, for she is kind and honorable, but even if she did overcome her nature to shoot someone, she would do it face to face. In the back of the head is the coward's way, and if there is one thing I can say unequivocally about Miss Lark, it is that she is not a coward."

Shocked to hear the name of Fortescue's former headmistress, the dowager gasped, "Good God, the Wraithe!"

It was, Bea thought, an appropriate reaction, for she was also taken aback by the victim's identity. After discovering Miss Lark's connection to Kesgrave, she had read the *Gazette* articles exposing the veniality and cruelty at the orphan asylum and marveled at the evenhandedness of the journalist's prose. Despite the suffering she had endured as a result of the board of supervisors' corruption, incompetence, and general indifference, the tone she had employed was cool and matter-of-fact. She relayed the vital details of the scandal without once betraying her personal involvement.

If Miss Lark still seethed over the abuses of her childhood, she revealed none of it in her writing.

Her restraint, however, indicated little.

Just because anger did not pervade the series did not mean its presence did not roil her blood.

That was true, yes, but Bea could not fathom why Miss Lark would seek further revenge against her former tormentor. She had brought the Wraithe's reign of terror to an end six years before with the exposé, which outlined in startling detail the corruption at the heart of the asylum's governing body. Fortescue's noble patron, Lord Condon, had been enriching himself by selling the orphans under his care into indentured servitude and marriage. Girls as young as thirteen were given to aging roués to be either their wives or conveniences and boys were sent into chimneys or mines. Although unable to connect the board of supervisors directly to the rough trade, as it was Miss Wraithe herself who arranged the sordid business with procurers in Saffron Hill, Miss Lark established that they were aware of the practice and had bestowed their imprimatur. The only reason any member of the *ton* joined a charitable institution was to flagrantly display their benevolence—as opposed to performing genuine acts of benevolence—so it required no great leap of the imagination to believe they had eagerly pursued their own objectives at the expense of the children nominally in their care.

In the end, anyone associated with Lord Condon's regime was either summarily dismissed from their position or made to resign in disgrace.

Having routed Miss Wraithe so effectively, why would Miss Lark decide to pursue her now, so many years after she had gotten her revenge?

Something would have had to have changed—a stroke of luck reviving the reviled woman's fortunes—and Miss Lark, finding the prospect intolerable, shot her in the head.

The *back* of the head.

Here, Bea was inclined to agree with the cook's observation. Everything she had heard about Verity Lark led her to believe that she would look her victim in the eye without flinching, especially after decades of furious resentment. Indeed, making sure Miss Wraithe knew who was ending her life would be an aspect of the reprisal.

A chicken coming home to roost—that was the whole point.

Startled by the dowager's response, Cook stared at her aghast. "You knew her?"

Shaking her head firmly, her grace swore she did not. "I have only heard of her."

"But Miss Lark knew her, didn't she?" Lucy said with a flash of understanding. "She has a connection to her."

"Well, yes," the dowager acknowledged with a cautious glance at Bea, as if seeking her advice on how much information to reveal. "They knew each other a long time ago."

Having anticipated this answer, the maid received it stoically, but even as she nodded with quiet dignity, tears welled again in her eyes. "That is it, then."

Cook scoffed irritably and derided the other servant's attitude as unhelpful. "You may believe anything you want, but I choose to believe that there is reason to have hope. Miss Lark did not shoot this Wraithe person, and there will be some way to prove it. If anyone can do it, it is Her Outrageousness. She is already trying to figure out what really happened. Isn't that right, your grace?"

Warily, Bea agreed. As much as she loathed the thought of giving the servant false hope, she could not deny the truth. Even if she did not owe it to Kesgrave to discover if his half sister was a murderer, the prospect of a mystery was too alluring to forgo.

It always was.

"I shall do my best, although I cannot promise that my investigation will help Miss Lark," she continued. "If she is guilty, then my intervention might make the situation worse, or the real murderer might be diabolically clever."

Neither caveat concerned the cook. "I am sure Miss Lark will welcome your efforts, as will Miss Drayton and Mr. Somerset Reade."

Unfamiliar with the latter name, Bea repeated it.

"Frederick Somerset Reade," Cook clarified. "He is the owner and editor of the *London Daily Gazette,* the paper Robert Lark works for. Robert is Verity's brother."

Bea lauded the other woman's determination to keep her employer's secrets. "But it is not necessary. I know Robert is a fiction devised by Miss Lark to protect her identity."

A trifle smugly, as though this comment proved a significant point, Cook looked at Lucy and said, "You see, Her Outrageousness figures things out."

Impressed despite herself, the maid asked how Bea knew the truth about Mr. Lark. "None of the neighbors suspect it. They invite him to tea all the time, and several are determined to marry him off to their niece or cousin."

Unable to answer this question honestly without revealing secret information, she murmured vaguely about deductive reasoning and returned the conversation to Miss Lark's predicament. "When was she apprehended?"

"Yesterday morning," Lucy said, struggling to calm her agitation by laying her folded hands on the table. "Miss Lark had breakfast at eight-thirty, later rather than her usual seven, and then spent a half hour in the study with Miss Drayton. At around ten, she ran out of the house dressed as ... well ... as ... um ..."

Here, the maid faltered as she contemplated how to describe her employer's customary habit of assuming various characters. Bea, mindful of this quandary, exhorted her to speak freely. "I am also aware that Miss Lark regularly wears disguises."

"It is necessary for her work," Lucy said, a defensive edge to her tone. "Most men will not talk to a female reporter. They consider it beneath them."

"Oh, yes, I know," Bea replied mildly, adding that she had encountered the same problem more than once in the course of her investigations. "I assume this digression means that Miss Lark left the house in male attire?"

Despite being offered these reassurances, the maid blushed as she admitted Miss Lark had left the house dressed as a clerk. "It is a plain outfit and one she wears frequently."

"Where did she go when she left the house?" Bea asked.

Lucy shrugged and looked to the cook, who was removing the kettle from the heat to pour over tea leaves. "I don't know. She does not inform us of her plans, and only sometimes tells Miss Drayton. Wherever she went when she left, she wound up in Agnes Wraithe's home. That is, according to the Runner who found her standing over the dead body with the gun in her hand."

Hearing this development, the dowager sneered at the unlikely coincidence of a Runner appearing at precisely the moment he was needed. "I have tried to summon them at least a half dozen times to no avail. They are never around when one needs them."

Although Bea's experience with the cadre of officers had not been as fraught, she agreed that it was odd that a Runner just happened to appear when Miss Lark was staring at the body. If she was innocent of the murder, then her immobility implied she had just arrived at the scene.

Otherwise, she would have had time to gather her wits and respond.

The notion applied if she was guilty as well. Shooting someone in the back of the head was most likely an unsettling experience, and in the wake of it, Miss Lark might have found herself paralyzed with shock. Minutes might have passed while she stood there, insensible to everything but the horror of her actions, allowing a neighbor who heard the gunfire to summon a Runner.

Although the scenario seemed plausible enough, it did not align with the Verity Lark described by Kesgrave. Any woman who would don a footman's livery to demand Sidmouth order the British Army to stand down in the face of a brewing insurrection on the belief that the intelligence the home secretary had been given was intentionally false would not find herself undone by murder, certainly not one she had committed from behind.

And that was key, the placement of the bullet, for it meant that the killer had the opportunity to carefully consider his actions—to act in cold blood, as it were. If that condition prevailed, then Miss Lark would have planned her escape before pulling the trigger and would have been long gone by the time the Runner entered the house.

The only way Bea could imagine Miss Lark struggling to recover her faculties was if the pistol had fired unexpectedly, such as in a scuffle to gain control of the firearm. But such a tussle was unlikely to result in a neat shot in the back of the head.

Hoping to learn more information, Bea asked where Miss Drayton was. Presumably, as Miss Lark's companion, she had a better sense of what had transpired.

As the cook placed a teacup before the dowager, she admitted that they had no idea where Miss Drayton was at present. "The poor dear has not stopped moving since the moment word came of Miss Lark's arrest."

Lucy fetched a silver bowl with sugar from a shelf to the right of the hearth and brought it to the table. "I am sure she did not sleep a wink last night. I could hear her pacing the floor when I banked the fire in the parlor. If I had to guess, I would say she is at the newspaper office with Mr. Somerset Reade, pacing there."

"Or outside the walls of Newgate," Cook said. "I know she went there yesterday when she got word of what had happened and tried to see Miss Lark. I don't think she succeeded, so she would have tried again."

"She could be interviewing barristers to represent Miss Lark in court," Lucy suggested as she laid a spoon on the table next to the sugar. "She lamented not knowing the name of any reputable ones to contact."

Intrigued by the caveat, Bea asked if Miss Drayton knew the names of disreputable ones.

Unable to answer the question, the maid retrieved a cloth from a hook on the wall and drew it across the table as if gathering crumbs. There were none because the surface was already pristine, but it gave her something to do with her hands. "It is possible. Anything is, I think, because Miss Lark meets all sorts of interesting people in the course of her work. Speaking of, Mr. Somerset Reade will be able to help. He runs a business and must know a solicitor who can refer him to the right office."

The dowager, raising the teacup to her lips and sipping delicately, said Lord Colson would take care of the barrister. "An established family like the Hardwickes have a battery of lawyers on which they rely. You may tell Miss Drayton not to worry her head on that score. You may also inform her that the Duchess of Kesgrave will find the true murderer and have her friend home from Newgate by the end of next week."

Lucy paused in her wiping to look at Bea in surprise. "Really?"

Obviously not, no.

A murder investigation was a fickle enterprise, and Bea never knew where the evidence would lead her—or even if there would be evidence to follow. Every case was different, and although she had been successful in her career thus far, she knew her record could change at any moment.

Eventually, she would fail.

As Bea tried to figure out how to word a reply that was honest but not unduly negative, the dowager enthusiastically affirmed her granddaughter-in-law's triumph as inevitable. "You may depend on it! Her Outrageousness is an indomitable investigator and will not rest until the true culprit is in chains."

Daunted by the peeress's overly gushing praise, Bea felt the heat rise in her cheeks and sought to hide her embarrassment by peering down into her tea. Clutching the handle, she said she would do her best. "I cannot make any promises, but there are enough irregularities to indicate that the situation is not as it appears."

Conceding the necessity of keeping the servants' expectations in check, the dowager agreed that the challenge ahead was formidable. "But so are you, and while I recognize the wisdom in taking nothing for granted, I do not see the harm in maintaining a positive outlook."

Although inclined to list the many harms such an attitude engendered, Bea held her tongue and sipped tea while asking additional questions about Miss Lark's recent activities. The staff, when pressed, could not point to an unusual event or occurrence but were quick to note that much of the events and occurrences in the house were unusual.

"As her grace can attest," Lucy added. "We had a dog when she was here a few days ago, and Miss Lark pretended to have a limp, and then when she went for a walk with Pinkie and her limp, she was attacked by a coachman. I won't say things like that happen all the time, but they happen more than I was led to expect when I accepted the position."

Cook, who was confined primarily to the kitchens, did not have as many interesting tales to relate, but she had been tasked with making liver biscuits for their canine visitor, and although she did not consider it beyond her ability to bake treats for a dog, she did deem it beneath her dignity.

Aware of the service Pinkie had performed for her country, Bea nevertheless nodded in sympathy for the servant's plight, finished her cup of tea, and offered her arm to the dowager to escort her up the stairs to the carriage.

Chapter Three

The Duchess of Kesgrave could not visit Newgate alone.

Obviously, yes, Bea knew she could not stroll into the infamous prison as a lone female and ask to see Verity Lark. There was no need for the dowager to point it out once on their return drive to Kesgrave House, let alone four times.

At the risk of doing grievous harm to their relationship, Bea felt compelled to warn the other woman that she was drawing perilously close to the level of repetition employed by her aunt Vera.

"There is no need to be cruel about it," the dowager replied as the carriage turned into the drive in Berkeley Square. "I am only looking out for your best interest. And mine, as Kesgrave would skin my hide if he thought I had encouraged you to visit Newgate. Having just reconciled with him, I do not want to be persona non grata again so quickly. Do let me enjoy being in his good graces for at least a week."

Bea swore she had no intention of undermining the newly restored amity between grandmother and grandson by doing anything foolish, and as she climbed down from the carriage with the help of her grace's groom, she fully believed the statement to be true. A great deal of latitude was given to a woman of her elevated status, especially one with her reputation for outrageous activities, but there were limits even for her.

She would wait until the duke returned from Watford with Hartlepool.

It would not be long now, for it was already one o'clock.

By Kesgrave's own estimate, he would be home by five, which left her four hours to enjoy a quiet interval in the library with the Culpeper book as she had originally intended. It would be a wonderful opportunity to catch up on her reading. She would enjoy the gimblettes de fleurs d'orange that she had arranged earlier with Mrs. Wallace and recline on the settee by the fire.

It would be lovely.

Time would fly.

Kesgrave would be home before she knew it.

Except he would not, she thought as she mounted the steps to the front door.

Five o'clock was an optimistic estimate based on the expectation of a journey free from incidents, and even if it proved accurate, it was naïve to expect the duke to climb down from his horse and promptly board the carriage. Dirty from his travels, he would desire an opportunity to remove the grime of the London Road before haring off to Newgate.

He might even insist they wait until morning.

Morning, which was eighteen hours away.

Twenty if she included breakfast, which she probably should, as Kesgrave would argue that he was not visiting the worst prison in the kingdom on an empty stomach.

The prospect of waiting nearly a whole day to talk to the imprisoned Miss Lark was intolerable, and Bea scowled with annoyance as Marlow opened the door. Not wanting to give unintentional offense to the stern-faced butler, she softened her features to present a serene expression as she bid him good afternoon.

"Your grace," he murmured in return, his smooth greeting in startling contrast with his formidable appearance: heavy black brows, broad shoulders, thick neck. "Mrs. Wallace was not sure how hungry you would be when you returned, so she took the liberty of asking the chef to prepare a light collation of pickled salmon and mayonnaise of cold fowl."

In fact, Bea was starving, which she only realized now that a meal had been offered. Grateful for the housekeeper's prescience, she asked for the food to be delivered to the library. Marlow acquiesced with a slight nod of his head and held out his hand to take her spencer, his customarily blank visage revealing nothing of his thoughts. Although it had been several weeks since she had felt the full weight of his disapproval, he had not warmed up to her the way many of the other servants had. She assumed that was because his history with the duke stretched decades, when Kesgrave was a small child with a murderous uncle and Marlow was a bareknuckle brawler whom the dowager had hired to protect her grandson. It would make sense that he—

Hold on, she thought, staring at his inscrutable features.

The Duchess of Kesgrave could not visit Newgate *alone.*

But in the company of a former bareknuckle brawler who was currently in her employ—surely, that was permitted. Not even the meanest stickler could take exception.

Marlow would, of course.

He would be appalled by the request.

And he would not need to say a word: His slashing black brows could convey the disapproval of a hundred vociferous men.

Despite its one minor drawback—having to actually ask

for the butler's assistance—it was an ideal solution, and Bea stood in the hallway scraping together the nerve to say the words. The best way to proceed was with authority: She should simply announce that he was accompanying her to Newgate and they would leave presently.

She must not pose it as a question.

To imply in any way that compliance was optional would be fatal.

Bea could easily picture the contempt with which he would refuse the appeal, his thunderous eyebrows barely moving as he coolly said, "No, thank you."

And the "your grace," which he would affix to the end—that would be brutal.

Taking note of her lingering presence in the hallway, Marlow asked if there was something else she required.

Well, there she was, at the sticking place.

Nowhere to go but forward.

Pulling her shoulders back, she raised her chin slightly and immediately lowered it again so that she would not appear overbearing. Then she replied in what she hoped was a blithe but commanding tone. "Yes, there is an interview I must conduct at Newgate"—damn it, she had not intended to provide an explanation—"and you will accompany me. I am ready to leave now but understand if you need a few minutes to prepare. I shall wait in the drawing room."

It was another misstep, for in truth she was not ready to leave. Ravenous, she would rather have a bite to eat before running off to the wretched prison. But she was anxious about issuing the demand and did not want to allow the butler time to come up with an excuse to decline the commission.

Strike while the iron is hot, she thought, as her stomach gave a mortifying rumble.

Despite the provocation, which was considerable,

Marlow's expression did not change, and he calmly replied that he would require a half hour.

"All right," Bea said stiffly, resisting the urge to thank him profusely for agreeing to her madcap scheme. "I shall be in the drawing room. Do let me know when you are ready."

"Very good, your grace," he murmured.

Bea's stomach growled again as she sat down on the settee, and she turned to look at the bell tug pensively. If they were not leaving for another twenty-five minutes, then she had time to eat the pickled salmon and cold fowl. Both were already prepared, after all.

She had no sooner decided to request the meal than Mrs. Wallace strode into the room carrying a tray with several dishes. Greeting her cheerfully, the housekeeper set the food on the low table next to the sofa and placed a serviette with utensils beside it. A moment later, Joseph entered with a pot of tea and decanter of barley water.

A veritable feast, Bea thought as her mouth watered.

"You must keep up your strength for the challenges ahead," Mrs. Wallace said as she removed the tray to make room for the beverages.

The challenges ahead.

Was that an oblique reference to Newgate?

Of course it was, she decided impatiently. The only reason the housekeeper knew to bring food to her in the drawing room was that Marlow had given the instruction. Evidently, he had mentioned their forthcoming errand as well. Despite the comment, Mrs. Wallace did not seem unduly troubled by the prospect.

If there was an advantage to having a murderous earl try to smother one to death in the comfort of one's own sitting room, it was the odd sanguinity it produced in the servants. Having witnessed how capably she had fended off her attacker, they knew full well she could protect herself in most situations. In the months since the wedding, they had grown accustomed to her strange flights and resigned themselves to the fact that she had corrupted the otherwise sensible duke with her freakish ideas.

How else to explain the way he had returned from the Kempton ball covered in vomit?

She had assumed the staff's attitude would undergo a slight alteration once they discovered she was with cherub and possibly carrying the Matlock heir. Judging by Mrs. Wallace's demeanor now, however, Bea realized it had not. Neither servant appeared particularly concerned about her visiting the most famously grim and gruesome prison in the entire country.

Grateful for their forbearance, she sampled the salmon, which was divine, as expected, and hoped Kesgrave would feel the same way. Given the urgency of the situation, he would not take issue with her visiting Newgate in his absence. He was an intelligent man who would recognize the necessity of responding quickly. Even if he considered the infamous pit of anguish and despair an eccentricity too far, his disapproval would be tempered by the fact that the accused was his sister.

He would understand, Bea was certain of it.

Well, perhaps, merely hopeful.

Nevertheless, there was nothing she could do about it now.

Reading Culpeper while an innocent woman languished in prison was intolerable.

Bea finished the last bite of fowl, wiped the corners of her mouth with the napkin, and proceeded to the entry hall, where Marlow was waiting for her. He had already arranged to have the carriage brought around, and as she climbed down the steps to the drive, she was met by Jenkins's censorious glare. He did not approve of the excursion and would make no attempt to hide it.

Indeed, as she stepped onto the floorboard, he muttered, "Business at Newgate. Nobody has business at Newgate."

Although Marlow did not affirm this opinion by either look or deed, Bea knew he agreed with it, and as she watched him settle on the bench across from her, she thought about thanking him for accompanying her despite his personal objections.

Would he be mortified?

Very likely, yes.

The butler had firm ideas about how a duchess should comport herself, and if she was going to defy convention so drastically as to enlist a servant to take her to Newgate, then she better not compound the breach with a display of gratitude. Bea held her peace, which was a familiar experience, for it was often on the tip of her tongue to thank Marlow for foiling Lord Miles's efforts and ensuring the young dukeling survived his childhood. Time and again, she restrained herself by imagining the look of horror on his face.

Or, rather, the lack of horror.

His visage would be as impassive as ever.

And yet somehow his contempt would be palpable.

The impulse to offer her thanks was not the only urge she suppressed. Early in her tenure as duchess—on the morning of her first full day, in fact—she had heard Marlow squeak at the mention of Mrs. Wallace being courted by a neighboring servant. It was sudden and brief, more like the yelp of a small animal in pain, and although she was convinced the fleeting sound was merely annoyance at mundane staffing considerations, she sometimes liked to imagine it was the product of a thwarted passion.

To be sure, it was not, for the butler would never allow the indignity.

Even so, she tried to imagine what a besotted Marlow would look like as the carriage turned onto Carey Street. The closer they drew to the prison, the more anxious she grew, and when the horses stopped in front of Newgate, she felt a chill pass through her. She pressed her back against the cushion, as if to hide from the building itself, and if she had been in the duke's company, there was a very good chance she would have changed her mind.

Obviously, she could not permit such cowardice in the presence of Marlow.

She took several steadying breaths as she waited for Jenkins to open the door and realized she was as anxious to meet Kesgrave's half sister as she was to enter the ill-famed prison. Presenting herself as the lady Runner who was going to save Verity Lark from the gallows was not the first impression she had hoped to make.

It sounded pompous and ridiculous.

Furthermore, she did not even know if it was true.

The more honest introduction would include a caveat: I am the lady Runner who will try to save you from the gibbet.

Try, perhaps fail.

The prospect terrified her.

Stepping down from the carriage, she got her first glimpse of the edifice, a severe monolith of granite and mortar, its gloominess deliberately imposed by the architect in an attempt to discourage criminality. Although elements of classical design could be found in its symmetry and grandeur, the building was heavy and oppressive, with small exterior windows to minimize light and accentuate despair. In drafting Newgate, George Dance the Younger employed the principles of *l'architecture terrible,* a theory posited by Jacques-François Blondel in his nine-volume treatise, *Cours d'Architecture,* which asserted that a prison's appearance should embody its purpose.

In that endeavor, Dance had succeeded, for there was nothing appealing about the structure and she felt a sense of doom as she drew closer. At the same time, she thought it was all a little overdone, for the chains that were carved in the stone above the entrance seemed cartoonishly simplistic in their symbolism, like a pirate ship flying the Jolly Roger.

Yes, yes, we get it, Bea thought cynically. You are a very menacing edifice.

Despite the moment of irreverence, Bea acknowledged that all that austerity served its purpose, inspiring dread in the beholder, and yet it did not instill terror in her. There was something too blatant in its intentionality to unsettle her, not like Fortescue's, whose gothic towers strove for a sort of benign horror, as if to lull you into complacency only to surprise you with its misery. Her equanimity could be attributed to the fact that she had never feared winding up in prison. The specter that haunted her childhood was an orphanage.

Marlow waited beside her as she examined the entry, hoping, no doubt, she was reconsidering the wisdom of her visit. He did not say anything to that effect, which was hardly shocking. Attempting to influence the behavior of his employer was against his usual style.

Ah, but Newgate was not his typical milieu.

Regardless, he made no comment and immediately followed when she resumed walking toward the keeper's house. Arriving at the door, she raised her fist to knock, then wondered if one observed the niceties at a prison or brazenly entered like at a shop.

The butler, noting her hesitation, said, "Please allow me, your grace," before giving three sharp thumps. A servant answered at once, and Marlow heralded Bea's presence in a clear, stentorian tone, as if announcing her arrival to a ball. Startled, either by the loudness or her identity, the man took a half step back before inviting them inside and leading them to a room on the right. Small but tidy, it looked like nothing so much as a lawyer's office, with wainscoting, shelves, a desk with stools, thick books, and a clock on the wall that ticked with unsettling precision. Two clerks worked diligently at the desk, and Bea would swear she was in Tucks Court again, calling on the solicitor who oversaw Lord Miles's business matters.

Continuing with the same air of command, Marlow explained their business and asked that the prisoner whom her grace desired to see be brought to that very room. Then he glanced at Bea to discover the name of that person and repeated it with authority. "The duchess will consult with Miss Lark here."

The servant protested, as that was not protocol. If the duchess wanted to meet with the prisoner, then she must proceed to the visiting box. "There are no exceptions."

Marlow received this disappointing news calmly, noting how aggrieved the Duke of Kesgrave would be to discover that his wife had been made to walk the despoiled passageways of Newgate, dodging filth and vermin, to arrive at a small room occupied by disease-ridden inmates—so aggrieved he might feel compelled to contact the governor of the jail to air his dissatisfaction. "On the other hand, he would be grateful for your consideration," he said, withdrawing two guineas from his pocket. "A token of his appreciation."

It was smoothly done, the offering of the bribe, its effectiveness heightened by the threat that preceded it, and the servant accepted the coins with a darting glance at the clerks at the desk. Whether they were aware or not of the exchange, they appeared oblivious and did not stir as the servant said he would see what he could do to please the duke. Then he left the room.

Bea, who had not contemplated the particulars of how the visit would be conducted, felt a wave of intense gratitude for Marlow's intervention. She had grown quite bold in the months since she had discovered the bludgeoned corpse of Mr. Otley in the library of Lakeview Hall, and yet she knew there was a refined element to her audacity.

She could, for example, throw herself bodily against the door to prevent the *ton*'s most illustrious members from leaving Lady Abercrombie's drawing room before she had an opportunity to question them about Lord Pudsey's murder, but that was on an entirely different scale from issuing orders to Newgate workers. She had been prepared to bear witness to the ugliness of the prison, to trudge into its depths, enduring the deprivation and despair. To allow Miss Lark to rot because she could not endure the squalor was an intolerable abdication of decency.

Nevertheless, she was relieved to be spared the ordeal.

"Thank you, Marlow," she said softly.

He nodded.

The clerks in the room scribbled diligently while they waited for the servant to return, which he did twenty minutes later followed by a man dressed in a black suit. Bearing a striking resemblance to a member of the clergy, he was in fact a turnkey, and although he had been apprised of the situation, he required more information.

By "more information," he meant five guineas.

Marlow produced the payment without comment.

Bea, who had only a few pounds in her reticule, felt like the veriest greenhorn for coming to Newgate without enough scratch to ensure a constructive outcome.

The turnkey, slipping the coins into his pocket, promised to be back with the inmate soon, and although Bea settled in for another long wait, he returned promptly. Only a few minutes later, he crossed the threshold again, this time with a woman in tow, and Bea's heart skipped painfully as she beheld the figure in the doorway. She was grimy and tall, with short brown hair matted to her head and dirt caked on her face.

Splotches of dried blood adorned her forehead, and a fist-size mark darkened to bluish purple on her cheek and eye. Her dress was torn, revealing a jagged wound in her forearm, and welts from the manacles festooned her wrists.

Bea, who had not expected to encounter such brutality, found herself at a loss for words as the turnkey dragged the prisoner farther into the room. Impatiently, he tugged the irons binding her hands, carelessly slamming her body against the doorframe as though she were a valise or a chair.

"You will take care!" Bea barked at her most imperious.

Only it was not hers, not really, for she did not know this haughty creature, this supercilious duchess demanding that a hardened turnkey abide by her wishes.

Even so, she continued. "If you do not, then I shall be forced to discuss your manners with Lord Sidmouth, which his lordship will find so pleasant, he will be moved to thank the governor of the jail for providing him with the opportunity to discuss his staff over lemonade at Almack's. I am sure the governor will be equally delighted."

The turnkey loosened his grasp at once, allowing Miss Lark to regain her balance, and dipped his hands into his pockets, doubtlessly to feel the compensatory press of the guineas he had extorted. "My apologies, ma'am."

Bea, nodding with pompous self-regard, kept her eyes focused on Miss Lark as she said, "Marlow, give us the room."

He did.

With his customary efficiency, he swept all the men from the office, even the clerks who had studiously kept their heads down, and although she did not witness money change hands, she assumed he purchased their compliance. It was simply the easiest way to settle the matter.

When the door was shut behind the butler, Bea turned to Miss Lark and invited her to sit down, gesturing to the pair of recently vacated stools as though they were plush chauffeuses beside a cozy fire.

'Twas ridiculousness itself, treating any space in that hellish monstrosity with the elegance of a drawing room, and yet she could do nothing else. Deeply unnerved by all aspects of the situation, she instinctively defaulted to the courtesies that had been ingrained in her as a child.

Aunt Vera would be so proud.

After she recovered from her faint, of course.

The notion of a Hyde-Clare setting foot in Newgate for any reason, however banal, was anathema to everything her relative believed.

Only unrepentant beasts had any business inside these walls.

As if to demonstrate how the act of sitting worked, Bea assumed the stool first and resisted the urge to pat the one across from her. Clearly, Miss Lark had been through a horrific experience in the hours since her arrest and her wits were dulled by pain and fear. She would respond in due time, and until then Marlow would keep the hordes from the door.

There was no need to rush.

And yet Bea felt her anxiety increase with every second that passed.

Although she had been in this situation before—only two weeks ago she had saved Mrs. Taylor from the gibbet by proving her innocence—there was something fundamentally different about being surrounded by the consequences of her failure. Despite the architect's best efforts to discourage crime with an ominous facade, the building itself did not serve as a deterrent, but if all future criminals could be brought inside its walls, if they could be allowed to walk its rat-infested hallways in chains, then perhaps the prison would achieve its goals.

Bea, for her part, planned never to enter the fetid pit again.

After a moment of hesitation, Miss Lark proceeded to the table, her movements impeded by the manacles that bound her ankles, and Bea wished that she had ordered the restraints removed before dismissing the turnkey from the room. Undoubtedly, the brief respite would have cost Marlow another handful of guineas.

Well worth the expense, however exorbitant, Bea thought as Miss Lark lowered onto the stool, her movements cautious as the heavy chains clanged loudly in the silence. At close range, the bruise on her cheek appeared darker, more tender, with swelling that overtook her eye, and Bea, who had sustained a pair of black eyes in the scuffle that followed her flight down the staircase, winced in sympathy. Despite the injury, Bea could see the resemblance to La Reina, whose portrait hung on the first-floor landing in Kesgrave House. She did not have her mother's delicate frame, for Miss Lark would have towered over the tiny creature, but her features had the same angularity, the same sharp beauty.

Kesgrave had it too: the square jawline, the cheekbones that could cut glass.

As Miss Lark settled on the stool, Bea contemplated the best way to proceed. Her impulse was to tut-tut over the abuse the poor woman had suffered and ask if she was all right, but an innate sense told her that would be the worst way to approach her. From the descriptions Kesgrave and the dowager had given, she knew the woman before her was proud, and a display of sympathy would only heighten her misery and discomfort.

The more productive tack was to be straightforward and matter-of-fact.

A woman of Miss Lark's ilk, who donned whatever identity had the most likelihood of succeeding with the sapheads in the Home Office and continued with her business, no matter how daunting, would have little patience for fussing or fretting.

To that end, Bea would get right to it.

No gentle preamble.

Just a brusque introduction and a request for information.

As if to confirm this conclusion, Miss Lark spoke first, her tone curt as she thanked the duchess for making the visit to Newgate. "I am aware of your investigative prowess and assume you are here to offer to employ these skills on my behalf. It is, however, unnecessary, as the matter is already being handled. Now I suggest you return to Kesgrave House before your husband realizes you are gone. He is unlikely to be pleased with your visit."

A dismissal!

Of all the ways Bea had imagined Miss Lark would respond to her offer of help, outright rejection before she had even uttered a syllable was the very last. And yet she should have anticipated it, for the woman had to feel the degradation of her situation keenly and would seek to compensate for the perceived weakness with a show of strength.

Resolved to step lightly, Bea kept her own voice cool as she replied, "You are referring to your friends' efforts: Miss Drayton, Mr. Somerset Reade, and Lord Colson Hardwicke, I presume. I understand they are capable and devoted to your welfare. I have no intention of interfering in their endeavors. My investigation would be supplemental."

"Thank you but no," Miss Lark said firmly.

Understanding the reason for the other woman's refusal, Bea was nevertheless frustrated by it but revealed none of her exasperation as she gently pressed the issue. "May I ask why?"

The manacles clanked as Miss Lark shifted her position slightly, her expression inscrutable as she considered how to answer, and Bea braced for the inevitable rebuff.

No, your grace, you may not ask,

After an extended silence, however, Miss Lark said stiffly, "The Duke of Kesgrave performed a very great service for me, and I will not repay his kindness by embroiling his wife in a sordid affair."

Bea felt the impulse to laugh.

The notion that anyone had to embroil the inordinately curious Miss Hyde-Clare in anything sordid was deeply funny to her. She had spent the past several months shabbily thrusting herself into one disreputable circumstance after another—precisely as she was doing now.

And yet she restrained her humor because it had no place in the somber room. Miss Lark's formality, the way she had referred to her brother by his title, made it clear that she perceived him at a remove. He was an august aristocrat on whom she had no claim despite their kinship.

Piercing that rigid decorum would be the real challenge.

To that end, Bea lauded Miss Lark for her scruples, then insisted they were unnecessary. "As my presence here demonstrates, I am perfectly capable of embroiling myself in sordidness without anyone's assistance. Furthermore, it is you who performed a great service for our country by preempting a senseless massacre that could have led to widespread violence and unrest, and to pretend that you personally benefited from Kesgrave's interference is disingenuous. Indeed, if anyone here owes a debt of kindness, it is I."

The comment confused Miss Lark.

It was fleeting, of course, only a flash of bewilderment that darted across her face before the blankness descended again.

Clarifying, Bea added, "For Mr. Twaddle-Thum."

Now Miss Lark blanched. "What?"

Seeing the other woman startle, Bea wondered what had

unsettled her more: that her Outrageousness had figured out the connection or that she had boldly brought it up.

"I know he stopped writing about me as a personal favor to you," Bea said, her tone deliberately bland in an attempt to convey her utter lack of interest in pursuing the subject. Miss Lark's discomfort, already acute, would only deepen at the reminder of Lord Colson's insolence, the existence of which she was likely to find incomprehensible. Only someone born into wealth and privilege could treat both with so much mocking contempt.

It was another point in his lordship's favor.

"As I said before, I do not believe you owe Kesgrave anything," Bea continued. "Your actions were in the best interest of our country. Nevertheless, I appreciate your intercession. It is the reason I learned of your predicament. I called on your home to express my gratitude."

Miss Lark appeared to relax slightly as the topic veered away from the rapacious gossip. "My staff told you I had been arrested for murder and imprisoned in Newgate?"

The hint of disapproval was unmistakable, and Bea rushed to add that the servants had been extremely reluctant to speak. "But I was with the dowager duchess, whom Lucy knew from her visit earlier this week, and it was obvious to both of us that something was amiss. I pressed for answers and embroiled myself. You see, you really have no reason to refuse my assistance unless you find it unseemly for a woman to presume to investigate a murder. If that is the case, then I would beg you to overcome your disgust long enough to allow me to help. I cannot promise to prove your innocence or find the true killer, but I have had much success in this arena and consider the odds favorable. In closing, I would point to the family connection. Its significance is not dependent on the existence of a bond, and even if Kesgrave never sees you again, I think it is better for his sister to be in the world than not be in the world."

Even if, Bea repeated silently in disgust.

Well, that qualifier was more revealing than she had intended.

If Miss Lark noticed the implication, she did not linger over it, preferring instead to correct the assumption that she had asked Twaddle to cease writing about her. "I never said a word to him."

"Noted," Bea said briskly, keenly aware that the statement was most likely true in the strictest sense. Lord Colson would inevitably know enough about Miss Lark's preference without her making a direct appeal, especially if he discovered her relationship to the duke in the wake of the dowager's visit. "Any implication that I was offering my help as a way of settling a debt is withdrawn. In its place, I offer the scarcity of murder victims in London and my gratitude for the opportunity to ply my craft. I hope that is acceptable."

Here, of course, Kesgrave would argue for the abundance of fatalities, for it seemed to him as though there was a new corpse every time they turned around.

Patently, that was not true.

After a brief spate in the middle of spring, the cadavers had fallen off.

Although Bea did not explain further, Miss Lark appeared to accept the argument as valid—or she simply realized that Her Outrageousness would continue to press the issue until she got the outcome she desired. Regardless, the prisoner nodded tersely and said, "Very well, your grace. I accept your offer. Thank you."

Bea acknowledged her acquiescence with a sober dip of her head.

Chapter Four

Although more than fifteen minutes had passed while they wrangled over her participation, Bea did not feel the press of time. Marlow would hold the men off for as long as she required, and if the governor of the jail himself appeared at the door demanding entry to the room, the former bareknuckle brawler would overcome him as well, most likely with money but possibly with threats of physical violence.

Consequently, Bea took a moment to order her thoughts before launching into her questions. The most logical place to begin was the crime scene, not the suspect's decades' old history with the victim, even though that was the more interesting aspect as far as she was concerned. Accordingly, she said, "I understand from your staff that the victim had been shot in the back of her head."

Correctly interpreting her tone, Miss Lark replied that the description was accurate. "The ball entered her brain near the lower portion, toward the bottom of the skull and must have killed her instantly. Based on where I found the gun, I believe the killer shot from close range, about three feet away, perhaps even closer. That means he managed to enter the house and draw close to the victim without her being aware. Either he is adept at creeping silently or the victim was not fully alert. As it was eleven in the morning, I suspect it was the former, but she might have been drinking or sitting down for a midmorning rest. Alternatively, she might have had a hearing problem, as she was sixty-two now."

Miss Lark shifted again, raising her elbow to rest it on the table, and the manacles scraped her wrist. New scratches caused fresh beads of blood to dot her skin, and although Bea knew they had to hurt, the other woman did not flinch. Instead, she continued, calmly offering a comprehensive description of the gun, which was a silver-mounted, single-trigger, over-under pocket flintlock bearing an intricately carved feathery design on the ivory handle that vaguely resembled the fleur-de-lis and the maker's mark of Bernard Michaels.

Impressed by the level of detail, Bea could only conclude that Miss Lark had considerable experience with guns, which was the cause of some envy. Her own firearm instruction had been distinctly underwhelming, and although Prosser had finally allowed her to discharge a loaded pistol after weeks of making her fire dry, he regarded her with a look of consternation that bordered on fear.

An armed female was a terrifying prospect!

What precisely did he think she would do—inadvertently shoot him because she was too hen-witted to realize the flintlock was loaded or intentionally maim him in a burst of rage?

"The muzzle was still warm, which indicates that the firearm had just been fired," Miss Lark continued. "I would say within the previous five minutes."

Oh, yes, Miss Lark had considerable experience with guns, Bea thought, struck by the certainty with which the pronouncement was made. Despite several weeks of lessons, she could not conceive of knowing such a specific detail, and contemplating the particular now, she wondered if the murderer had dropped the weapon in his haste to leave the scene or carefully laid it down as a lure for the next person who entered the room.

Finding both prospects likely, she decided the latter was the more plausible explanation simply because the firearm as described by Miss Lark was of significant value. Few killers would be inclined to linger after shooting their victim, but none would be in such a hurry that they would abandon a well-made pistol with a carved ivory handle. Retrieving it from the floor would take only seconds, and Miss Wraithe lived alone. They would have no reason to expect that an inopportune visitor would saunter into the room.

Unless, of course, that was the whole plan—which, according to the dowager's comment regarding the difficulty of summoning a Runner, seemed plausible.

"It was a trap," Bea murmured.

Miss Lark, her lips twisting with a faint hint of cynicism, answered evenly, "I believe so, yes."

"The killer knew you were coming and waited until you were near to shoot," Bea said thoughtfully, her mind already breaking the scheme down to its component parts. "And the Runner—the killer arranged for him in advance. He had him on hand to come upon you at the ideal moment."

"The gun was in my grasp," Verity confirmed. "I had just turned it over to examine the other side when the Runner—he is called Cyrus Thimble—bounded across the room and wrenched my arm."

"He is in the killer's pay," Bea noted thoughtfully.

"I believe so, yes," Miss Lark said again. "But it is also possible Thimble was coerced—if he owed the killer money or if the killer had harmful information about him or threatened his family. Regardless, he is part of the scheme."

"How does he explain his remarkable timing?" Bea asked.

"He claims he was answering a summons to a house nearby when he heard the pistol discharge," Miss Lark replied, adding that she had been unable to get useful information from the Runner, who had not felt obliged to answer her questions. "You will want to talk to him first. If you can convince him to tell you who hired him, then you will be one step closer to finding the killer. If he refuses to talk, then you must keep watch of him for several days and learn everything you can about him, which means interviewing his employer, colleagues, and family as well as searching his house."

Although Bea had already decided to seek out Thimble at the first opportunity, she was disconcerted by the itinerary Miss Lark proposed, which was unnervingly thorough. Despite her many investigations, she had never monitored a suspect for a prolonged period of time and was not convinced she would excel at the practice. "Why were you there, at the house?"

"The Wraithe invited me to her home to discuss terms," Miss Lark said cryptically before adding, "She was under the mistaken impression that she could blackmail me over my taking a male name as a reporter for the *Gazette*. She convinced herself that I would pay to keep Robert Lark a secret. I would not. He is a valuable persona that I have taken pains to make believable, and if given the opportunity, I would continue to use him for years to come. But I would gleefully reveal the truth myself on the front page of the newspaper to deprive her of a single moment of joy."

Readily, Bea believed it—and not because Miss Lark's loathing of the dead woman was almost tangible. The notion of yielding to another person's will seemed utterly alien to her. "Why go at all if you had no intention of discussing terms?"

"I had to discover how she knew. I was not called Verity

Lark during my time at Fortescue's, at least not as she would know, so there is nothing linking me to Mary Price. Yet somehow she figured out who I was. I say this with no malice —" She broke off with a shake of her head, and a smile appeared briefly. "Well, I say it with *some* malice. But the Wraithe was not the sharpest tool in the shed. Indeed, she was duller than a butter knife. There is no way she figured out my identity, let alone Robert's, on her own. That meant she was working with someone far cleverer than she, and I could not rest until I knew who he was. An unknown enemy with access to secret information is a danger to me."

Although delivered without emotion, the statement sent a slight shiver down Bea's spine because Miss Lark made it sound so menacing and she wondered if the other woman went through life expecting vengeful foes to pounce out of every dark corner.

It was not, Bea allowed, an entirely irrational way of perceiving the world. She herself had an archnemesis from her earliest days of her first season, and although she knew Mrs. Norton despised her, she had never thought to worry that the society matron would cause her actual harm, an oversight that allowed the spiteful heiress to come perilously close to ruining her.

Clearly, Bea could benefit from adopting some of Miss Lark's distrust.

"Your staff said you left the house dressed as a man," she said.

"I did, yes, but not really," Miss Lark replied confusingly. "The Turnip is more of a boy."

The addendum did not fully clarify the matter, but Bea felt she had a general sense of what she meant and asked if the Turnip was one of her characters.

"Formally, he goes by the name Joseph Pope, but I think of him as the Turnip, as he has only recently arrived to

London and he is earnest and sweet. Prone to making a cake of things and yet agonizingly sincere in his intentions," she said with so much sympathy Bea could almost believe he were real. "As he is a bungling ninny, he makes everyone he interacts with feel superior, so I thought he would be useful in ferreting out the identity of the Wraithe's accomplice."

"The Turnip was to be your emissary?" Bea asked, grappling to understand how the roster of personae worked. "He would represent your interests?"

"He would try, the dear boy, but fail utterly," Miss Lark explained patiently. "I wanted to frustrate the Wraithe *and* earn her contempt. When I arrived at the house, I knocked on the door and it swung open. The Turnip assumed he had broken the frame by knocking too hard and called out an apology. I did not receive a reply."

"But you entered regardless," Bea said, marveling at how blatant the plan was when examined in retrospect. The open door was patently a trick.

"Cautiously and with much curiosity," she replied as if making a significant amendment. "But, yes, I did enter the house. It was not as I was expecting. It is in a neighborhood called Brompton Grove, which is on the edge of St. Giles and almost as run-down as the rookery. From the outside the home is as dilapidated as its neighbors, with chipped paint and broken stones and rotted casings. But the condition inside is much different: The floorboards are sturdy and the walls have been recently painted. Halfway down the hallway was a door on the right, and I could hear the crackle of the fire. I called out again as I turned into the room. I saw the Wraithe immediately. She was slumped over in her chair and even before I noticed all the blood, I knew she was dead because she was pitched at an unnatural angle. Still, I confirmed she had no pulse. Then I examined the gun, which was positioned halfway between the door and the chair. I knew something was off right away, not just because of where it was but because the craftsmanship was so fine. As soon as I saw the maker's mark, the whole thing clicked into place. I knew it was a trap because nobody who would murder a disgraced headmistress in Brompton Grove would leave it behind. Something much deeper was afoot and I was a lackwit for not realizing it sooner. The Runner grabbed me by the collar and yanked my wrist just as I was about to drop the gun."

The threadbare dress Miss Lark wore bore no resemblance to the Turnip's attire, and Bea suppressed a shudder as she imagined how the rough men who oversaw the inmates discovered her true identity and compelled her to change clothes.

As her dismay served no purpose, Bea pushed these thoughts to the side and asked Miss Lark when she received the letter from the victim.

"Two nights ago, Wednesday," she said. "It was addressed to Robert Lark at the *Gazette*'s offices on the Strand, and Freddie delivered it to the house when he came by for dinner. I read it an hour later when I retired to Robert's study to work on an article. It was brief and to the point: She knew my secret identity and if I wanted it to remain a secret, I would call on her Thursday morning at eleven to discuss the terms of her silence."

"Were you surprised?" Bea asked.

Miss Lark, arching an eyebrow cynically, replied that nothing the Wraithe did could surprise her. "She was greedy and cruel, with a highly developed instinct for survival. I assumed she nursed a profound hatred for Robert Lark for ruining her comfortable existence and dreamed up vicious acts of reprisal. I would not have expected her to seek financial compensation because it is so cold-blooded, but she was at heart a practical creature despite her maliciousness, and revenge, which offers other compensations, does not pay the creditors. Based on the condition of her house—sturdy on the inside, falling down on the outside—I think she had run through the funds she had squirreled away during her tenure at Fortescue's and was in need of a new source of income."

"You think the blackmail scheme was her idea?" Bea asked.

"I do, yes," Miss Lark replied.

"Earlier you suggested she was working with someone far cleverer than she," Bea reminded her. "Why do you not think it was his idea to blackmail you?"

"It might have been the idea of a shadowy figure," Miss Lark allowed with a pensive press of her lips. "But blackmail feels like the Wraithe. It is simplistic and obvious, which is what would occur to someone with her limited abilities. And she loved money, so squeezing me for coins would feel like retribution to her. To devise a punishment that was equal to the one dealt her would require a creativity that she lacked. Perhaps the shadowy figure wanted her to do something else with the information and she refused, and that is why he killed her. The shadowy figure is your best suspect. The Runner will lead you to him. You just need to determine the best way to make that happen: surveillance, manipulation, or bribery."

There was, Bea thought, some merit to Miss Lark's theory of the shadowy figure directing the action from a safe remove. Someone *had* arranged for the Runner to appear at precisely the right moment, and that person was almost certainly the murderer. At the same time, she could not believe he had expressly sought out Miss Wraithe to present her with the information about Robert Lark to ultimately kill her after her usefulness to him was at an end.

She assumed the sequence of events was messier and

more chaotic, entailing an argument or a betrayal or several of both.

Bea asked about the letter's current location. "Where may I find it?"

Startled by the query, for it indicated her answers would not be accepted without scrutiny, Miss Lark furrowed her brow briefly before replying that it was in the top drawer of Robert's desk in his study.

"Very good," Bea said, then pressed for details regarding her plan for the visit itself. "You said you went dressed as the Turnip. In this scenario, who was the Turnip to you that you would send him to deliver a message on your behalf?"

"A clerk at the newspaper office, recently hired and anxious to prove himself to his employer," she replied. "The Turnip is nonthreatening, the sort of person you leave alone in the front parlor while you fetch teacups from the kitchen cupboard."

"And that was how you intended to discover information about the shadowy figure, by searching the front parlor?" Bea asked.

"It was one of the ways, yes," Miss Lark replied with a faint smile. "The Turnip has various means at his disposal. His sweeping ineptitude has a way of disgusting his targets into careless indiscretion, and as the Wraithe overvalued her intellectual gifts, I was fairly confident she would make a revealing boast. If she did not, the Turnip was tasked with requesting more time to meet the blackmail demand. He was, you see, an opening gambit. How I ultimately handled the Wraithe depended on what I discovered. Under normal circumstances, I would have done extensive research before attending the meeting, but I got the letter too late in the evening and Delphine waylaid me the next morning as I was leaving to discuss one of Robert's articles. I did not want her to worry about the Wraithe, so I said nothing and addressed her concerns without revealing my own impatience to depart. As a result, I arrived with no time to spare before the meeting and could not get a lay of the land in advance."

A development that was deeply uncomfortable for her, Bea realized. If the interview had revealed anything about Verity Lark, it was that she was a meticulous woman. She noticed details, and noticing details gave her a semblance of control.

In that way, she was just like the duke.

"Do you have any idea who the shadowy figure is?" Bea asked.

With a regretful shake of her head, the prisoner admitted that she had not had an opportunity to gather the information that would allow her to draw conclusions. "After meeting with the Wraithe, I had planned to watch her for a few days and see with whom she met. I expected her to still have dealings with Lord Condon, who is Fortescue's disgraced former patron. He has the resources and a motive to look into Robert Lark more closely. Furthermore, he and the Wraithe were as thick as thieves. Neither one would have been able to perpetrate a complex scheme without the other. As far as I know, he has been in Ireland since the scandal broke, but maybe he decided it was time to return."

"Lord Condon," Bea repeated with a thoughtful nod. "Who else?"

Miss Lark sighed with frustration and raised an arm as if to sweep her fingers through her hair, but the manacle clanged and dug into her wrist. She dropped her hands to the table with a thud. "It is impossible to say. Any one of the hundreds of orphans who passed through Fortescue's would have good cause to kill her, as would the dozens of underlings who reported to her during her years as headmistress. Or it could be someone she interacted with regularly now, such as the fishmonger, the collier, the bookseller. Well, not the bookseller, for she was all but illiterate. I never saw her touch a book except to thwack one of her charges over the head with it. But in general, the principle holds: She was a detestable human being who made enemies as easily as breathing."

As it was impossible not to be overwhelmed by the prospect of so many suspects, Bea was grateful to have Thimble as a place to start. Hopefully, he would lead them to the shadowy figure who coordinated the murder and spare her the necessity of looking farther afield. Daunted by the enormity of the undertaking before her, she felt a sudden impatience to begin and announced that she had enough information for now. "I will return if I have more questions. Before I go, is there anything I can do to increase your comfort?"

There was not, no, for Lord Colson had the matter well in hand. "I was given my own room in the state area this morning, which can only be his doing, as neither Delphine nor Freddie have the consequence to arrange it. And a behemoth of a man who calls himself Big Fist Johnston pledged to keep me safe during my confinement and instructed me to let him know if I run into difficulties. I assume he is an associate of Hardwicke's. I also assume Hardwicke is trying to use his influence to secure my release. I do not expect it will bear fruit because the home secretary could not care less about the plight of a lowborn nonentity, and Under-Secretary Grint will wring his hands into knots worrying about the appearance of impropriety of freeing a murderess. My only hope is to find the real killer. If you can do that, your grace, then I will be in your debt," she said with a faint smile.

Oh, but it was not a smile, Bea thought.

It was an upturned grimace, a scowl compelled by obligation to appear hopeful, and Bea realized Miss Lark did not believe she would succeed. Even with all the information she had provided, the inmate did not expect to leave her prison, and despair pressed on Bea in a way that was disheartening and unfamiliar. Two weeks ago, she had saved Mrs. Taylor from the exact same fate, and yet somehow it felt different now.

Because it was not the same fate, she realized. Despite the courtesan's status as chief suspect in her friend's murder, her life was never in danger. Her outlandish claim to being safest in Newgate—state side, of course!—was naught but an act performed for an admiring audience. The moment imprisonment became an actual possibility, she would have fled London for a country village and lived the rest of her life in obscurity, the odiousness of milking cows amiable punishment in lieu of hanging.

Miss Lark did not have the option of escape, and as such she could not treat any part of the investigation as a frolic or a caper. Her pessimism was justified by circumstance, and Bea felt her own sanguinity fade in accordance, for it was difficult to sustain her optimism in the face of so much negativity.

Oh, yes, how very churlish of Miss Lark to allow her spirits to dip when her legs were encased in irons and she had to rely on an individual known as Big Fist Johnston for her safety. Do make a note of it, your grace, Bea thought in grim amusement. Condemned prisoner fails to adequately prop up the flagging spirits of investigative duchess.

Disgusted with herself, she struggled for a response that did not reveal her own insecurities.

Miss Lark had mentioned a debt.

That was a good topic. She should make a comment about that.

And still she foundered for the correct thing to say. She

could not reiterate her gratitude for convincing Mr. Twaddle-Thum to stop writing about Her Outrageousness because Miss Lark had already renounced all involvement.

But surely there was some other way to establish a balance between them.

Miss Lark had so many skills and could perform any number of harmless services in exchange.

Indeed, she did, and there was one Bea envied in particular.

"Let us say shooting lessons, then," she announced.

Taken aback by the remark, Miss Lark said, "Excuse me?"

"After I find the real killer, you may give me shooting lessons to settle the debt," she explained. "My current instructor does not believe women should be armed and as such has provided me with very little practical tuition. Given your thorough description of the gun that killed Miss Wraithe, I can tell that your skill level is quite advanced and would ask for lessons. Then we may consider ourselves even."

For the first time since she had entered the room, Miss Lark appeared flummoxed as she struggled with how to articulate her dismay at the proposal. "I am not. ... That is, I am not really familiar with. ... Whomever the duke hired is more qualified."

She was, Bea thought with genuine mirth, as horrified as Kesgrave by the prospect of an ongoing relationship, and although she had not made the suggestion in a bid to distract Miss Lark, it had that effect.

Lightened by it, Bea asked if there was anything else she should know before she left. "Do you have messages for me to convey to Miss Drayton or Mr. Somerset Reade? If you do not object, I will inform them of our meeting and assure them of your continued good health. All things considered, Miss Lark, you look well enough."

The chains clanked as Miss Lark raised her hand to brush the bruise on her cheek. "You mean you will not mention my black eye?"

"I won't, no," Bea confirmed with a sympathetic wince. "I hope it is not too painful. I suffered a similar affliction a few weeks ago, in both eyes, and the discoloring has only just gone away."

Miss Lark, who did not appear startled by this revelation, asked if she had also offended a burly inmate by glancing at him out of the corner of her eye.

"No, I tackled a killer at the bottom of a staircase as he was trying to escape a darkened house, and he punched me several times in his effort to free himself," she replied.

"The Taylor affair," Miss Lark said knowledgably.

"Yes, the Taylor affair," Bea confirmed. "It is the type of thing of which Mr. Twaddle-Thum would ordinarily make a meal, so I am grateful for his lack of interest. You have already disavowed all responsibility for his sudden inattention, and yet I cannot help but believe you have exerted influence over his decision in some unintentional way. I am grateful for it."

Receiving credit for something she had not done flustered Miss Lark, whose cheeks turned a light shade of pink at the praise, and she agreed to the firing lessons seemingly as a way to distract from her own discomfort. "Provided his grace approves," she added.

Confident Kesgrave would not object to anything if she saved his sister from the noose, Bea rose to her feet. "I am going to open the door and let the others back in. I am sorry you cannot remain in this room indefinitely."

Miss Lark insisted she should not be. "I know the bruise looks bad, but, as they say, you should see the other fellow. I made a pretty decent showing for myself before Mr. Johnston lent his assistance. And with a room in the state area, I am reasonably comfortable. I shall be fine. Please tell that to Delphine and Freddie. They have nothing to worry about." But that was patently absurd, given her current situation, and she chuckled lightly in acknowledgment of its preposterousness.

Opening the door, Bea found Marlow standing on the threshold blocking the entrance, his folded arms pressed against his chest in a menacing fashion. As a deterrent, it proved successful, for none of the men seemed the least bit interested in crossing him. Instead, they leaned against the opposite wall with varying degrees of annoyance.

Bea thanked them for their patience as well as the loan of the room. Then she darted a look at Marlow and proceeded to the entrance, grateful for the fresh air and weak sunlight that greeted her the second she stepped outside. Closing her eyes in relief, she inhaled sharply, then instantly felt guilty for the intensity of the feeling. She opened them again and spotted Jenkins, anxiety etched into his features, walking toward her.

Approaching at a rapid pace, he chastised her for disappearing for an hour. "A full hour! I thought something terrible had happened to you in that hellish place. I didn't know what I was going to tell the duke."

Instantly contrite, she apologized for being so thoughtless. "It simply did not occur to me that you would worry because I was with Marlow. You know he would never allow anything bad to happen to me. Now do let us leave this place. It is indeed hellish, and we have been here long enough."

Mollified by the rebuke, which was not how Bea intended the remark, Jenkins led them to the carriage, which was on an adjacent block. A young minder kept watch of the horses, and the groom handed him several farthings in gratitude for the service. Then he opened the door and helped her climb into the conveyance. Settling on the bench, she watched Marlow ascend, and although the butler showed no signs of weariness she imagined the experience was just as exhausting for him.

Consequently, she said, "Thank you, Marlow."

He nodded as if accepting his due for a routine duty, such as locking the doors at night or selecting wine from the cellar.

"No, Marlow, thank you," she repeated, this time with particular emphasis, so he would understand how much she valued his assistance. Without his intimidating presence and purseful of coins, she would have accomplished nothing.

The only thing worse than visiting an inmate at Newgate was failing to visit an inmate at Newgate.

Comprehending the difference in her tone, the butler replied with gravitas appropriate to the situation, "You are welcome, your grace."

A wheel dipped into a hollow in the road, causing the carriage to lurch to the right, and Bea grabbed onto the strap. As she steadied herself, she contemplated what else she should say to Marlow. Obviously, it was bad *ton* to explain oneself to one's servants, and yet she felt some truth was owed to him. He had endured the filth and stench of the notorious prison and deserved to know why.

But even as she opened her mouth to provide a modicum of context for the experience, he removed the need for it by noting how curious it was that a woman with no decency had managed to produce two upstanding children. "I suppose her lack of involvement in their rearing is responsible."

He knew!

Well, yes, of course he knew, she thought derisively.

The resemblance to La Reina was so pronounced Kesgrave recognized the woman as his mother's daughter at a glance from several feet away. Marlow had stood considerably closer to her in the same room for more than a minute. The shocking thing would have been if he had not detected the likeness.

Even so, the realization startled her, and before she replied to his remarkable statement—and the generosity he displayed toward an incarcerated stranger *was* remarkable—she had to pause for several moments to regain control over her emotions. It was also terrible etiquette to elaborately praise one's butler. Coolly, then, she said, "Yes, I expect that is right."

The carriage drove over another hole as Marlow nodded again, and Bea tightened her grip on the strap. As he seemed disinclined to continue the conversation, she turned her attention to her investigation to figure out what her next steps should be. After depositing the butler at Kesgrave House, she would return to Bethel Street to collect the letter from Miss Wraithe as well as give Miss Drayton her friend's assurances. Bea trusted that she would pass along the information to Mr. Somerset Reade.

Next, she would visit the scene of the crime to make sure it aligned with Miss Lark's description, then call on the neighbors to try to locate the one who had summoned the Runner. She had little hope of succeeding, as she did not believe the person existed. Thimble was complicit. Whether he reported to the shadowy figure of Miss Lark's conjecture remained to be seen.

Having settled on her list of items to do, Bea allowed that only the visit to Bethel Street was a viable option for the afternoon. Brompton Grove, however, was not. Bordering one of the worst rookeries in London, it was not a suitable neighborhood for her to visit alone, especially if she planned to knock on doors to pester the locals. Having promised just that morning to behave responsibly, the least she could do was request an escort to a questionable neighborhood.

But not Marlow!

The poor butler had done enough for one day.

Jenkins was a viable option, she thought, but the kindly

groom fretted so much about her safety it would be cruel to put him in the position of having to help. Even if she did, he would in all likelihood agree and then dawdle until the duke returned in hopes that he would have the good sense to refuse her request.

He would not, of course.

By some inexplicable stroke, the duke found the investigative process as gratifying as she did, although presumably for different reasons. He certainly did not need the approbation or external validation that identifying murderers bestowed. As a wealthy peer, he had never lacked for approval, either from society or strangers. Unlike a tongue-tied spinster of six and twenty years, he did not have to prove his worth to anyone.

And perhaps that was the thing, she thought.

He was proving something to himself.

And to her.

Kesgrave quite ardently craved her admiration.

It was at once utterly baffling and sweepingly mundane.

Regardless, she was confident he would be as eager as she to save Verity Lark from the hangman's noose. Even if she was not his half sister and someone he seemed to respect despite himself, he could never stand by and allow anyone to swing for a crime he knew she had not committed.

As the carriage turned into the drive at Kesgrave House, Bea calculated their possible arrival time in Brompton Grove if the duke returned at five as he had planned. After having something to eat and washing off the travel dust, he would be ready to leave at seven, which was still early enough to conduct interviews.

Reminding herself to cancel dinner with the dowager and send her regrets to Flora, Bea released the strap as the horses pulled to a stop in front of the large manor in Berkeley Square. As eager as she was to commence her investigation, she felt compelled to observe the proprieties for Marlow's sake. She could not very well shove him out of the carriage and continue to Bethel Street.

Accordingly, she restrained her impatience and waited as Joseph darted forward to open the door. She accepted his hand to disembark, and as she stepped onto the gravel drive, she advised Jenkins to be ready to leave again in thirty minutes.

"I trust that is enough time to feed and water the horses," she added.

Frowning fiercely, the groom nevertheless nodded in assent, and as he walked away to fetch one of the stable boys, he muttered, "And where are we off to next? Horsemonger Lane?"

As it was the principal prison for Surrey, the answer was obviously no.

Bea held her reply, however, out of deference for the groom, whom she had no wish to embarrass. Instead, she followed Joseph up the front steps and learned that the duke had returned almost an hour before. Delighted by this unexpected turn, for now they could begin at once, she hurried into the house as the footman called after her that the duke was in the drawing room entertaining a caller. Although it was not the most welcome news, she decided it did not matter, for the visitor was likely Lady Abercrombie or Aunt Vera coming in person to pester her about the removal to Haverill Hall, and she would move them along quickly.

If the caller was Hartlepool, then the situation was trickier, for he tended to stand on ceremony. But he and Kesgrave had just spent several hours together. He would have no need for further contact. His time would be better spent in Lexington Street, chastising his nephew for his latest scrape.

And if it was someone else—well, then, she would just have to be rude.

A life was at stake!

With these thoughts in mind, Bea strode into the room, her lips already open as she prepared to bid the caller a brisk hello and even brisker goodbye, and came to a sudden halt when she encountered the duke's stormy gaze.

Chapter Five

Kesgrave's brow cleared immediately.

Bea had barely drawn a surprised breath before he was smiling warmly and bidding her hello. Smoothly, he gestured with his right hand, which was holding the stem of a wineglass, and introduced her to their caller: Lord Colson Hardwicke.

"He was just telling me about your excursion to Newgate," the duke added, making her aware of the source of his displeasure, for certainly he had not expected to return home from his own outing—early, no less!—to find his wife off visiting the country's most squalid institution.

Having allowed for the possibility of his disapproval, Bea assured herself she was not unnerved by it. Frequenting prisons was not among the list of commonly approved activities for young women in the capital, and he would have been shocked indeed to find out where she had gone.

Even so, his own sister's life hung in the balance, and he would have to adjust his expectations accordingly. She could not have just twiddled her thumbs while he was negotiating the London Road.

But *why* was he not negotiating the London Road, she thought as she turned to greet Lord Colson, who stood in the center of the room, a tall figure with high cheekbones, a prominent chin, and blue eyes with a touch of green in them. By any account, he was an arresting man, not quite handsome but striking, and contemplating him in her own drawing room, she decided there was not a hint of the Twaddle about him.

Whatever embarrassment or shame or awkwardness he might have felt in meeting Her Outrageousness after months of ridicule was subsumed by anxiety for Miss Lark. "Good afternoon, your grace. I know you have arrived home just this minute and I do not mean to hound you, but I would be grateful if you could tell me how you found Verity."

Although she had failed to anticipate his lordship's immediate call, she realized belatedly that she should have expected it. If he could arrange for Mr. Big Fist Johnston's protection, then he had access to any number of wardens, turnkeys, and guards. He had probably been sent word of her presence at Newgate only minutes after she had entered the keeper's house.

No wonder Mr. Twaddle-Thum was such an omniscient gossip.

He had spies everywhere.

Smothering the sharp sting of resentment that rose at the thought, Bea smiled warmly and informed him Miss Lark was faring reasonably well in her confinement. "She is slightly the worse for wear, as to be expected, but she is apparently holding her own, even without the assistance of Mr. Big Fist Johnston. I trust your spies have told you the same thing."

The relief was visible on Lord Colson's face as he confirmed her supposition. "That is the report I have been given, but I find it difficult to trust their assessment, as they are turnkeys and warders and doorkeepers, rough men who see violence and destruction every day. As long as Verity has not lost a limb or had her eye gouged out, they will tell me she is fine."

He stood rigidly in one spot as he spoke, his body fairly vibrating with anxiety, and Bea found herself doubting her deduction for the first time since conceiving it, for the depth of his feelings for Miss Lark seemed at odds with the rapacious gossip's mendacity. Struggling to contain his apprehension, Lord Colson Hardwicke, the infamous wastrel and the Marquess of Ware's ne'er-do-well spare, struck her as a fundamentally decent person.

Well, yes, but even Mrs. Ralston managed to feel genuine affection for her daughters.

"You may be assured Miss Lark has both her eyes, albeit one is swollen from a recent tussle," Bea said. "But she has been moved to the state side, as you had arranged, and is satisfied with the accommodations. You will still worry, of course, but I think you may temper it with the knowledge that she is in the best position possible for her situation. I can also report that her spirit remains intact. We had a fruitful conversation about the murder. She believes she was entrapped, and I agree the idea has merit."

His lordship's features grew lighter still as he digested this account. "I am sure the hardest part of imprisonment for Verity is not being able to tackle the problem herself. Inactivity is painful for her."

Kesgrave, who had observed the exchange silently, suggested they all take a seat. "I had just convinced Lord Colson to have a drink while we waited for you to return," he explained as he handed the glass he was holding to the other man and crossed to the sideboard, where several decanters of dark-colored liquids were arranged in a neat line. "We are having a young claret."

Bea hailed this as an excellent plan and sat down on the

settee with an encouraging gesture to their caller, who lowered onto the chair next to her. Turning to look at him, she asked how his meetings at the Home Office had gone.

Although his countenance remained neutral, his lordship's frustration was palpable as he issued a terse reply. "Terribly! I felt as though I were talking to a brick wall. The Home Office cannot be caught interceding on the behalf of a murderess," he announced in a pompous, clipped tone that bore no resemblance to his previous speech, doubtlessly because he was mocking his subject. "We cannot risk the scandal!"

"Spoke to Sidmouth, did you?" Kesgrave asked as he carried two glasses to the settee and sat down beside Bea. He placed her glass on the adjacent table and drank deeply of his own claret.

"Spoke to, swore at, threatened," Lord Colson said bitterly. "He could not be persuaded."

"And Mr. Grint was no help?" Bea asked.

"Worse than no help!" he growled with snapping anger. "He owned himself greatly concerned and pledged to do everything within his power to help, even call on the governor of the jail himself to demand her release—upon approval from Sidmouth. He could do nothing without his superior's sanction, which he knew he would not get. Sidmouth would never lift a finger to help a commoner. Indeed, he would be hard-pressed to care about a baronet. I am furious that Grint thinks I would be fooled by his facile pantomime."

"That was not a particularly deft way to handle the matter," Kesgrave observed mildly. "One expects more from the former head of the Alien Office, whose success depended on managing and manipulating the egos of his underlings."

"Since his promotion to under-secretary, I have found Grint to be more lackey than leader, which I have defended as a necessity due to the pressures of his position," he replied. "But no more! I have made it very clear that I will not provide the Home Office with any further help. My willingness to cooperate ended the moment Sidmouth called Verity a murderess. He is an imbecile."

"He is a smug imbecile, which is worse," Kesgrave added.

"It is true," Bea said. "If they had any sense at all, they would have appeased you with lavish promises of assistance and then appeared mystified when all their efforts came to naught. Naturally, I expect little of Sidmouth, for if it cannot help him suspend the writ of habeas corpus, then he does not even know it exists. But Grint is famous for his machinations during the war. That he is too shortsighted to see the value in keeping you in his stable is troubling."

For several long moments, Lord Colson regarded her steadily, thoughtfully, broodingly, and as she returned his unwavering gaze, she realized his eyes were more green than blue. Then he leaned back in the chair and took of sip of claret, determined, she decided, not to be troubled by how much she did or did not know about his wartime activities.

If he was indeed Twaddle, then he should have little cause to wonder at her failure to accept that folderol about Kingsley's heroic pursuits. His reports about Her Outrageousness were equally as ridiculous.

Driving the point home, she added, "Grint should also recognize a conspiracy when it is presented to him by a trusted agent. I assume you explained that Thimble had been placed there to catch her with the gun in her hand?"

"I did, repeatedly," replied Lord Colson, his expression dour as he recalled the conversation. "He did not care. Tomorrow morning, I will seek out Thimble and learn the truth. He will not lie to me."

His tone implied dire things for the Runner if he refused to talk, and Bea, who did not believe brute force always had its desired effect, volunteered to conduct the interrogation that evening. "But first I want to talk to the neighbors in Brompton Grove to confirm Thimble was not summoned as he claims. Having that information in hand will be more persuasive."

She expected Lord Colson to argue because his glower deepened, but he agreed, noting that the sooner the interview was conducted, the better. Then he rattled off the Runner's address, which Kesgrave wrote down before asking why Miss Lark was in Brompton Grove in the first place.

Briefly, she outlined the particulars, starting with Agnes Wraithe's letter and blackmail attempt. She described the scene as Miss Lark found it, noting the quality of the gun, and explained the theory regarding the shadowy figure. Lord Colson, who had been made cognizant of some of the details but not all, also suggested Condon as a primary suspect and for many of the same reasons as Miss Lark.

"I plan to call on his representative in England tomorrow," she said.

"His name is Edmund Ellis," his lordship replied.

Kesgrave, recognizing the barrister, said he had a sterling reputation. "I do not think he would be involved in anything disreputable, but we will find out what he knows of his client's recent activities."

"Thank you," Lord Colson said.

Gratified by the level of trust he had placed in them, Bea said, "At present, we are going to Bethel Street to collect the letter from Miss Wraithe. Will you accompany us?"

He would not, no.

Determined to remove Miss Lark from the misery of Newgate by nightfall, he would call on the warden next to arrange for her to stay with him and his family for the duration of her confinement. It was a simple enough matter to settle, requiring only a generous donation, for the warden was not selective about to whom he exposed his wife and children. "I was on my way to his home when I received word of the duchess's visit and changed my direction. But I must go now if I am to have any hope of dislodging his current tenant before nightfall."

"His current tenant," Kesgrave said with a curious press of his lips. "That is Bentham, is it not?"

Bea, who had not expected to hear the name of her would-be killer, turned to the duke with astonishment. "That is where he has been this whole time? I assumed he was in a cell awaiting trial."

"He struck a bargain with the lord high steward because nobody wanted to deal with the ugliness of a trial before the House of Lords, least of all the prince regent, who knows it would not benefit him to have his nobles' grievances aired in public. Bentham pleaded guilty to a lesser crime, which preserves his title and lands for his children, and will spend the rest of his life confined to prison," the duke explained with a hint of disgust in his voice, noting that he had not been consulted on the decision and that the general assumption had been that he would also be grateful to escape the coarse interest of the public. "I am not sure I agree with that assessment, but there is nothing to be done now. In any event, Bentham will spend the rest of his days confined to a small room without a single toady to fawn over the cut of his coat, which is what gave his life meaning. As I see no reason why he will not live a great many years in silence and obscurity, it is a fitting sort of justice."

In principle, Bea did not object to the arrangement. Lacking a strident vindictiveness, she did not particularly care what punishment the murderous earl endured—as long as he endured some degree of retribution and was denied the opportunity to do more harm. The thought of his traipsing off to the Continent to spend decades in repose on a Greek island à la Lady Skeffington infuriated her.

"If I prevail, he will be confined to a fetid cell by bedtime, which strikes me as even more just," Lord Colson said, adding with a flash of amusement that Bentham would encounter dozens of men who would admire the cut of his coat right off his back. "I must go. After giving the warden two months' worth of wages for a week's stay, which I have been assured is the going rate, I am calling on the lord mayor, who agreed to meet with me at my father's behest, to make sure a date is not immediately set for her trial. He prides himself on the rapid dispensing of justice, which I cannot have. I will kidnap him, if necessary, but I am confident a bribe will suffice. I have a bottle of 1789 Château Lafite that will almost certainly interest him."

Knowing little about vintages and vineyards, Bea was nevertheless familiar with the reverence which with wine enthusiasts discussed years. Uncle Horace still talked in hushed tones about the robust, silky character of the 1802 bottlings.

Kesgrave hailed the plan as likely to succeed, as the lord mayor was generally averse to conflict and would follow the easiest course. "In this case, that is appeasing the formidable Marquess of Ware. He has no interest in causing an upset."

"That is my understanding as well," Lord Colson replied smoothly, and yet this statement, like all the others, was said with an undercurrent of unease, a tightness that belied his composed demeanor. Pushing the trial date back a week or even two was a temporary measure, and if evidence to support Miss Lark's innocence failed to emerge, then no court delay would save her life.

If it came to that, Bea had no trouble imagining the daring prison escape his lordship would implement, with Miss Lark being smuggled out of the fortress in a cart filled with dirty laundry or climbing down the gloomy walls of the building on an improvised rope of bedsheets.

Lord Colson was not going to allow Verity Lark to go to the gallows.

Clearly, his emotions ran much deeper than respect among colleagues.

After the besotted lord left with a promise to keep them apprised of his progress, Bea waited for Kesgrave to sit down again before trying to ascertain why he had returned so early. "I hope neither you nor Hartlepool suffered an accident en route to Watford?"

"Nothing so dramatic," he replied, clasping her hand in his and raising it to his lips for a gentle kiss. "Hartlepool had a note from his nephew this morning announcing his plan to go to the seaside for the week, and knowing how much Netherby hates the beach, he spent half the ride puzzling over what it meant. Unable to suppress a sense that it spells disaster for the family, he insisted we turn around."

"On the contrary, a dark premonition is highly dramatic," she said with an amused lilt. "I suppose this is because Mrs. Taylor consented to allow Netherby to escort her to Vauxhall last week? She has been less discriminating with her favors since discovering the nest egg she thought she had saved had been pilfered by a trusted friend."

"I suspect Hartlepool only proposed the outing to take his mind off the courtship, which worked for the twenty minutes it took to get through the knot of carriages around Covent Garden," he said, adding that his lordship's sister was arriving early next week. "And he is increasingly worried what she will think of his stewardship. Alice does not know that Netherby took his own house in Lexington Street. She thinks he has been tucked under her brother's wing for the season."

The image of the officious lord cowering in anticipation of his sister's displeasure delighted her, and she smiled as she took another sip of her wine. "I am surprised Hartlepool does not plan to decamp to the seaside himself."

"He also hates the beach," Kesgrave said absently before tightening his grip on her hand and saying, "Tell me about Newgate."

It was not what she had been expecting, a calm request for information, and she tilted her head as she looked at him, trying to find some evidence of his earlier irritation. "Marlow is a treasure, and whatever you are paying him is not sufficient."

Kesgrave, who knew the salary of every person whom he employed at Kesgrave House, down to the boy who carted food scraps out to the compost heap, replied that it was indeed quite sufficient. "And the reason why he fell in readily with your plan in the first place. But I am glad he proved so helpful. By and large he is very good in situations requiring brute force."

It was, Bea thought, an oblique and most likely unintended reference to the violence of his early childhood, and rather than allow herself to stew in fury and pity, she said, "Marlow recognized your sister."

The duke revealed no discomfort at the revelation.

He did not wince or flinch or recoil.

And yet Bea could see his muscles tighten in response.

Nevertheless, his tone was matter-of-fact when he noted that it was only to be expected, given how pronounced the resemblance to his mother was. "Anyone who knew La Reina would see it."

Struck by the lack of inflection in his voice, she wondered at his ability to appear so untroubled by his sister's incarceration and impending trial. Surely, he felt some alarm at her situation.

Providing him with the details of her visit, Bea distilled the one-hour call into a ten-minute summary. She did not mention the rough way the turnkey had dragged Miss Lark across the threshold or how the prisoner initially refused Bea's assistance. The majority of the explanation was focused on the scene at Miss Wraithe's house: the open door, the position of the body, the placement of the pistol.

Kesgrave, listening without comment, had only one question at the end of the narration and it pertained to Miss Lark's physical condition: Was the report she gave of the prisoner's injuries to Hardwicke accurate?

That was it.

He did not raise the possibility that his sister might be guilty.

Astonished by the display of trust—in her as much as in the accused—Bea admitted that Miss Lark had skirted the worst of it. "The bruise on her cheek is actually quite fierce, and her eye is so swollen it is almost shut. She has a jagged wound on her forearm and angry scrapes on her wrists from the manacles. I imagine her ankles are in much the same condition. But that is the extent of her injuries, as far as I could see, and she did not move gingerly, as though she were in pain. She is fine enough for the present and likely to stay that way if Lord Colson succeeds in arranging lodging with the warden, which I think he will."

"That is good," the duke said with a nod before advising her to dash upstairs to change her clothes before they left for Bethel Street.

Startled, Bea glanced down at her dress, which was wrinkled with blotches of dirt clinging to the hem. That was peculiar because she could not recall walking in puddles of sludge.

Amused, she asked if she looked too bedraggled to leave the house.

"On the contrary," he said as he tugged her to her feet. "You do not look bedraggled enough for a lane that borders

St. Giles. Tell Lily to pick out a plain frock in a muted color and dull fabric."

"She will adamantly refuse," Bea predicted with an amused grin. "The last time she allowed me to wear an unadorned dress, I sauntered downstairs to find your former mistress in a stunning gown. She is still sewing rosettes on the hem of my walking dresses two weeks later."

"As intimidating as your maid is, I am sure you will figure it out," Kesgrave said confidently. "You managed to persuade Marlow to take you to Newgate, so I know what you are capable of. I trust you were also going to bring him on your excursion to Clement Lane as well."

"Oh, no," she said, drawing an angry glare before she clarified. "I had no intention of visiting Miss Wraithe's neighborhood without you. After collecting the evidence at Bethel Street, I planned to come back to Kesgrave House, pace the entrance hall with growing frustration until you finally deigned to return, scold you like a fishwife for arriving so late, and then lead you outside again so you could call on the neighbors in your travel grime. Be glad for Netherby's inexplicable yearning for the seaside, your grace, for it has spared you an extremely uncomfortable evening."

Kesgrave, delighting in perversity, swore he had always wanted to be upbraided by a harpy and begged for a demonstration even as she strode out of the room. He called after her as she climbed the stairs to her dressing room, where Lily regarded her with the expected dismay when she requested her most bedraggled gown. Her maid complied only after Bea swore with one hand on a Bible that she would hide behind the largest available object if she caught a glimpse of any member of the *ton*.

Forty-five minutes later, she and the duke arrived at the Lark residence and Jenkins opened the door to the carriage with tart disapproval. The last time the duchess had called on this location, she had proceeded almost immediately to Newgate, and he shuddered to think where she would wind up next.

"Probably the Tower," he muttered.

Unable to decide if this dire prediction was an improvement on Horsemonger Lane Prison, Bea lamented to Kesgrave how highly strung his poor groom was. "Maybe we should send *him* to the seaside to take the waters. A restorative plunge would do wonders for his nerves."

"Fewer corpses would do more good," Kesgrave replied blandly.

"I am certain he is not so unjust as to believe it is *my* fault the residents of our fair city keep killing each other," she said, raising her hand to knock. Her knuckles had barely grazed the door before it swung open to reveal a rosy-cheeked woman with a wild mop of blond curls. She apologized at once for her indecent haste, but it felt as though she had been waiting an age for them to arrive.

"Lord Colson sent a note, you see, so I have been looking out the window, which is the first activity I have been able to focus on for hours. Usually, I am able to calm my mind with needlework, but in this particular circumstance knitting blankets feels like playing the fiddle while Rome burns. I am Delphine Drayton, your graces," she said, dropping into a brisk curtsey, then promptly resuming her monologue as she stepped back to allow them to enter. "Come, let me show you to Robert's study. Lord Colson mentioned you were looking for a letter, but he did not say which one. It should be easy to find because Verity is so organized. Everything in its place!"

Miss Drayton paused for a shallow breath as she led them into a comfortable room with windows facing the road. Its dark molding and rich colors gave it a masculine cast, as did the desk near the back wall, with its breadth of gleaming mahogany wood. Bookshelves lined the wall to the left and opposite hung a circular board for throwing darts.

"I am grateful you are here, your graces," she continued, lighting a pair of sconces next to the doorway even though it was bright enough in the room without them. "I know you take an academic interest in murder, but I like to think you also take a personal one as well given the connection, to which I will allude only this once. Here is the desk."

As her aunt was given to nervous chatter, Bea knew the benefit of letting someone talk until they ran out of words. As soon as Miss Drayton fell silent, she confirmed it was personal. "Even before I met Miss Lark, I was impressed by her exploits, and there is the connection, which we do not take lightly. You may be assured we will do everything within our power to free her from the suspicion of murder, and although I would never be so foolish as to make a promise I do not know if I can keep, I can say that I am optimistic we will succeed. Now, to that end, we are looking for a letter from Agnes Wraithe."

Thunderstruck, Miss Drayton widened her eyes as the color left her face. "From ... from the *Wraithe*?"

Having stood outside the walls of Fortescue's and felt an ominous dread wind through her as the nightmares of her childhood besieged her, Bea understood the wave of terror that swept through the other woman at the mention of her childhood tormentor. Gently, she explained, sparing no details.

Miss Drayton, her color returning slowly now that the worst of the shock had passed, snapped impatiently, "How very like Verity!"

Startled by the bite of anger in her tone, Bea drew her brows together and, darting a look at Kesgrave, said, "It is like Miss Lark to be incriminated in a murder?"

"It is like her to rush into a situation alone without telling anyone about it because she is convinced she is aware of every possible outcome and has accounted for every factor that might possibly go awry," Miss Drayton explained wearily as she lowered into a chair. "Verity has an inflated sense of her own competence, and it is compounded by the fact that she is not wrong to have an inflated sense of her own competence. Verity *is* excessively capable. There are few things she cannot do with aplomb, but as this predicament illustrates, it is impossible to account for everything."

It was, Bea thought, a valid point.

Miss Drayton pressed her palm against her forehead as she closed her eyes briefly and sighed. "I do not mean to sound harsh. Obviously, I do not truly believe Verity is in any way at fault. I am merely frustrated by this sense of helplessness I feel, which has been made worse by the return of the Wraithe. Of course Verity did not mention her. She did not want to worry me or Freddie. She could have told Lord Colson, but she does have funny ideas about strength and independence. And I imagine it unsettled her as well. Although she pretends to be invulnerable to fear, she had to feel some tremor of alarm at seeing that scratchy handwriting again after all these years. We had believed the Wraithe was well and truly routed," she said, then abruptly shook her head as she apologized for rambling again. It was just that she had had so very little sleep.

And the Wraithe, of course.

Having resolved to say no more, Miss Drayton could not stop herself from marveling over the unexpected turn. "The specter of our childhood come back to haunt us. I know I should feel some pity for the way she died, shot in the back of the head like a highwayman escaping down a dark road. But I am just so angry that even in death she is still managing to plague us. Why could she not have keeled over from apoplexy like a proper old harridan?"

As Bea had encountered many inconvenient deaths in the course of her career as a lady Runner, she had no answer to that question. It was the nature of murder to make life difficult for the survivors. Rather than engage the exhausted woman in a philosophical discussion, Bea murmured sympathetically as Kesgrave walked to the other side of the desk. He opened the drawer on the right and removed the packet of papers that were lying on top. He sifted through the sheets to gauge their contents and identified the letter, which he handed to Bea to peruse.

It was, she noted, precisely as Miss Lark had described. Rather than engage in pleasantries, its author launched into the business at hand, explaining the situation as it stood and requesting her presence on Thursday, June 18, at eleven in the morning to arrive at the terms of her silence. She did not use the word *blackmail,* per se, but the implication was clear. She also refrained from including a preliminary sum, so it was impossible to know what she was thinking in terms of an amount.

Miss Drayton, hearing the contents of the letter, let out a strangled snorting sound that was somewhere between a snicker and a scoff. "Good gad! The Wraithe must have been doddering indeed if she thought she could squeeze one farthing out of Verity—or any of her former charges, for that matter! We detested her with every fiber of our being, even the most docile among us, and would rather starve in the streets than yield to any of her demands as an adult. She was the essence of cruelty personified, and I was so very pleased when Verity and Freddie toppled her and the board of supervisors. They were all rotten to the core. And Lord Condon, who always brought us candy. I remember him well, a jolly grin on his face as he pulled lemon drops from his pockets. He had an endless supply, and we were so grateful and all along he was a fiend."

As Miss Lark had mentioned Condon, the former patron was already under suspicion, but Bea had yet to consider other members of the supervisory board. They were, as far as she could remember, a genteel assortment spanning ages and genders, and she asked Miss Drayton to write down their names.

"It is not exhaustive," Miss Drayton said as she handed the slip to Bea. "In as much as it is a list of people who loathed the Wraithe, it is not complete. She was just as cruel to the teachers and clerks and porters who worked at Fortescue's. I could not begin to recall all their names, but I am sure the records would be available to you if you ask the current head matron, Mrs. Caffrey."

"That is an excellent suggestion," Bea said with a glance at the sheet. It contained five names. "Unless you can think of anything else we should know, we will be on our way."

"My mind is blank right now, but the murder is all I can think about, so I am sure I will come up with something. If I do, I will send you a note. And in the meantime, I will do my best to recall the names of some of the people at Fortescue's."

Bea, hailing this as a good use of her time, handed the list to Kesgrave, who slipped it into his pocket with the letter. Miss Drayton escorted them to the door and thanked them again for taking an interest in her friend's plight. "I do wish I could do more to help you. It is torturous remaining in this house, pretending to knit while I really pace the parlor waiting for word from Hardwicke or Freddie. I almost wish I were in Newgate myself so that I could be distracted by its abject misery and deprivation. No, that is a horrible thing to say. Obviously, I do not mean it. Please pay no attention to me. I am unmoored without Verity to chastise for her recklessness. You will send word, won't you, when you discover something?" she asked soberly, then let out a self-conscious giggle. "Listen to me: Exhorting dukes and duchesses to do my bidding. I am sorry, your graces. It has been a peculiar two days."

Bea assured Miss Drayton she had done nothing that required an apology. "Even if your request were an exhortation, it would be a reasonable one. We will of course apprise you of anything pertinent. And I would urge you to try to be a little less worried about Miss Lark. Lord Colson seems to have her welfare firmly in hand."

Although the sentiment had the air of a platitude, it nevertheless soothed some of Miss Drayton's anxiety. "You are right. I know you are right. Hardwicke would move heaven and earth for Verity. She will be fine. She did not do it, so she will be fine," she said as she grasped the handle on the door. Opening it, she expressed amazement at Bea's loveliness. It was not what she had expected from Her Outrageousness, she confessed, then closed the door with a sharp clap—presumably before she could make another less than gracious comment, Bea thought.

Chapter Six

Agnes Wraithe's house was precisely as Miss Lark had described: dilapidated on the outside, well-kept on the inside. With its cracked facade and crooked shutters, it looked no different from the other homes on the road, a development that ensured few passersby would give it a second glance.

It was, Bea thought, a reasonable strategy for concealing her prosperity. As an older woman living alone, she would not want to advertise her comfort, and although nothing in her front parlor indicated excessively deep pockets, she lived considerably better than the average resident of the adjacent rookery.

The chair before the fire, for example, the one that bore evidence of the victim's murder—it was made with a lovely silk brocade. The cushion was worn, yes, but just barely. If the seat were in the drawing room in Portman Square, Aunt Vera would not start bemoaning the high cost of reupholstery for at least another five years.

As she noted the quality of Miss Wraithe's possessions, she recalled Miss Lark's cynical assumption that the former headmistress had feathered her nest nicely with the proceeds from her corrupt activities at Fortescue's and had recently run out of funds, necessitating the need for blackmail.

Surveying the room, Bea decided the notion had merit and imagined that Verity Lark's secret must have struck the victim as heaven-sent. She could squeeze the reporter for a modest sum and continue to live comfortably enough. As was typically the case, the solution to a seemingly intractable problem arrived at the precise moment it was no longer necessary.

Did the killer know what Miss Wraithe had planned?.

If Miss Lark's theory of the shadowy figure was accurate, then it did not matter what the killer knew because he was merely a minion hired to perform a job. He bore his victim no animosity.

"The most pressing question in regard to the shadow figure theory is the size of the conspiracy," Kesgrave said as he surveyed the room from the doorway. "As I see it, there are three options: The shadowy figure employed both the gunman to shoot Miss Wraithe and the Runner to find her. We shall call that proposition one. How does the first proposition strike you?"

"As the riskiest," Bea replied, drawing closer to the chair and noting its position before the hearth. "The more people involved in a scheme, the greater the chance something will go wrong. Furthermore, there is the challenge of coordinating the timing and the possibility that one of your minions will betray you. If the shadowy figure is clever enough to arrange this, then I think he is clever enough to realize that."

On a curt nod, the duke agreed. "Proposition two is the shadowy figure killed Miss Wraithe himself and hired the Runner to find her."

There were, Bea thought, several appealing aspects to this second possibility: Requiring one person fewer, it was a simpler scheme costing its architect less money while giving him greater control over the outcome. "But it does not address the coordination challenges, and now the minion, whose morality has already been proven to be extremely flexible, possesses evidence against his employer. I find it hard to believe that anyone who devised such an elaborate plot would make himself vulnerable to blackmail or coercion, especially in light of the Runner's role, which is known. All we would have to do is apply pressure to Thimble for him to point us toward the real murderer. Or keep him under surveillance until he leads us to him, per Miss Lark's suggestion. No, I do not think the second proposition is viable. It must be proposition three."

"In which the shadowy figure employed the Runner both to kill Miss Wraithe and discover Miss Lark in a damning situation," he said.

Although it was the explanation that made the most sense, Bea nevertheless found it difficult to accept, for she could not fathom how a man could devote his life to enforcing the laws that held together English society and then break them himself—and in such an ugly way.

Shooting an elderly spinster in the back of the head!

It was too corrupt.

To be sure, yes, but the nature of a villain was to be villainous.

On this deeply profound revelation, she pointed out that the third proposition solved the problem of coordination. "It is the simplest plan, which is an advantage. But it puts Thimble in the neighborhood for the entire course of the crime. After leaving the house the first time, he would have had to stay in the general vicinity to wait for Miss Lark to arrive. Loitering increases the likelihood of someone spotting him. We will have to ask about that when we look for the neighbor who issued the summons."

"There will be no summons," Kesgrave said confidently.

Of the same general opinion, she could not quite smother the part of her that expected the shadowy figure to have arranged for someone to corroborate the Runner's story. As a criminal mastermind, it behooved him to ensure that every aspect of his scheme could withstand scrutiny.

Even so, it would still be a lie, she reminded herself, and lies were difficult to sustain in both detail and demeanor. The dissembler had to keep a tight grasp not only on the threads of his fiction but also his manner. Appearing confused or embarrassed or generally uncomfortable was as revealing as misremembering a fact, and she could not believe that the scheme's architect, as thorough as he appeared to be, had not taken the neighbor's ability to sustain a prevarication under prolonged questioning into consideration.

The duke, hearing these thoughts, assured her that the shadowy figure, if he did indeed exist, would not have accounted for any of it. "The only reason he would have taken pains to create a deep framework for his fiction was if he anticipated your interest, and I am certain he did not. Even with your remarkable rate of success in recent months, I do not think every murderer in London is taking a rear-guard action against the Duchess of Kesgrave."

"Bentham did," she said, compelled to mention the notable exception.

"Yes, and look how well that turned out for him," he replied amiably. "Nothing about the story will hold up, I promise you. The notion that the residents of this neighborhood could afford to buy a warrant, let alone prosecute a crime, is risible, and I defy anyone on Clement Lane to produce an item of enough value to justify the expense."

"You are right, of course," she said, circling the chair to stand a few feet behind it and focusing her attention on the crime scene, trying to picture how the room looked when

Miss Lark entered. "The gun, with its maker's mark and elaborate ivory design, was about here. An extravagant piece. That is significant. A cheaply made gun would have been just as damning, and yet the killer or the shadowy figure made sure Miss Lark was implicated with a high-priced flintlock. Why?"

Kesgrave, asserting that he could not pretend to know how much a Runner made per annum, hazarded that it was similar in range to a domestic servant's income. "If that is the case, the pistol cost as much as Thimble's annual salary."

"Not Thimble's gun, then," she observed softly.

"I do not believe so, no," he replied.

"The shadowy figure gave the valuable flintlock to Thimble to leave behind because it points away from Thimble. If Thimble owned a pistol equal to his annual salary, he would have taken it with him. Its very presence invalidates proposition three," Bea said, drawing her eyes together as she contemplated the fiendishness of the plot. The attention to detail was most unsettling because it indicated that the shadowy figure had anticipated further interest and might have gone so far as to persuade a neighbor to actually summon a Runner.

The duke, however, took the opposing view, seeing the flintlock itself as reassuring evidence of a deft hand at work. "It supports the existence of the shadowy figure, which, I will remind you, is still only a theory."

It was a salutatory reminder, and considering it, Bea proposed a fourth proposition: The Runner acted alone. "If there is a connection to Fortescue's, he could have been planning her murder for years, slowly saving enough money to buy the gun. Or he might have stolen it or acquired it from a crime scene. Miss Lark and Miss Drayton both said the list of suspects is infinite if you include all the former charges and staff at the asylum. Maybe Thimble is one of the children whom Condon and Miss Wraithe sold, or he could be a former worker, perhaps a porter or a gardener."

"A daunting assortment indeed," Kesgrave said calmly.

Determined to take everything in order, she walked to the fireplace to continue her examination of the murder scene. On the mantelpiece were sundry items that hinted at the presence of children: two toy soldiers, a ball, and a carved wooden horse. Coated in a thin layer of dust, they had sat there untouched for several weeks at least. Brushing the grime from her fingers, she turned around and studied the room from the other perspective. In front of her was the chair in which Miss Wraithe had died. Several paces to the left and toward the long wall was a blue floral settee with a white-painted frame. A dark-stained cabinet was next to it, an assortment of empty vases, half-finished embroidery samplers, and books displayed behind its glass. The mahogany piece pressed against windows streaked with dirt and overlooking the road. Opposite them, on the other side of the seat, was a table, sturdy and square, and although it accommodated four comfortably, it had only the one other chair, an indication that the recently deceased did not entertain often.

Struck again by the placement of the chair, she thought it was strange that the victim would calmly sit before the fire when she was expecting the arrival of a former charge whom she had not seen in almost two decades and who had ruthlessly maligned her in print, ensuring the loss of her employment. "If I were she, I would be pacing with a mixture of excitement and anxiety, reviewing how I planned for the scene to unfold. And I would orchestrate the seating, deciding where I would sit or stand and where my caller would sit or stand. Ideally, I would sit Miss Lark on the settee while I occupied the chair, which is a little higher, thereby giving me the advantage of height. In matters of crime such as blackmail, you do not want to have to look up at your target and Miss Lark is so tall."

In the middle of the table was a teapot, which Kesgrave opened. "It is just dregs."

"So she had no intention of playing gracious hostess," she observed, her eyes resting on an assortment of pages next to an ink bottle, a pair of quills, and a ledger. Miss Wraithe had not even bothered to gather the papers into a neat pile. Bea read one of the sheets and saw it was a shopping list. Flipping it over, she found it was a copy of the letter she had sent to Miss Lark.

"It is a version," Kesgrave amended, withdrawing the one they had taken from the study in Bethel Street and putting the two missives side by side. "This draft is wordier. You see how she bids her good day and makes a benign comment about her health? In the one that was delivered, she offers no pleasantries or conclusion. She just affixes her name. Here, she writes 'your obedient servant.'"

Sifting through the pages on the table, Bea found a second iteration, which contained a briefer salutation and was signed "yours truly." "You can see the progression but not the direction. Either she started with the simplest and tried to add flourishes or it was the other way around. Regardless, she gave the tone of the message a lot of thought. Alternatively, her associate—aka the shadowy figure—had lots of thoughts about the message's tone. I suppose the answer depends on how involved he was in the scheme," she said, folding the two messages in half and handing them to the duke to put in his pocket with the third.

Finishing their inspection of the front parlor, they walked through the rest of the house, noting the pantry was small but well stocked and the bedroom upstairs was tidy, with a plum-colored counterpane neatly folded at the foot of the bed and a pair of pillows fluffed nicely at the head.

Peering out the window at the narrow street, Kesgrave suggested they conduct their interviews with the neighbors before it grew much later. "The house is situated in the middle of the block, so I suggest we start to the left and proceed in a circle like the hands of a clock."

Soberly, she agreed with his proposal and regretted they did not have time to make a table to record their progress. "As you are so fond of charts, your grace."

His lips twitched with amusement as he pointed out that he had made only the one.

"That is true, yes, but what a chart it is," she replied, imbuing her tone with more than a modicum of awe. "The epitome of organizational splendor: eight columns, four dozen rows, information coordinated by color, subject lines written in all capital letters."

"Five dozen rows, brat," he corrected. "Haverill Hall employs fifty-eight servants."

Inevitably, it did, yes. An estate as large as the Matlock family seat would inevitably be twenty-five percent larger than her provincial mind could conceive. Although she had understood the immensity of his holdings from the moment they had met at Lakeview Hall because the air of reverence with which the introduction had been made could only denote massive wealth, she had never really contemplated it in material terms.

Doing so now, she felt overwhelmed, for nothing in her upbringing had prepared her to be mistress of a large manor house. Slotted for spinsterhood by the end of her second season, she had been trained to satisfy the demands of a few ornery relatives, not to issue orders to dozens of servants, many of whom respected the dowager's confident hand or even La Reina's commanding one.

Presumably, there would be no murders in the country. How, then, was she supposed to impress the staff if there were no killers to thwart, especially in the confines of her own sitting room?

"Stephens took it upon himself to add color," the duke continued. "I merely asked him to sort the servants by title, responsibility, and sphere of influence. I know how intimidated you were by the size of the London household and thought seeing everything in one place would ease your anxiety."

"You mean knowing the worst of it all at once," she muttered.

"Actually, the chart does not include workers from the village whom we hire from time to time," he admitted, a grin flashing across his features.

Of course there were more. Any schoolroom miss with a shred of hope in her heart knew a horde of fifty-eight maids, footmen, gardeners, stable boys, cooks, gamekeepers, and grooms was simply inadequate to running a vast ancestral estate.

She could not bear to think about it.

"Let us go," she said firmly, striding to the staircase.

They stepped out of the house and began their canvas of the block with the house to the left. The duke knocked on the door, which was a bright shade of blue with faded patches, and as they waited for someone to answer, she wondered how out of place they looked. Although not dressed in finery, they had an elegance about them that could only come from money, a development that applied doubly to the duke, whose tailcoat was ruthlessly tailored. The quality of the cut was unmistakable.

Her supposition was confirmed a few seconds later when the door suddenly swung open and an angry woman wielding a broom with threatening ferocity abruptly dropped the implement. As the wood handle clattered to the ground, she bowed her head in embarrassment and begged their pardon.

As they were not expected, she had assumed they were someone else. She kept her eyes tilted down and spoke so softly Bea could barely hear the words, the other woman's mortification was so acute.

Seeking to put her at ease, Bea said she had done the same thing herself on more than one occasion, but rather than extend the neighbor's discomfit by providing examples, she explained that she and the duke were investigating a report that a Runner had been summoned to her house.

Confounded by the charge, Mrs. Cox stared at Bea with astonishment for several seconds, then she slowly shook her head and said someone was having her on. "We ain't never called for a Runner here. Want nothing to do with them. Was it Aggie the Haggie who said it?"

Fascinated by the term, at whose meaning she could easily guess, Bea leaned forward and said, "Excuse me?"

"Aggie the Haggie," she repeated, tilting her head to the right to gesture at her neighbor's home. "That's what my sons —they are six, eight, and twelve—call Agnes Wraithe next door. Aggie the Haggie because she is a mean old hag. She yells at them all the time. Whenever she sees them, she yells at them for ruining her shutters or playing too close to her windows. She steals their toys and after the nails on her door knocker rusted, she had the nerve to accuse my Jimmy of pulling it down. She is a witch and a harridan, and I bet she lies all the time. Is she the one who said it?"

As the woman's use of present tense made it clear she did not yet know that her neighbor had been murdered, Bea informed her of the development and asked if she had noticed anything amiss the day before at around eleven in the morning.

Taken aback by the news, Mrs. Cox owned herself stunned. She had always assumed Agnes Wraithe was too mean to die. "It is good to know she was as human as anyone."

"And did you notice anything unusual yesterday?" Bea pressed.

The woman furrowed her brow. "Strange how?"

"An unfamiliar person loitering in the area or trying to hide?" she added.

"Oh, I see, then, no, nothing like that," Mrs. Cox replied, adding that her son Billy liked to watch carriages go by the window. "He would have called me if anything unusual happened. He was beside himself with excitement last week when a horse threw a shoe."

"How thrilling," Bea said and thanked the woman for her time.

Calling on the next house, they had a similar conversation. Although Mr. Douglas's children were too old to invent denigrating nicknames for their neighbor, they also detested her. When they were younger, she would chase them away from her front window with a poker.

Regarding the Runner, he was sorry he could not be of more help, but he had not summoned one the day before or ever. He would not know how even if he wanted to.

House after house, they got the same general response, although the farther they walked from Miss Wraithe's door, the fewer personal complaints about her they heard. By the time they finished their last interview, Bea felt reassured by the shadowy figure's lack of rigor. Having failed to make sure the Runner's story could be substantiated if scrutinized, he bolstered Miss Lark's claim to innocence. Now when they confronted Thimble about his summons claim, they could confidently accuse him of lying.

Climbing into the carriage, she instructed Jenkins to take them to Willow Place so they could do just that.

Chapter Seven

Cyrus Thimble had nothing to hide.

A man of medium height with a muscular build, a broad nose, and dark brown hair that tumbled into his eyes no matter how often he brushed it aside, he had a straightforward way about him, a sense of honest dealing that nobody had ever had the temerity to question before—certainly not to his face!

To be fair, Bea had not questioned it now.

All she had done was introduce herself and the duke.

Standing at the top of the third-floor staircase in the cramped building in which he lived, she had knocked firmly on the door and waited for it to open. When it did, she found herself presented with a pleasantly disheveled father of approximately five and thirty years old holding his toddler son. Affably, she had identified herself and Kesgrave.

Thimble stiffened and said, "I have nothing to hide."

But an evasive look crossed his features as he glanced over his shoulder and lowered the boy to the floor. He stepped around the small child and said in a quiet voice, "Here, let us have our conversation in my office."

And then he shut the door behind him.

All three of them were in the hallway now.

It was not the behavior of a man who had nothing to hide.

And yet he repeated it.

Silence followed this pronouncement as he tightened his jaw, and Bea wondered if he was smothering the urge to say it yet again. Compelled to assert his innocence, he seemed to realize the futility of the claim: Only the guilty sought to counter an unspoken allegation.

When he managed to restrain the impulse, Bea explained that they were there to investigate the murder of Agnes Wraithe in Clement Lane the morning before. She made no mention of their interviews or indicated any doubt of his honesty. Nevertheless, his shoulders grew more rigid with every syllable she uttered and she began to fear he might do actual harm to his spine if he stiffened further. "The duke and I have come from the scene of the crime and have a few questions regarding your investigation. I am sure they will not take long, and you can return to dinner with your family."

"*My* investigation of the crime consisted of identifying the killer by the fact that she was dressed as a man to disguise herself and was holding the murder weapon as plain as day," he replied crisply, adding that the gun was still warm from being recently discharged. "So there can be no mistaking who is responsible for Agnes Wraithe's death. I took the suspect into custody and brought her to the magistrate's office in Bow Street. If you are familiar with the murder, as you claim, then you know everything I have relayed represents the events accurately."

A loud bang echoed throughout the hallway as the door to another flat in the building slammed shut. Raising her voice slightly to speak over the patter on the staircase above them, Bea reassured him that his account aligned with the one she had heard. Her point of interest, however, was in his timely arrival. "According to the report I received, you were in Clement Lane responding to another crime."

He stated that was correct.

But his poor back—tightening further!

"What was the nature of that crime?" she asked.

The Runner snapped, "I know who you are!"

Blandly, she replied, "Well, yes, you do know. I introduced myself and the duke not ten minutes ago."

But he shook his head as though she were trying to trick him. "You are Her Outrageousness, prancing around London solving murders with all your clever ploys and ruses. I think it is rubbish! Maybe you even make them up, like with that Dugmore business. There was nothing suspicious about his death. Just another old man dying in an old man way. The coroner was not even called! And yet you found a killer. I think it is quite curious, maybe even suspicious. Go ahead, ask me all the questions you want. I have nothing to hide!"

He spat the words defensively as the neighbor who had been trundling down the steps walked past with a look of naked curiosity. Thimble returned his interest with an angry glare.

As Bea knew he had several things to hide, including the fact it was he who pulled the trigger if proposition one proved correct, she was not surprised by his belligerence. Clearly, he had an inkling that his lie had been discovered and was responding with anxious aggression. It had always been a risk, accepting money for murder, but the threat had never felt real. He assumed he would get away with it.

Calmly, she repeated the query. "What was the nature of the crime that brought you to Clement Lane?"

"You want to know the nature of the crime, do you?" he asked with growing ferocity. "The nature of the crime, is it? I'll tell you what it was."

But he did not.

Thimble stared at the wall opposite, a pensive line deepening between his brows as he foundered for a credible answer. He should not have been at a loss—anyone who invented a story was obliged to come up with supporting details—but having failed to anticipate doubt or suspicion, he had not bothered to embellish his fiction. And now, in the moment, he had too many factors to account for, and after eliminating the crimes that did not make sense for the neighborhood or the situation, such as theft or murder, respectively, he had few options.

What was left when you removed the most popular offenses?

Abduction, forgery, molestation, sorcery.

Bea waited to see which one he would pick.

"Treason!" Thimble announced.

Fascinated, she murmured thoughtfully, "Treason, was it?"

"Yes, treason," he repeated more assertively the second time, determined to brazen out the lie. "Daft old bird thought we was still at war with Boney and reported her grandson for drinking French brandy."

Bea glanced at Kesgrave to see how he was receiving this nonsense and assumed the look of bland interest on his face mirrored her own polite expression. Returning her focus to Thimble, she nodded sympathetically and noted that the transition to peace after so many years of war no doubt confused many of their older citizens. "What is her name?"

A name, yes!

He should have expected that question as well and had a name at the ready, but again he grappled for a response. "Her name is ... well, I ... it seems like I didn't get her name because ... because of the gunfire. I ran out as fast as possible when I heard the gunfire. I have an obligation ... I can't let people shoot each other without trying to. ... Well, it's not right that people shoot each other, and French brandy isn't treason. And ... and it wasn't even French! She had read the label wrong."

Beads of sweat gathered along his hairline as the exertion of fabricating details extemporaneously began to take its toll.

Good, Bea thought, pressing for yet another particular. "Ran out of where?"

Thimble's jaw moved but no words emerged, and he turned to Kesgrave with beseeching eyes, as though to plead with him to intervene on his behalf. The duke smiled at him faintly as a door on one of the landings below opened and angry voices carried up the stairs. They were arguing about mud on a newly scrubbed floor.

Thimble curled his hands into fists, clenching his fingers into taut knots while the rest of his body slackened, and he leaned against the wall as if seeking its support. Rapping his knuckles against the plaster, he glared at her with intense loathing, and in his sneer, Bea saw a murderer twisting in his own impenetrable web of lies. Caught, captured, condemned, he would cling to his hatred and resentment, and she stood there quietly, allowing him to consider his options. They were limited, of course, and consisted of only two: attempt to escape, beg for mercy.

The silence in the hallway deepened as the downstairs quarrel ended with a slamming door, and the Runner raised his chin as he pushed off the wall. Slipping his hands into his pockets, he admitted there had been no report of treason, no old biddy, no summons. "That was a story. I had to have some reason why I was already there."

Bea was struck by his insouciance.

Her own shoulders tensed in anticipation of a confession; she could not fathom why he was suddenly so calm. At the very least, his voice should quiver as he made the confession. His family was just on the other side of the door, his wife and toddler son, and in a few moments he would say goodbye to them, possibly forever.

Bea hoped for his son's sake that the shadowy figure who hired him to shoot Agnes Wraithe gave him enough money to compensate his son for growing up fatherless.

"I'm sorry, I'm sorry, but I had no choice. I had to lie! The truth would have gotten me in trouble because we are not allowed to accept payments. We are not thief-takers!" he explained in a rush, his tone equal parts abashed and pugnacious. "My boss can't know I had an arrangement with her for that morning. I have had several with her over the years, and it was always something trivial and harmless. She paid me a pound here, a guinea there, to frighten the children who lived nearby. She was convinced they were constantly tyrannizing her in small, sneaky ways, like breaking her door knocker and throwing pebbles at her windows, and once she insisted they had stopped up her chimney, although it was obvious that a poor bird died in it. Another time she swore the Cox boy next door had broken into her house, but she could not name a single thing that was missing. Still, she was convinced he had been there because he is a wicked child who loves tormenting her. She was a bit daft, but I went along with it because she paid me and it was harmless. And it never hurt a child to be reminded to respect his elders. I would be grateful to any man who did the same for my own sons. It was a little different this time because she wanted me to intimidate a grown woman. All I had to do was be in the room when the woman arrived and loom aggressively if she argued with Miss Wraithe. I mean, it was nonsense, wasn't it? I can't arrest a woman for pretending to be a male journalist, but Miss Wraithe said it was fraud and false representation, and the woman wouldn't know the difference if I used terms that sounded legal. It was harmless, but I would be turned off without a notice if my boss found out."

He punctuated the torrent of words with a sharp inhalation of breath, then stared at Bea with an almost defiant glower, as if daring her to question his veracity—a strange stance to take given the subject of his speech. He had just confessed to lying and now sought to claim the high moral ground.

Unfortunately for him, it did not work like that.

To his credit, Thimble had managed to marshal a cogent argument in his defense, rather than stuttering incoherently about treason. Her questions and the doubt they espoused had convinced him of the severity of the situation. All at once, he had perceived that something vitally important was at stake and with that revelation had come clarity. The lazy thinking he had employed previously would not suffice now that Her Outrageousness had pranced onto the scene.

Thimble finally understood that.

After his dismal showing earlier, Bea was impressed with his ability to devise a new narrative with actual details and lauded his quick wit. "I am sure it will stand you in good stead in Newgate."

In response to this ominous statement, Thimble drew his brows together and explained that Runners did not work inside the prison. "It is not our territory. I suppose I could get employment as a turnkey or a guard if I was so disposed, for the pay is reportedly quite good, but I have no interest in working there. I don't want to come home every day smelling like piss and excrement."

Although Bea generally respected a bold strategy, she was more than a little insulted that the Runner believed she was so facile. "I meant as an inmate."

"Why would I be an inmate at Newgate?" he asked curiously.

It was startling, his nonchalance, in light of his previous

trepidation. He did not appear to comprehend that the jig was up. "Because you murdered Miss Wraithe."

Calmly, displaying no alarm, he denied it. "Verity Lark killed her. Remember, she was in the room with the dead body when I arrived? She had the gun in her hand? She was dressed like a man so that nobody would suspect her?"

His tone was slightly bemused, as if startled to discover her memory was so poor, and Bea marveled over his composure. Where had this seemingly deep reserve of equanimity come from? Only minutes ago, he had been nearly hysterical at the prospect of coming up with a female name. "You are still lying. You were hired to kill Miss Wraithe and make it appear as though Miss Lark were responsible. It was a trap and you sprung it."

Pursing his lips, Thimble scratched the side of his neck as he said, "No, I am sure that is wrong. I would never kill someone no matter how much money was offered to me because I find murder morally repellant. Do you know how many boys I have inside my home, your grace? Three. I am raising three sons, and what kind of example would I set for them if I went around killing old women for money? And I would have to be beetle-headed to make a deal with the type of reprobate who is ruthless enough to pay for murder. A clump like that would not live to see sunrise."

Bea found his poise maddening. "You may deny it with all the amused condescension you wish, Mr. Thimble, but I know you are a liar. You have already admitted it to me."

"Of course I lied! I was afraid of losing my job," he replied evenly. "But you ferreted out the truth and now there is nothing I can do but discuss it candidly and hope you are kind enough to keep the business between us. It is only a small fib, and to show my repentance, I will donate the guinea Miss Wraithe pledged to give me to charity. And you may choose! Do you have a favorite one, your grace?"

Agog at his airy confidence, Bea growled, and Kesgrave stepped forward and asked him to relate a credible sequence of events. "So far all you have managed to do is contradict yourself. In one statement you claim you were already in the room when Miss Lark arrived and in another you entered the room after Miss Lark."

Generously, Thimble conceded he had jumbled the explanation by not drawing a distinction between what Miss Wraithe requested and what he had actually delivered. "She wanted me to come at ten fifty-five so I would be there when Miss Lark arrived at eleven, but I was delayed on my walk there and got to the house a little *after* eleven."

"Delayed?" the duke asked.

"By a scuffle on the pavement just around the corner from Clement," he said with a huff of disdain. "Two women were scratching at each other like feral cats over an enamel brooch they both claimed was theirs. It was a pretty bauble with a design similar to the Prince of Wales emblem with gold filament and a mother-of-pearl coronet. It was a fancy piece, so I knew it didn't belong to either of them. When I took possession of the brooch to bring to the rotation office, they turned their claws on me, and I could not free myself for several minutes. I told them to come to the office with proof of ownership and the item would be immediately returned."

Although highly reluctant to abandon the shadowy figure theory, Bea had to concede that there were aspects of this story she found persuasive—namely, the brooch. "It is still in the rotation office?"

Amused by the question, Thimble jeered lightly and asked where else it would be. "You think her nibs came around with a receipt proving her purchase? Neither of those women can scrape together the shillings to buy a tin of Prince of Wales biscuits. They don't have the scratch to buy a fancy brooch that looks like one. Visit the office in Great Marlborough

Street. They'll confirm this. All of it! You can also ask the neighbors if they saw the scuffle. It was a noisy one and might have drawn attention."

Bea, assuring him that they would indeed verify the brooch's current location, contemplated how difficult it would be to confirm other aspects of his account. The ledger on the table had contained entries for rudimentary provisions such as eggs, gammon, and tallows. There was no line item for bribing the local Runner. Although the neighbors had made Miss Wraithe's dislike of children plain, none had mentioned tussles with law enforcement.

Recalling the feebleness of his previous lies, she sought details. "Tell me about the first bribe. How much did she give you and what did she ask you to do?"

"One guinea to arrest the eldest Cox miscreant for stealing a bottle of milk from her doorstep," he answered easily. "The second time she offered me a guinea to arrest Miranda Jones for making scratches in her front door. I don't know what happened to the milk—maybe someone did steal it—but the door was fine. It had some scratches in it by the handle, which could have been caused by someone missing the keyhole a few times. I pointed that out to Miss Wraithe and she tripled the offer to three guineas because the girl had an evil look about her, she said. If she had not destroyed her door yet, it was only a matter of time. So I took the money and arrested the girl. I put her in a cell overnight and returned her to her parents in the morning unharmed."

As the boy in question was only twelve years old, Bea felt a frisson of alarm for the girl, who was probably just as young and still plagued by nightmares from the experience. It was all well and good for Thimble to say the child emerged from the ordeal unscathed, but that was only in the physical sense, and his disregard for whatever terror she must have suffered was yet another gross violation of his duty. He was supposed to apprehend dangerous criminals, not help a vicious harridan carry out acts of petty revenge against the neighborhood children, whom she seemed to despise for being juveniles.

The brooch, Thimble's lack of fear, and the specificity of his account were fairly persuasive, and yet Bea resisted the explanation because it decimated the theory of the shadowy figure. If Miss Wraithe invited him into her home, then there was no mastermind directing the action. All the motivations she had ascribed to the killer were meaningless, and far from Miss Lark being the target of an elaborate scheme, she was merely the victim of horrible luck.

A few minutes earlier and she might have witnessed the murder itself.

A few minutes later and she would have found Thimble holding the gun.

Aghast at the revelation, Bea realized the shooting might have nothing to do with Fortescue's at all. Exasperated by Miss Wraithe's abusive treatment of the children, one of the neighbors might have decided to put an end to her cruelty. If that was the case, then they had an entire lane of suspects, including Mrs. Cox, Mr. Douglas, and little Miranda's parents.

It was a daunting prospect.

"And the third bribe?" Bea asked when the Runner fell silent. "Whom did she target that time and for how much?"

Thimble lost some of his assurance as he reworded the question. "You want to know the amount of the third bribe, do you? The third bribe. I'll tell you what it was."

But Bea recognized the evasiveness from earlier in their conversation and begged him to spare himself the trouble of lying. "There was no third bribe, was there?"

The Runner lowered his eyes to the floor and said no.

"Because it was not necessary by that point," she said assuredly. People were so predictable in their habits. If they did something once, they did it a dozen times. "She had you in her pocket by then, did she not? If you refused, all she had to do was threaten to tell your superior about the bribes."

"She used my own argument about the door against me!" he growled. "She said the magistrate would be interested in knowing how cheaply the Bow Street Runners could be bought. I had no choice. I had to agree. And I know it sounds bad to you, but it really was insignificant. I would just frighten the children. No damage done! And with Miss Lark, I was just there to threaten to arrest her. I was not actually going to do it. It was just a little harmless intimidation!"

Bea was not sure the parents would agree.

Kesgrave, seeming to follow her line of thought, asked for the names of all the children the Runner intimidated. "List them one by one along with their offenses."

Thimble complied with a petulant grimace, pointing out when he reached the end of the catalogue that there were not that many. "Only six! You see, it *was* harmless."

Only six, yes, because half the names were repeated several times. Poor Miranda Jones bore the brunt of Miss Wraithe's delusions.

As the duke secured the addresses of the six children, Bea pondered the validity of her new theory. The notion that Miss Lark was merely the victim of wretched misfortune rather than a masterful conspiracy overseen by a shadowy figure struck her as both more and less plausible.

Unquestionably, there were few true coincidences with respect to murder scenes.

But masterful conspiracies were rarer still.

If Bea had to place a wager on which unlikely event had occurred, she would put her money on the former. Happenstance required less coordination.

How, then, to account for the gun?

None of Miss Wraithe's neighbors in Clement Lane could afford to own a firearm by noted maker Bernard Michaels.

Ah, but what if it belonged to the victim? It would not be unreasonable for an elderly woman who lived alone in a ramshackle road to take the precaution of securing a weapon. She did, after all, frequently antagonize her neighbors by terrorizing their children. One of them could have reached a breaking point. Little Miranda's father, for instance, infuriated by the abuse of his daughter, might have called on Miss Wraithe to demand the end of the cruel treatment and the conversation grew heated. In a moment of rage, Mr. Jones reached for the first thing he could find—the pistol, which Miss Wraithe had put on the table in anticipation of her confrontation with Robert Lark—ordered her to sit in the chair, and shot her in the head.

A not implausible sequence of events, Bea thought, and it would explain why the gun had been left behind. It was a damning piece of evidence, and trying to extract its value by selling it would expose the culprit to the charge of theft or worse.

Examining the theory from the other side, she wondered if Miss Wraithe had money to spend on the ornate weapon. She had enough scratch to furnish her home with quality pieces, such as the settee and the chair, and to keep its interior in good repair. But it would be pure foolishness to buy something so extravagant without a regular source of income.

Or even an irregular one, Bea thought, recalling Miss Lark's speculation in regard to the former headmistress's finances becoming only recently strained. Given the comfort in which the woman had lived, her ill-gotten gains should have run out much sooner.

But they had not.

Because people were predictable in their habits, she thought again.

And it was true: Already, she had two instances of blackmail.

After giving the addresses to Kesgrave, Thimble eyed her warily and asked if their conversation could be kept between them. "It doesn't seem fair that I should lose my job for taking bribes from Miss Wraithe *after* she is dead. It was just the two. No real harm. Maybe I could buy treats for the children? My boys love comfits."

Although she did not think a handful of mint-flavored pastilles would compensate Miranda Jones for the terror of passing a night in the cells beneath the Brown Bear, Bea endorsed the plan, further noting that his sons probably also enjoyed playing games such as chuck farthing. "You could supply the coins. I recall from my own childhood crowns work best."

Unstintingly, Thimble agreed and promised to reward the children for their virtuous behavior the very next day. He also reminded her to call on the rotation office in Great Marlborough Street to confirm his story about the brooch. "You will see that everything I have said is the truth—apart from the lies I told previously. I did arrive moments after Miss Lark shot Miss Wraithe, and she was holding the gun. That is the God's honest truth. You can look all you want for the real killer, your grace, but I believe she is already in Newgate."

Another door snapped shut in the hallway, somewhere on a floor below them, and Bea listened to the shuffle of footsteps grow faint. Noncommittally, she assured the Runner that his opinion had been noted but refrained from making a spirited defense of the accused. Time would show him the error of his ways.

Until then, all she had were theories.

Stepping outside into the June night air, she shared her current one with the duke, who agreed that the deceased did indeed seem unduly fond of blackmail. If it was the first idea that occurred to her upon discovering Robert Lark's true identity, then perhaps that was because it was the idea that always occurred to her. It would certainly explain how she could spare the extra coins to torment the local children.

"Four guineas is nothing to sneeze at when you have no income," Bea said.

Kesgrave cautioned her against growing overly confident. "She might draw a pension from her time at Fortescue's."

She could not believe Miss Lark would allow such a thing to stand. "There would have been a dozen articles against it and possibly an act of Parliament to prevent it."

Well, naturally, no, for a bill could be introduced only by a member of Parliament, and no reporter, no matter how successful in rousing public opinion to his cause, could propose legislation—and even if by some deft political maneuvering such a thing could be done, it would not be done by a *female* reporter, the duke explained.

Amused by the earnestness in his voice, as though profoundly troubled by her lack of basic understanding of parliamentary procedure, Bea climbed into the carriage to return to Brompton Grove.

Chapter Eight

As they entered the small house in Clement Lane for the second time that evening, Bea reiterated her belief that it would not be difficult to find Miss Wraithe's blackmail ledger. Now that they knew there was something to look for, discovering its hiding spot would be child's play.

"It will be under the floorboard or behind a painting or under her mattress—all of the places people commonly conceal things," she continued, briskly turning into the front parlor, with its sparse furnishings. "According to Miss Lark, the victim was not bright or creative. She would make the simplistic and obvious choice."

Kesgrave, finding this statement credible, removed the painting option from contention on the grounds that the walls contained none. "There are no decorations of which to speak. I saw a mirror in her bedchamber. We can check behind that."

Looking around her now, she realized he was right. The walls were bare, the room absent of ornamentation aside from the fireplace, whose surround featured acanthus leaf capitals atop reeded side posts. Intrigued by the possibilities, she strode across the room to the hearth to begin poking and prodding. Gently, she tapped the lintel.

The duke, his head tilted to the side, asked her what she was doing.

It was, Bea thought, an unexpected question given the most recent topic of conversation. Even so, she explained that she was testing the mantel to see if it was hollow. "If so, Miss Wraithe might have hidden the ledger inside."

"Yes, Bea, that much was readily apparent from the way you were rapping your knuckles against the wood. I mean, what are you doing over there? We will start here, at the north end of the room, and work our way across to the south side in a methodical fashion. If it is under the floorboards, then we must proceed plank by plank," he said.

He spoke solemnly, soberly, his manner faintly disapproving, as though slightly aghast at her failure to instinctively comprehend the correct approach to the problem. Behind him, daylight was fading, the rays of the sun too far to the west to illuminate the room fully, his blond curls bright against the wretched pickle green of the drapes.

Somehow it was still striking, the perfection of his features, the gorgeousness of his pedantry. Of course there was only one way to search for the ledger itemizing bribery payments in the home of a venal former headmistress.

How silly of her to believe otherwise!

"You think I am being unduly rigid, but I have done this before and if you do not go quadrant by quadrant, you will eventually wind up in a fountain arguing with Poseidon about the cost of mackerel and wearing a wool skull-cap," he added matter-of-factly.

"Literal Poseidon or Hartlepool carrying a trident at a fancy dress ball?" she asked, crossing to join him near the window. As they could not inspect the same area, she positioned herself in the opposite corner.

"Worrell in our classics tutor's wig trying to make a point about the futility of studying for exams during my second year at Oxford," he replied as he lowered to his knees to examine the first board. "He stole my notes and hid them somewhere in his rooms. I was aided in my search by an excellent bottle of French brandy, and while it did little to help me locate the missing pages, it did alleviate my frustration. It also persuaded me I should always wear a fez."

"Potent stuff," she murmured.

Nodding, he slid forward as he tested two planks at a time for looseness. "Three weeks passed before I even considered taking it off. I had become convinced it was a good luck charm, as I did brilliantly on all my exams despite being egregiously ill prepared. I do not know who was more surprised: Worrell or I."

It was, Bea discovered, impossible not to be charmed by the image of the young duke assiduously applying himself to his studies as if his exam results mattered. Possessing wealth and status, he did not require an education so much as the patina of intellectual rigor, which his diploma would have conferred regardless of performance.

"I do not recall a Worrell," she said as she progressed swiftly through her own row of boards. "Have I met him?"

"He is Redhill now," Kesgrave replied, reaching the other side of the room and beginning his return.

Bea pictured a stout man with pale cheeks and a protruding front tooth with whom she had had a few brief exchanges. Apparently, age had subdued him.

Once they finished the floor, they moved onto the furniture—cabinet, settee, table—before scrutinizing the fireplace. Next, they turned their attention to the pantry and larder. Finding nothing, they headed upstairs to the bedchamber, a modest-size room with a square of red matting at the foot of the bed.

"It is here," Bea announced confidently, dropping to her knees to lift the floor covering. Beneath it were well-worn planks of a dark-stained wood, with one slightly more pock-marked than the others. She reached down to pull it out but could not establish a firm enough grip to dislodge it.

The gap between the slats was too narrow.

Rising to her feet, she examined the items on the clothes-press and spotted a narrow strip of wood. It was splintered on one end from wear.

"There you are," she said with an air of satisfaction as she clutched the slim device and carefully slipped it into the slender fissure to the left of the scarred board. The plank wiggled and popped out, revealing a deep cavity. "Eureka, as they say."

Kesgrave leaned back on his heels as Bea withdrew a small daybook from the compartment, then a stack of letters secured with a thin length of twine. "Nicely done."

"And yet still not as impressive as Flora's gargoyle discovery," she replied modestly, for Miss Wraithe had really made it as easy as possible. Even the placement of the hidey-hole in the bedchamber was evident in retrospect. She would have wanted the secret information to be close to her while she slept and inaccessible to the public.

Placing the letters beside her, she opened the daybook to the first page and noted the date: January 1, 1810. That was ten months before Robert Lark's exposé appeared in the *London Daily Gazette* and toppled the corrupt management of the asylum. As she had expected, the book contained a more truthful accounting of its owner's income and expenditures. "It goes back six years, so it begins when she was still at Fortescue's, where her costs were lower. She barely spent anything. In June, she bought chocolates and hair ribbons.

Her salary was fairly generous at ten pounds per month, so not as much as a housekeeper but more than a butler on average. Furthermore, it was supplemented by bonuses from Lord Condon. They are indicated with a little star," she said, laying the book on the floor so he could see for himself. "They appear frequently and in varying sums, as little as a few shillings in July and as much as ten guineas in September."

"Payments for the children they were selling," he said.

"Business was brisk in the fall," she noted, flipping ahead until she found the page where the pattern changed only a few days after the first devastating article appeared. "The bonuses from Lord Condon are still here. You see, look"—she pointed to a particular line, then flipped to the next page and the next—"the amount is steady at five pounds and so is the date of payment, which is the first of the month. It is the same on every page: December first, January first, February first, March first. She was blackmailing him."

"I am surprised by her restraint, for sixty pounds per year is a trifling amount for a man like Condon, who probably spends twice that on lemon ices. If she knew damning information about him, she could have collected a lot more," he said, shifting his position to get a better look at the daybook. "What does that say? The name is too long to be Condon."

Bea leaned forward to read the tight scribble at the very bottom of the page, which detailed the expenses for May. "It says Wigsworth. Charles Wigsworth and he has two stars next to his name. Let's see if he is mentioned again." She turned the page and perused September. "Yes! Here he is. He also paid Miss Wraithe a bonus of five pounds on the first of the month. Her handwriting is a little difficult to decipher, but I think it says, 'Compensation for services rendered above and beyond expected performance.'"

Kesgrave, repeating the name thoughtfully, insisted that Wigsworth was familiar to him. "But why is it so?" he asked softly with a scowl of consternation. Then his features lightened as he realized the answer. "It is on the list of supervisors given to me by Miss Drayton. Charles Wigsworth was on Fortescue's board and was made to resign along with the rest of the members."

"And what about Caroline Knowles?" she asked.

As the duke retrieved the slip of paper from his pocket, he inquired as to the extent of Knowles's gratitude.

"Also five pounds per month, starting in July," Bea replied. "No stars. One heart."

Kesgrave confirmed she was on the list of supervisors. "I trust Pritchard Dibdin and Alicia Beveridge also provided a bonus for superior service."

"Let us see," Bea said softly, starting her search from the beginning of the book. "Here is Dibdin. He began paying in July as well. A busy month for our blackmailer. Mrs. Beveridge makes her first appearance in December 1810, and that is her only appearance. She does not appear in January or February or ever again. I suppose she could have actually paid Miss Wraithe a bonus for work above and beyond, but that seems highly out of character for the victim. But if she had done something that made her vulnerable to blackmail, then she somehow managed to convince her extortioner not to bleed her."

The duke proposed a case of tit for tat. "If she had compromising information on Miss Wraithe, then their threats might have canceled each other out. Miss Wraithe's own history seems rife with opportunities for blackmail."

Bea allowed that it was a reasonable explanation, as the former headmistress was earning twenty-five pounds per month. "That is three hundred annually, and her expenses were low. The house is three crowns per month, and she spent about twenty pounds on coal. She did not require the extra money she would have gotten from Alicia Beveridge, and if she found her pockets to let, she could always increase the amount she charged her victims. Condon, per your estimation, could pay twice as much and not feel the pinch. But she did have plenty, and if she wanted to spend lavishly on an item—say, for example, a pistol from the esteemed firm of Bernard Michaels—she had the funds."

Mildly, he agreed, noting her theory regarding an irate neighbor seemed just as valid as the one positing an angry former associate. "I know how much the idea of a shadowy figure secretly controlling the action appealed to you and am impressed by how readily you are moving on to other notions despite your disappointment. That said, I think you are underestimating the extravagance of the Bernard Michaels gun while overestimating Miss Wraithe's appreciation for beautiful things. As you noted, her furniture is sturdy, presentable, and made with quality materials. But that is all it is. The design is not exceptional, and the craftsmanship is merely competent. She invested in reliable pieces that serve a useful function, and if she did own a gun, I would expect it to be an equally practical purchase."

Trusting his judgment, she suggested they task Lord Colson with investigating the neighbors while they interviewed the former supervisors. "Let us start with Alicia Beveridge. She is the anomaly, which makes her the most interesting."

Kesgrave, gathering the letters and daybook into a neat pile next to the hole, said they would call on the woman first thing in the morning, before Condon's solicitor, a pronouncement that startled Bea, who insisted there was no reason they could not visit her right then.

"It is after eight-thirty in the evening," he replied as he snapped the wood plank back into place. "That is the first reason. I am hungry, which is the second reason. The fact that you are hungry as well is the third. The fourth is you are tired. Number five is I spent a significant part of my day traveling back and forth on the London Road, suffering Hartlepool's ceaseless droning and the dust of travel, which I have yet to wash off sufficiently. Do you want me to go on? Because I can go on."

"I do not doubt it, your grace," she said with amusement as she rose to her feet and stepped to the side, allowing him to replace the floor covering. "I am certain you have reasons six through ten organized by alphabet."

He scoffed at the simplicity of the notion. "They are organized in descending order of importance, starting with number six: I have yet to speak to Marlow about your visit to Newgate."

"Aha!" she exclaimed with an air of triumph, earning a curious look from Kesgrave, who had lowered to his haunches to pick up the documents recovered from the floor. "I knew you had an issue with my going. You had a fierce grimace on your face when I entered the drawing room, and now you are going to put a prohibition on all future prison outings."

Kesgrave shook his head as he regarded her with a mixture of delight and exhaustion. "You really should hear yourself speak sometimes, Bea. *All future prison outings.* Just how many do you imagine there will be and who are you planning to visit? Or is this your scheme for securing new murders to investigate once you've exhausted your acquaintance?"

Delicately, she advised him to watch his pronouns. "For I do not think there is any arrangement of people and places that puts your former mistress in my stable."

Unable to refute the accuracy, he bowed his head docilely and said, "Touché, brat."

"But please do not take Marlow to task for accompanying me to Newgate," she added as they exited the bedchamber. "As everyone delights in reminding me, I am mistress of

Kesgrave House, and he was only complying with my request."

"I have no intention of chastising him," he said following her down the staircase. "I would like to get his impression of the situation. His perspective is different from yours—and Lord Colson's, for that matter—and might add something useful to the conversation."

A perfectly reasonable explanation, to be sure, but it failed to account for his ferocious frown, a point she made as they stepped outside. Although it would remain light for at least another hour, the sun had begun to drop in the sky.

"Well, yes, that I would attribute to the damning case against Miss Lark," he replied, smoothly locking the door with the same slim implement he had used to unlock it. "When Colson told me she had been arrested for homicide, I did not expect to hear that she had been found with her hands literally on the murder weapon. You entered only a moment later, as I was still digesting the information."

Bea felt her face flush as she realized the mortifying fault in her logic: She was not the center of his every thought. Sometimes he contemplated other things.

Of course he does, your grace. You are not that *interesting!*

Nobody was.

To hide her embarrassment, she greeted Jenkins with more enthusiasm than the circumstance required—she had last seen him forty-five minutes before, not forty-five days—and accepted his help in boarding the carriage. The heat in her cheeks began to recede as she sat down, and when Kesgrave settled on the bench across from her, she asked him if he still felt unsettled by the damning case against Miss Lark.

Taking issue with her description, he owned that he had been concerned, then gently but noticeably changed the subject by noting that the information they had found was encouraging.

Amiably, she agreed. "A cohort of blackmail victims is always a comfort."

His lips twitched faintly as he rested his head against the back cushion, the weariness he had alluded to earlier readily visible in his drawn features. "Is it?"

"Second only to a cadre of corrupt government officials," she said with a cheerful confidence she did not quite feel. Although it was a relief to have viable subjects, she knew names in a daybook were a long way from a confession, and she could not bear to think what would happen if she failed in her endeavor. There was something about the circumstance—Verity Lark's flittery existence, the way she had fluttered into the duke's life on seemingly gossamer wings—that made the investigation feel alarmingly fraught. But for an absurd provincial puppy seeking to exploit his grandfather's death to gain the attention of the worst gossip in London, Kesgrave would have lived his entire life without knowing he had a sister.

And not just any sister—a fearless adventurer who swashbuckled and spied.

The discovery itself was so disconcertingly random. People slipped by each other in the dark of night or the bustle of a crowd all the time, and there was a looming sense that it might yet happen. Verity Lark could vanish as suddenly as she had appeared.

That terrified Bea, who wanted this for the duke: a sister, family, Verity.

Even though her own relatives had been a source of pain, strife, and disappointment for the vast majority of her life, she still believed it was better to have more family than less family—doubly so when your uncle was a murderous fiend who tried to snuff out your life as a young child, your father was a cruel despot, and your mother was a self-absorbed coquette who exploited her beauty for power and spared no thought for anyone who could not further her ambitions.

They were a merry assortment indeed, a trio of cackling villains, and into this thieves' den strode Miss Verity Lark.

And it was precisely that, Bea supposed.

Something to even the scales.

Aware that the duke would continue to resist the relationship, Bea decided it would be prudent to mention her pact with the accused now so that he would not be surprised later. "Miss Lark was extremely reluctant to accept my assistance because she did not want to be beholden to me, and after a somewhat protracted negotiation, we settled on shooting lessons as the way to discharge the debt. I think it is an excellent idea, as she is an expert shot and less inclined to harbor a prejudice against armed females like Prosser. But if the prospect makes you uncomfortable, I shall take instruction at Bethel Street, and tell you I am interviewing physicians with the dowager. That is the proper parlance, is it not, for sneaking out of the house to meet Miss Lark?"

She was teasing.

It was a jest!

But rather than smile, Kesgrave tightened his jaw.

"No, Bea, no," he said firmly, his tone surprisingly genial for the flare of anger that burned in the depths of his cerulean gaze. "You do not get to tease me about the single lie I told you when you have told me half a dozen. You swear and you swear not to do something, and then you do it. One time it was even a wedding vow, a wedding vow you broke on the first day of our marriage. You could not go a full four and twenty hours without breaking your word to me, and given the great disparity in our records, I will not be subjected to raillery on the subject, however good-natured or gentle you think it."

Bea's heart collapsed.

It simply disintegrated into a million tiny specks of dust, and the hollowness inside her chest cavity made breathing oddly difficult.

Inhale, she thought.

You must inhale.

But she did not want to gasp.

A gasp would indicate something was wrong, and that would never do.

Kesgrave was allowed to criticize her.

He was allowed to object to what he correctly perceived as hypocrisy.

Determinedly, she rested her back more firmly against the cushion, both to preserve her dignity and to try to calm the tremor that shivered through her. To still her left arm, she pressed it between her body and the door. Striving for amiable, she said, "You are right, Damien. I am sorry."

It was good, she thought.

A little breathless but also sturdy, not distraught.

And she smiled.

Not brightly, for that would reveal too much, but faintly, as though vaguely amused by her own predicament.

Yes, that was it.

She was amused.

And now all she had to do was hold the pose for the rest of the carriage ride.

It would not be long now.

Maybe another twenty minutes.

If she was overwrought—and she rather thought she was, given her inability to stop the tremor no matter how much pressure she applied—it was only because she was so taken aback by his anger. She recalled in perfect detail the instances to which he referred, and what she remembered most vividly about them was his affable acceptance.

Their quarrel over her wedding vow in the Mayhews' drawing room—she thought it was banter. Truly, truly, she thought he found her absurdities charming. And when she had barged into Mr. Jordan's office to find the duke standing over his uncle's freshly slain corpse after expressly promising to stay away, she had genuinely believed his relief at her timely appearance outweighed his annoyance.

That she had mistaken his gracious resignation for whole-hearted support was clear to her now, and she would not mind being so egregiously wrong if she did not feel so wildly misled. He was welcome to his resentment. She had broken her word, and he had every right to ring a peel over her head—when it happened. The display of temper now so many months later meant he had been stewing over the insult.

And that was why she could not still her arm no matter how tightly she squeezed it against the door, because Kesgrave suddenly felt unfamiliar. He had such a gorgeous way about him, such an easygoing manner, such an appealingly light touch, but maybe that was just the gloss.

Maybe underneath it all, he seethed.

"Goddamn it, Bea," he muttered irritably as he reached across the space between them, clasped her right hand, and tugged her onto his lap. "I am tired and hungry, and it is possible that I might feel some anxiety about Miss Lark's safety, although I do not understand why you are so blasted determined to talk about it. All of that apparently makes me out of sorts, and although it is not fair of me to take my ill humor out on you, there is no reason why a flash of pique should set off a fit of vapors. How are you trembling?"

Honestly, she had no idea.

The heat from his body should have been more than enough to warm her.

Ah, but that was the rub: It was fear, not cold.

But the fear should have subsided as well.

She allowed herself one minute to burrow, pulling her limbs toward her chest as she curled her body into his. She closed her eyes and relished his reassuring solidity.

Her arms steadied.

Her heart rebuilt itself.

She pulled back, noting the wrinkle of concern between his brows, and protested the inaccuracy of his description. "I did not have a 'fit of vapors.' I was smiling, faintly, to be sure, but still smiling."

"If you mean that ghastly grin on your face, then I must disabuse you of the notion, for you looked as stiff and ghostly as a Grödnertal doll," he said flatly. "And you were pushing yourself into the corner of the carriage as if to make yourself disappear into the door. It was all very disconcerting to watch and out of proportion to the situation. Why are you so agitated? Not because I snapped at you. I am certain I have done *that* before."

Picturing the frozen smile on the popular children's toy, Bea winced and allowed that her reaction might have been immoderate.

"Might have been?" he repeated with vague amusement. "You withered, Bea, and I did not even raise my voice."

She acknowledged the truth as she struggled to explain the strange panic that had overcome her. "It felt to me as though you were airing an old grievance, something long since resolved, and I thought, Oh, no, he seethes. And then I wondered what other resentments you held and if they too would suddenly snarl with fury out of seemingly nowhere and would I always have to be on my guard against them."

"Your mind, how it races," he murmured, laying a gentle kiss on her forehead.

"I can assure you, the great galloping leaps it takes are no pleasure for me either," she replied with sardonic hauteur.

Kesgrave pressed another kiss on the top of her head as

his arms tightened around her. Then he shifted her position so that she was next to him on the bench, his blue eyes somber as he considered her silently for several seconds. Then he admitted that he might seethe. "Not very often and not over minor slights. But some insults smart long after they should, and I am as vulnerable to the sting as the next man. In this case, I do feel some guilt about lying to you and as such it is a poor subject for teasing. I did lash out briefly, and although I could have aired my objection differently, I find myself more troubled by your tendency to think the worst. It is of a piece with the mistress conversation, I think, and it feels as though you are looking for some great flaw to validate a prior conception, which I do not think is fair."

Well, naturally, yes, Bea thought.

Of course one part of her brain was tensed and ready for the next, seemingly unbearable blow. He was the Duke of Kesgrave: a pompous pedant whose wealth and status afforded him every advantage, whose handsome visage and pleasing form earned him fawning praise from every quarter. He had been pampered and petted and assured of the correctness of all his opinions, and yet he was somehow the most delightful human being she had ever known.

By rights, he should be a monster.

"I thought you would make an excellent murderer," she said.

Showing no alarm at this unsettling non sequitur, he demonstrated his astonishing affability by saying with only a hint of interest, "Did you?"

"When we met, at Lakeview Hall, you were my first suspect," she continued in the same neutral tone. "That was inevitable because you *were* standing over Otley's slain corpse, and an impertinent spinster does have to begin her investigation somewhere. But I was also unnerved by your perfection, and I do not mean just your physical appearance. I barely knew you and already your sense of humor, your ability to laugh at yourself, took my breath away. Something about your flawlessness struck me as inhuman, and I wondered if you might seek out horrible things as a way to counter your own insufferable perfection. And here we are, all these months later, and I am still unnerved."

It was harder than she had expected, maintaining her equanimity while he contemplated her with those cerulean eyes wide with amazement. Then concern glimmered in their depths, and she resisted the urge to stare down at her hands.

Staunchly, she said, "I know it is unfair to you and promise to do better. The good news is, we are making steady progress, Damien. It has been almost a year since I feared you might be a fiendish murderer. And we ticked inconstant husband off the list earlier in the month, and now we can remove seether. At this rate, I predict that we will have exhausted all the options by the new year."

At this encouraging report, he displayed no amusement. If anything, his frown deepened and he said, "It is the same for me, Bea."

"Obviously, your grace," she said with an amiable nod. "I was standing over Otley's murdered corpse as well, and you had to begin *your* investigation somewhere."

Now he smiled faintly. "No, brat, I mean trusting my good fortune. It serves no purpose, but sometimes I tease myself by imagining a world in which we never met. It seems a little too capricious to me, the way we both happened to be in the library at the exact right moment, and I picture the dour Miss Hyde-Clare who sat across from me at the dinner table and think that might have been it. I would have forgotten her existence before my horse had even left the drive and lived my entire life without seeing your impish grin."

Bea's heart, so recently mended, seemed to rupture from fullness as she grappled yet again to comprehend the breadth of his perfection. Effortlessly, he had responded to her revelation in kind, somehow making her feel as though the outrageous fortune was not all on her side.

Dizzy with happiness, she flung herself at him, her lips capturing his as her hands slid up his chest to wrap around his neck. Her desire for him felt oddly voracious, as though it had been months since she had touched him instead of mere hours, and she shifted her position, climbing back on his lap to draw as close as possible.

It was lovely, so lovely, the warmth of him under her hands, the clever play of his lips, and she sighed in expectation of pleasure.

But it would not do.

No, it would never do.

And not just because they were in the carriage minutes from home.

Jenkins's blushes must be spared, to be sure, but Kesgrave was tired and hungry and she owed letters to Lord Colson, Miss Drayton, and the dowager.

Satisfaction could wait.

They would have dinner in the library, within fumbling distance of the settee, and they could resume their activities as soon as other obligations had been met.

But they were not home yet, she thought, tilting her head back as the duke's lips wandered from her ear to her jaw to her neck, continuing downward.

Gasping for breath as wonderful sensations danced through her, Bea trembled again.

Chapter Nine

By nine-thirty the next morning, the duke's steward had not only found Alicia Beveridge's address but also gathered a dozen relevant facts about her, which he compiled in a brief report: She was two and thirty and of the Essex Gielguds. She had been married to William Beveridge for eleven years and had served as a supervisor for Fortescue's for three and a half before ignominiously resigning with her fellow members of the board. She had two children, both girls, ages five and nine, and was distantly related to Lord Castlereagh through her mother's side. She had been presented to society by Mrs. Pardoe and received five proposals of marriage.

Finding this detail extremely dubious, Bea raised her eyes from the sheet Kesgrave had handed her upon her arrival to the breakfast room. "How could Stephens possibly know the number of marriage proposals she had? He is just making up things now, is he not? He fears falling short of your outsize expectations and thinks it is better to write any old thing than to present a sparse account."

Untroubled by the accusation, he refilled his mug with

coffee before procuring a slice of gammon. As he passed the platter to her, he said, "One of the pleasures of employing a competent steward is not having to question the competence of my steward. If you doubt the accuracy of the information, then you are encouraged to question him about his sources. But do leave me out of it. Stephens knows exactly what I expect of him, and it is in line with his abilities."

"Yes, your grace, I noticed your use of the passive 'are encouraged,' as though it were not you who offered the encouragement," she said with a lilt of amusement. "Your fear of offending the servants has been well documented and does not require mention."

"And yet you persist in mentioning it," he replied with an air of disapprobation. "Whatever Stephens's methods are for gauging the social success of a young woman, I am sure they are impeccable."

Bea, whose queasiness was most intense upon rising, decided she could stomach the ham and placed a thin slice next to her shirred eggs. "Did his research reveal the ideal time to call on Mrs. Beveridge or are we to try our luck with a morning visit?"

The duke, dabbing gently at the side of his mouth with a serviette, said the latter. "The report notes that her activities remain curtailed by the scandal, although not as severely as when news of it first became public, so I think we may reasonably expect her to be at home."

"Yes, I see," Bea said as she glanced down at the sheet and perused the next item on the list. "She enjoys a regular Wednesday evening game of whist, at which she takes an average of eight tricks. Eight tricks, Damien, really?"

Kesgrave returned her skeptical gaze with a blank stare for several seconds before gesturing to the envelopes at her elbow. "You have missives from your aunt and Tilly."

Her lips tightened into a scowl as she glared at the

envelopes, of which she had been perfectly aware. She had recognized both her relative's handwriting and Lady Abercrombie's cloying perfume the moment she had entered the room. Rather than acknowledge either his comment or the letters, she asked if he had received a reply from Lord Colson, to whom she had sent a lengthy missive sharing their progress and assigning him tasks the evening before.

Kesgrave admitted he had heard nothing, then added that he did not expect a response. "He has all the information he needs to find out if Thimble was telling the truth about the brooch and Miss Wraithe's treatment of the neighbors' children."

"And Miss Drayton?" she asked, curiously inspecting the table for another envelope or small card. "There is no word from her either?"

Highly entertained, he said there was not, but he could send Joseph to Bethel Street to request a detailed response to the informative missive Bea had sent the night before. "So you will have an excuse not to read the notes from your aunt and Tilly."

Bristling, she said she did not need an excuse. "I can simply not read them."

"Of course," he murmured amiably, making no attempt to hide his mirth.

"I do not need to read them because I already know what they say. They're more questions about our stay at Haverill Hall," she complained with a petulant moue. "Aunt Vera keeps asking how I am going to manage various aspects of overseeing the stately home, such as the pinery and Turkish bath, as Welldale House has neither and she cannot fathom how both would not require an overwhelming amount of care and attention. And Lady Abercrombie has been pressing for a week to see a plan of the nursery so she can advise me on the staff I will need for the cherub."

"That is easy enough. Just ask Stephens."

Her peevishness turned hostile as she snapped, "I did! And he gave me drawings for an entire wing. I do not see why an infant requires an entire wing."

"To be fair, the nursery occupies only one floor of the wing," he said reasonably.

Bea did not appreciate the clarification. "Your house is obnoxiously large, your grace. Nobody should own a home so colossal that an infant has an entire floor to himself, and if you had any decency at all, you would donate it to the village and live in a cottage with a normal-size nursery."

"But think of the staff!" he said provocatively. "If you are already tripping over Marlow in this house, which you have described on several occasions as a palatial concern, just imagine how awkward it would be in a cottage. Here, have some berries."

She glared at him.

Kesgrave resumed eating gammon.

James entered with a cream-colored letter and held it out to Bea.

"Now, that is more like it," she said, eagerly accepting the note, which she immediately unfolded and began to read. "It is from Mr. Somerset Reade, Miss Lark's friend and the editor of the *London Daily Gazette.* He wanted to introduce himself and thank us for our efforts on Miss Lark's behalf. He also appreciates our kindness and consideration in informing Miss Drayton of our progress. He remains hopeful of a satisfactory conclusion to his friend's ordeal and begs us to send word if there is anything he can do to aid our investigation."

"That was very well done," Kesgrave said as he raised the mug to his lips.

"Indeed, yes, his manners are excellent," she agreed with a light sneer in her tone as she expressed surprise that a man who knew how to act with civility would not only employ an odious gossip but also give him an opportunity to spread his abhorrent lies.

It was on the tip of her tongue to add her theory regarding Lord Colson, for it dovetailed nicely with her previous comment and even suggested an answer: It would be the height of folly and perhaps even professional malfeasance to refuse the services of the Marquess of Ware's son. If the offspring of a powerful lord proposed to contribute to your newspaper, you accepted his offer with alacrity and asked how many column inches he required.

She held her peace, however, because she still could not decide if her hypothesis was inane or insightful, and there were other, more pressing issues to discuss.

Finishing their breakfast, the duke called for Jenkins to bring around the carriage and Bea tucked the pair of unopened letters in the escritoire in her bedchamber, where they joined the chart, other unopened letters, and a brief missive from Flora asking if Haverill Hall really had a hammam. Although amused by her cousin's display of erudition, for she could have learned the foreign word for "Turkish bath" only through extensive research, she was nevertheless unnerved by the insidious subtext. Flora was clearly angling for an invitation, and Bea could not bear the thought of having to make another person feel at home in a place where she herself felt like a trespasser.

But that was another problem for another day, she thought, sliding the drawer shut with perhaps more force than necessary.

Outside, she found Kesgrave waiting beside the carriage, and she boarded with his help after bidding Jenkins a cheerful good morning. As Mrs. Beveridge lived in a neighborhood adjacent to Mayfair, the journey did not take long and twenty minutes later they arrived at a tidy redbrick on a corner lot. Their knock was answered by a properly dour butler who accepted Bea's card with a brisk nod and asked them to wait in the entry. Then he strode halfway down the corridor and disappeared through a door to the left. Only ten or so seconds later, a woman came flying out of the room, a scarlet shawl fluttering in the breeze as she raced toward them.

"Goodness gracious, we cannot do this here," she hissed, her eyes darting left and right with agitation. "Come, we must go somewhere he won't look. Not the dining room because he has not had his breakfast yet. The square?" She eyed the door consideringly for a moment before shaking her head. "The neighbors will see! Let us adjourn to the stillroom. He would never think to check there."

Although bewildered by the extremity of the response, Bea agreed to this proposal and followed her host to the servants' area.

Mrs. Beveridge was a small woman with a narrow frame, blonde hair, and light blue eyes. Her walking gown was plain and unadorned, with only a trim of rosettes along the bodice, but the simplicity suited her as did the deep pink color. Her manner was likewise without fuss, and as soon as she closed the door to the room, she said, "I must apologize, of course, for the abysmal treatment, for I know it is not the thing to entertain guests belowstairs. But I had to do something! After six years in exile, I have begun to claw myself back to respectability, and I cannot allow a visit from the murder duchess to undo all my good work. I hope you understand."

Whatever understanding Bea may or may not have extended to the situation was pushed aside by Mrs. Beveridge's description.

The murder duchess.

Good Lord, was *that* what people were calling her now?

It struck her as ten times worse than Her Outrageousness.

Appalled to discover she could ever be grateful to Mr.

Twaddle-Thum for his subtlety, she forced herself to focus on the situation and ignore her great unease. Considering Mrs. Beveridge's bizarre behavior, she assumed the woman knew about Miss Wraithe's murder and resented being counted among the suspects.

"My husband is determined to be unreasonable," Mrs. Beveridge continued as she fetched a chair from the corner and dragged it toward the table, where it joined two others. "He has a horribly suspicious mind and delights in thinking the worst of me. If he sees the pair of you, he will assume I have done something beyond the pale, and that will lead to weeks of recriminations. It is simply less painful for me to host the Duke and Duchess of Kesgrave in my stillroom than endure William's displeasure. Now let us sit down and get this over with. Who is dead, how were they killed, and why in God's name do you think it has anything to do with me?"

Although Kesgrave could not have spent much time in his own stillroom, let alone regularly conduct conversations in it, he accepted her offer with gracious ease and sat down on the hard wooden stool as though it were an elegant bergère.

Hesitantly, Bea followed suit, pitching slightly backward in the wobbly chair. As she shifted forward to counter the uneven legs, she answered the questions in rapid succession. "Agnes Wraithe, shot in the back of the head, you are not among the cohort of former supervisors from Fortescue's whom she was blackmailing."

Mrs. Beveridge's eyes widened first in surprise and then in horror before narrowing with confusion. "I am not being blackmailed by Aggie and *that* is why you are interested in me? I must marvel at the perversity of your worldview that you would find a woman's virtue cause for suspicion."

"You made one payment, in December 1810, which is anomalous to the other entries in her daybook," Bea explained as she wondered at the source of the other woman's defensiveness. It could be a sign of guilt. Having gone to some lengths to ensure Verity Lark hanged for her crime, it would be highly unnerving to discover her own head so close to the noose. But it could also indicate general discomfort at being interviewed by the murder duchess, with her perverse worldview. "And I find all anomalies suspicious. Furthermore, you *were* among the cohort exploiting the orphaned children in the care of Fortescue's for your own profit, so I am not sure how accurate the term *virtue* is as a description."

Mrs. Beveridge's cheeks turned bright pink at mention of her perfidy, and although her brows darkened with belligerence, she revealed no hostility in her reply. "I have no cause to argue with you, your grace, because I have done nothing wrong. I did not murder Aggie. You are correct to be suspicious because she made the same blackmail attempt on me as the others. After those awful articles came out and we were all forced to scatter to dark corners in shame, she threatened to share damaging information about me to my husband. She demanded five pounds per month to hold her silence, and although that is not a remarkably large amount, I simply could not pay it. William is particularly miserly with my pin money. He will not give me a farthing unless I tell him precisely what it is for and why and provide receipts. As you can imagine, it is intolerable to be kept on a tight leash. It is why I was forced to turn a blind eye to the exploitation of the orphans in the first place. I could not risk losing the opportunity to take a percentage of the donations I raised. It was only fair, as I was doing all that hard work of asking and cajoling and flattering—so much flattering! I once told Patricia Stock that her daughter was the embodiment of elegance and grace just as the clumsy girl was tripping over the hem of her own dress and spilling red wine on my carpet. A woman deserves compensation for all that as well as *some* small amount of money to buy fripperies. Asking my husband for five pounds a month would be tantamount to telling him I was being blackmailed. With that in mind, I proposed another arrangement."

Given how assiduously the victim pursued extortive payments, Bea found it difficult to believe she would be receptive to anything other than cash. "And what was that?"

"Friendship," she replied with a grin that was as amused as it was self-satisfied. "Aggie was a simple woman with an uncomplicated outlook on life: She was the victim. Perennially abused and ill-treated, she had no choice but to resort to blackmail to regain what had been taken from her by a corrupt system. All she was trying to do was reset the scales, which were tilted against her, and it was to my benefit to encourage these beliefs. Nobody ever had before, so it was easy enough to do. I let her rail against the various injustices she was forced to suffer and offered comfort when necessary and outrage when appropriate. All she really wanted was a warm body to listen to her. She was so lonely, the poor thing. I do not think she would ever admit it, but she missed those orphans dreadfully. Nothing gave her more pleasure than punishing a small child for a minor offense. I invited her here for tea a few weeks in a row, and after the third week, I never heard another word about blackmail. So I paid just the one installment, which was, I assure you, difficult to hide from my husband. I had to take money from a secret tin of coins my housekeeper keeps in her office to pay for minor expenses! But William is so impressed with the charitable impulse that led me to befriend a disagreeable, lonely woman like Aggie. He considers it penance for my sins, which I suppose it is. But of course he has no idea *which* sin. That would discomfit him hugely."

A weekly tea was no small commitment, and Bea felt confident her hostess would not mention it if her servants could not verify the information. As such, she assumed it was true and proceeded to ask when was the last time she had seen Miss Wraithe.

"Five days ago," she replied without pausing to review dates. "With a few exceptions, she came every Monday at one and stayed for about an hour, although sometimes she lingered for as many as two. It depended on how ill-used or imposed upon she felt. Some days were worse than others."

"How aggrieved did Miss Wraithe feel on Monday?" Bea asked.

"Fully," Mrs. Beveridge replied succinctly before adding, "The whole world was aligned against her, and she finally had proof. She was positively giddy."

Fascinated, Bea leaned forward in her chair, which lurched with the shifting weight, and wondered what conspiracy Agnes had discovered that validated her skewed understanding of the world. "Did she tell you what she had learned?"

"In great detail," Mrs. Beveridge confirmed. "I do not think she could have been coy about it even if she tried. She was bursting to tell someone. It had to do with the articles, the ones in that wretched newspaper that ruined us all. Aggie was convinced that she was the singular target of the stories, which was absurd, for Connie had gotten the worst of it, and it was no picnic for me, either."

"Connie?" Bea asked.

"Lord Condon, Fortescue's patron whose behavior was deplorable," she clarified. "Anyone who followed the scandal would agree that he suffered the most because his sins were the greatest. I think it is clear from the reporting that Aggie was merely his subordinate carrying out his dastardly scheme. But Aggie was determined to believe her suffering was greater because she was forced to flee to a drafty little house in a mean little road in London while he returned to his comfortable estate in Ireland. She had no comprehension of the social cost of the scandal. She understood it only in material terms."

"The information she discovered actually confirmed her supposition?" Bea asked. "Was she in fact the intended target?"

Mrs. Beveridge trilled lightly at the notion and shook her head. "But you could not tell Aggie a thing when her mind was made up to it, and I had nothing to gain by correcting her. As usual, I just sat quietly while she blathered about the crimes against her. I did, however, point out that blackmailing a reporter was perhaps not the cleverest response, as you know how those wretches are, always digging around in decent people's business. I told her if she tried to blackmail this Lark woman, then the reporter *would* make Aggie the target of her work and the truth would come out about her dealings with Connie and the others. I told her to leave well enough alone, but she would not. She had taken it into her head to open a school for children. It had been long enough since the debacle at Fortescue's and, as I said, she missed having children to order around, as well as a staff. Aggie adored being in charge! I told her it was a horrible idea. She was too old, for one thing. Aggie was sixty if she was a day. But also, I did not think enough time had passed since the scandal. She was adamant that she could find a little village in Surrey, which is where she was from, and nobody would recognize her name or question her expertise. She was sure the plan was a sound one, and I said nothing more. It was not my place to change her mind when she was set on doing something, especially when it would ultimately benefit me, but I thought both ideas were disastrous."

A horrifying prospect, Miss Wraithe's new school would have never come to fruition, Bea thought. Verity Lark would have come up with some way to scotch the plan even if it meant founding a newspaper in the area—*Surrey Daily Gazette*

—and relentlessly publishing articles about the venal headmistress.

Kesgrave, noting Miss Wraithe's certainty that she was the target of Robert Lark's reportage, asked what evidence she had cited as proof.

"It was this Lark woman," Mrs. Beveridge repeated, her smile tightening as she struggled, it seemed to Bea, to hold on to her patience. "The articles are credited to a man named Robert Lark, but Aggie learned that Robert Lark does not exist. There is only this Lark woman working with the editor of the newspaper who was bent on destroying her for some imagined wrong in her childhood. It was just more Aggie nonsense. She could rattle on for days. It could become quite tedious. Feathers says I should pay her. She says five pounds a month not to listen to her whining is a bargain. But it is easy for her to say because her husband is not a suspicious skinflint."

At this description of her spouse, Bea found herself wondering about the four suitors Miss Gielgud had refused. Had they been manifestly worse or had Mr. Beveridge represented himself as more liberal-minded than he actually was?

"Feathers?" Kesgrave asked.

"Harriet Featherstone-Haughton, kindred spirit and my sworn confidant. Our friendship was forged in the desperate fire of tragedy, and for three years now she has listened to me grumble about Aggie's visits. I do not know what I would do without her steady hand guiding me," Mrs. Beveridge said with a heavy, sentimental sigh. "And because she has been a patient and understanding listener, she knew it was a waste of breath to try to warn Aggie away from anything, let alone one of her beloved blackmail schemes. Even so, she said it was to my credit that I made the effort to protect Aggie from her own worst impulses. Dear Feathers! I wish I could have spared her all this drivel, but I had to tell someone and obviously William would never do. The truth is, I do not think she really minds because if she did, she would offer to pay the five pounds herself. She could well afford it, as *her* husband practically throws money at her."

Taking note of Mr. Beveridge's miserliness, as his spouse intended, Bea contemplated adding him to their list of suspects. Blackmail could very quickly become a costly proposition, and the implication was he would resent paying it. If he realized his wife's frequent caller possessed damaging information that could further harm his name, he might have come up with a more permanent solution than a weekly appointment for tea. Mrs. Beveridge was convinced he had no idea about the extortion, but she would not be the first woman who believed she had successfully hoodwinked her spouse.

Although the idea was worth exploring, Bea did not yet allow herself to digress. First, she wanted to understand the victim's frame of mind during her visit earlier in the week. "Miss Wraithe's proof was the fact that the reporter who wrote the articles was a woman, not a man? That was the extent of it?"

"Precisely!" her hostess exclaimed. "A woman named Verity Lark rather than a man named Robert Lark who could be traced back to Fortescue's. That is why she was convinced the newspaper stories were a conspiracy against her. But hundreds of children passed through the doors of the asylum during her tenure and they must be scattered across dozens of occupations. It would be stranger if none of them ended up working at a newspaper. It goes without saying that I did not make this observation, as it was not my place."

"Do you know how she found out about Verity Lark?" Bea asked, amazed that so many words had been said on the subject and yet that significant detail had not been revealed. "Did she tell you?"

Mrs. Beveridge raised her shoulders in a gentle shrug. "Some fussy old crone."

"Excuse me?" Bea asked, not comprehending.

But next to her Kesgrave stiffened.

He understood what she did not, and it was only when their host elaborated that Bea realized whom the words described. "That is what she said. Some fussy old crone sent her solicitor to ask her about the treatment of one of her charges. Aggie knew the child as Mary Price, the by-blow of one lightskirt or another, but the solicitor called her Lark, Verity Lark. Aggie recognized the surname immediately, and it was all she needed to uncover the truth. I know she explained in great detail how she arrived at all her deductions, but I won't sit before you and pretend I listened. Sometimes the only way I could get through a two-hour tête-à-tête with dear Aggie was to tune her out and make noises about something being monstrously unfair whenever she paused to inhale."

The revelation of the dowager duchess's part in the affair was stunning, and Bea looked at the duke to see how he had received the news. His expression, alas, was inscrutable, and she wondered if he was struck by the same wild implausibility as she: Every attempt his grandmother made to ease the misery of Mary Price's life only worsened it.

It all seemed strangely cursed.

Bea did not need to know the particulars of Miss Wraithe's process to perceive how she followed the trail of evidence back to Miss Lark. Realizing another former charge was editor of the newspaper, she would have easily imagined the rest. Knowing herself already to be the victim no doubt made everything instantly clear.

The validation would have delighted her.

No wonder she was giddy.

"You said your husband does not know about the blackmail. How can you be sure?" Bea asked.

Mrs. Beveridge smiled faintly and said, "Because I am here answering your questions, your grace, which I would not be able to do if William had an inkling Aggie possessed compromising information. Rather, I would be near Birmingham, in a hovel on the edge of his estate, growing my own potatoes and slowly starving to death because I do not know how to grow potatoes. He forgave three thoughtless dalliances and has no intention of forgiving a fourth. It is why my access to funds is so restricted. He is convinced penury will keep me out of trouble. It is also why we are talking in the stillroom. He must not have any cause to question the worthiness of all my choices, and the presence of the murder duchess in his own home would make him think I had somehow gotten myself entangled in a murder. For a man of breeding and wealth, he has a remarkably coarse mind. One would think he was educated at the village school rather than Eton and Cambridge."

Although this explanation was far from conclusive, Bea placed the husband at the bottom of her list. She would reconsider his guilt if all of the blackmail victims had alibis and none of the neighbors in Brompton Grove roused Lord Colson's suspicions. Before it came to that, however, she would have to discover what damaging information Miss Wraithe knew about her former associates.

"Wouldn't you like to know!" Mrs. Beveridge said with a light trill, then admitted she was in the same boat. "I made multiple attempts to discover what horrible things they had done and was rebuffed. Aggie would get a wary look in her eye and stop speaking for several minutes. The silence was always a little eerie because she was usually so loquacious. I think she thought I wanted to extort them as well because William is so clutch-fisted and I need some way to have money for myself. But it was mere curiosity. My own sin was tame, and I wanted to know if their peccadillos were also mild. Presumably, yes? I cannot imagine Wiggy—Charles Wigsworth, another former supervisor—stepping out of line, for he is an even-tempered man of science. Caro, my dear friend Caroline Knowles, is a kind and gentle soul, a widow well before her time. And Mr. Dibdin is old, too old to cause anyone harm. The person I do wonder about is Connie. The articles contained so much damaging information about him that I am astonished to know there is anything left to hide. So it must be very horrendous. She had just raised all the monthly payments to ten pounds—to raise the funds for her school as quickly as possible—and Connie is the only one who agreed without protesting. All the others argued. Aggie did not like that!"

"But she could not be surprised they resisted," Bea said, pointing out that ten pounds was double the original amount. "That is not an insignificant increase."

Mrs. Beveridge shook her head and said Bea misunderstood. "Aggie was angry about Connie. If he did not complain, then it must mean she had not asked for enough, which made her feel as though *he* had taken advantage of *her*. She spent at least a half hour complaining about it. I did not see what the fuss was about because she could raise the price again if it bothered her so much. It was blackmail, for goodness' sake, and not constrained by any dictates of decency. But that was Aggie, always the victim, as I said. And now she actually *is* a victim. I do not think she would appreciate the irony, but Feathers will. I must write to her immediately. Are we done, your graces, or do you have more questions for me? Please bear in mind it has been almost forty-five minutes, and William will soon begin to wonder where I am."

Thanking the other woman for her patience, Bea promised she was nearly done. "Given your comments, I assume Miss Wraithe had proof you were having an affair with someone unsuitable. Is that correct?"

Flinching, Mrs. Beveridge accused her of having a sordid little mind. "Andrew was perfectly suitable for an affair. The gardener at Fortescue's, he was young, handsome, and strong, which made him the ideal paramour. But Beveridge would bristle at the insult to his honor, as if *I* have none! He is a beast of hypocrisy, as you may be sure he dallies himself with enthusiasm and frequency."

Bea nodded and asked her where she was the day before at eleven in the morning.

Mrs. Beveridge did not like this query either, and her lips pinched in response to the murder duchess's impertinence. Nevertheless, she stated that she was at home at the time of dear Aggie's murder, attending to her correspondence. Where else would she be?

"And that is all, yes? You will leave now and spare me a scene with my husband?"

Graciously, Bea told Mrs. Beveridge that she was free to leave if she wished. "But the duke and I have to interview key members of your staff to confirm your alibi."

This information greatly disturbed her host, who begged them not to talk to her servants. "Please, please, you must not! If you do, I will never be able to keep your presence a secret. The butler will say nothing, but my lady's maid is a chatterbox. It is why William hired her."

"It cannot be avoided," Bea replied.

But Mrs. Beveridge, who had endured the discomfort of her own stillroom for almost an hour in an explicit bid to evade exposure, refused to accept that some sort of compromise could not be reached between them. They were all rational creatures.

Could the duchess perhaps disguise her identity?

"I shall fetch a scarf and you could throw it over your

head so that your face is partially hidden in shadow and the duke can hide in the butler's pantry," she suggested eagerly before recalling that the room had windows that overlooked a busy hallway.

The wine cellar would be ideal.

Would his grace object to passing some time in the wine cellar? "You may avail yourself of any of its contents save for the Martell, which is William's favorite. But I would beg you to enjoy any other vintage that takes your fancy."

His grace did object, quite stridently in fact, and, dismissing her proposals with flagrant contempt, he said the duchess would conduct the interviews without subterfuge. Then he called for Mrs. Beveridge to summon the housekeeper so that his wife may begin the process of confirming the suspect's account. "While that is happening, you will remain in the room. Do take your chair to the corner and sit there silently. Anything you say will be understood as an attempt to influence the proceedings. Is that clear?"

"As crystal," Mrs. Beveridge snapped, rising to her feet as she recognized the futility of either the gambit or further argument. She dragged the heavy wooden stool across the floor and settled it in the corner, as directed. Then she sat down, clasped her hands in her lap, and asked if her placement was acceptable to the duke. "You did not mean for me to *face* the corner, did you, your grace?"

Kesgrave assured her it was fine as Bea stepped out of the room to find the housekeeper, who had been hovering near the doorway, clearly puzzled as to why her humble stillroom was suddenly the site of so much illustriousness. Briefly, Bea explained, and although her account contained only the most pertinent details, Mrs. Beveridge whimpered. She otherwise held her peace and allowed Bea to gather the information she and the duke required.

A half hour later, they had confirmed every aspect of Mrs.

Beveridge's story except her claim to have been attending to her correspondence during the time of the morning. Her lady's maid said the mistress was an indifferent letter writer who spent more time staring blankly into space than composing replies.

"It drives her mother batty," she added, noting that all Mrs. Gielgud wanted was news about the welfare of her granddaughters. "She worries they are not getting a proper education because their governess does not speak fluent French despite what it said on her letters of reference."

A chatterbox indeed, Bea thought.

Thanking Mrs. Beveridge for her time, Bea proposed they leave via the servants' entrance, as it was more discreet than the front door.

The hostess's only response was a wan smile.

Chapter Ten

Lord Condon's solicitor, who could have no reason to anticipate a call from the Duke and Duchess of Kesgrave, greeted them with an air of placid expectation, as though they had arrived at the appointed hour, and invited them to tea.

"I have just laid it out," Edmond Ellis said as he swept them into his office, an elegant room with beamed ceilings and gilt mirrors. Gesturing to a cluster of chairs toward the right side of the room, he invited them to sit down as he strode to the sideboard and retrieved two more cups and saucers. "I wish I had biscuits to offer as well, but I am afraid I finished the tin last night. I should have returned home for dinner but was close to being done with something, so I stayed long after it was advisable."

Hesitantly, Bea lowered to the cushion and wondered if the solicitor had been warned of their visit in advance. Given the state of their investigation, the only person who might have known Ellis was their next call was Mrs. Beveridge and that poor woman had seemed too consumed by her own anxiety to worry about someone else's troubles. Furthermore, she and Kesgrave had come directly there from Bickenhall Street, which did not allow enough time for Mrs. Beveridge to compose a letter and have it delivered by her footman.

Lord Colson, perhaps? He might have decided to press the lawyer for information about the former patron before proceeding to Brompton Grove to question Miss Wraithe's neighbors.

"Here we go," Ellis said softly as he placed the china on the table and sat down across from Bea and the duke. Pouring the tea into the delicate cups, he observed that Grundy and Furst were extremely diligent. "I have had the pleasure of associating with them both socially and professionally, and I have a great deal of respect for them. I would never imply that the quality of their work has declined as their popularity has increased. Instead, I would wonder if their success has allowed some of their most important clients to feel a trifle neglected. It is only to be expected when a firm expands as quickly as theirs has."

Baffled by the direction of the conversation, Bea looked at Kesgrave, who apologized to Ellis for giving him the wrong impression. He remained satisfied with the men who oversaw his legal affairs in London. "Rather, we are here to inquire about Lord Condon."

Whatever disappointment Ellis might have felt at this reply was masked by the thoughtful look that swept across his features as he repeated the name. "It is true that I look after his business matters in England and he is satisfied with my work, to which I am confident he would be happy to attest if you require references before retaining my services. Or does my client own shares in a company or venture you wish to join? If so, I would advise you to have Mr. Grundy or Mr. Furst contact me—unless they are too busy to do that according to your preferred schedule. If that is the situation, then I must urge you to reconsider your representation."

The duke further clarified that they were gathering information about a former associate of Condon's, a woman called Agnes Wraithe. "She was headmistress at Fortescue's Asylum for Pauper Children during Lord Condon's tenure as patron."

"You do not have to identify her to me," Ellis replied tartly. "I am considerably more familiar with Agnes Wraithe than I have any wish to be."

"I am sure you are," Bea murmured, realizing the solicitor must discharge the monthly debt on behalf of his client. "You will be able to help us, then."

Ellis, pinning her with his dark gaze, said absolutely not. "I cannot discuss any matter that pertains to a client without his express permission. To that end, I advise his grace to have Mr. Grundy or Mr. Furst send a letter to Lord Condon detailing his area of interest and what he hopes to discover. We can resume this conversation when I have his lordship's authority to speak freely."

Even at its most expedited, this prescribed course of action would take at least a week to execute, which made it an unfeasible solution—and not only because it wasted valuable time. Lord Condon was unlikely to grant his approval. He had no motivation to expose himself to the ugliness of a murder investigation, especially if he was in some way involved in the shooting.

Aware of the futility of a protracted discussion, Bea asked the duke to name a minor legal concern that he could entrust to Ellis. "There must be something small that he can quickly settle for you, such as a dispute over a boundary line on one of your properties? Or he could send a letter on your behalf to Lady Abercrombie informing her that the plans to Haverill House are the private property of the Matlock estate and that, if she continues to press for them, you will be compelled to take legal action against her."

The duke, his lips twitching in amusement, insisted that

any lawyer who agreed to pursue such a frivolous and ill-conceived lawsuit deserved to be struck from the rolls. Nevertheless, her objective was clear, and he was certain there was some thorny issue among the estate's many dealings that could benefit from Mr. Ellis's care and experience.

"There," Bea said, turning back to the solicitor. "Kesgrave would like to hire you to represent him in an important legal matter. As he and Lord Condon are both clients of yours, I trust you will not mind answering a few questions regarding his lordship's arrangement with one of his former associates at the orphanage."

Oh, but Ellis did mind.

Benefiting himself at his client's expense was a violation of his ethical code, and his expression underwent several changes—from decisive to confused to annoyed to resigned—as he struggled to arrive at a solution that aligned with his conscience. Finally, he said, "I do not mind answering a few questions as long as it is only on the agreed-upon topic."

Appreciating a reasonable parameter, Bea said they were interested in Condon's relationship with Miss Wraithe. "You have already admitted to a familiarity with her."

"She calls on my office on the first day of every month to collect a payment of five pounds from his lordship, usually before I or my clerk has arrived," he said, his lips twisting in a moue of distaste either at the expenditure itself or the eagerness with which it was sought. "She is a volatile woman with unusual reactions to things. When I told her Lord Condon had happily acceded to her request for a five-pound increase starting in July, she grew irate. She even had the audacity to accuse me of trying to cheat her out of funds that were rightfully hers. That is when she smashed the lovely creamware vase on my desk. I do not think she meant to break it. She knocked it with her satchel when she spun around furiously on her heels and marched to the door, but it shattered all the same and she made no effort to apologize."

Having heard something of Miss Wraithe's dissatisfaction with his lordship's ready agreement to the new amount from Mrs. Beveridge, Bea was not surprised by this account—especially if the solicitor had actually used the word *happily.* It must have felt to the avaricious blackmailer as though Condon was taunting her.

Contemplating his choice of words, she said, "*Was* it a request, Mr. Ellis?"

With a fleeting smile, he admitted that it was not. "And I assume from your question that you are aware of Miss Wraithe's less than honorable proclivities. She has been applying pressure on his lordship since the day she lost her post at Fortescue's. At the time I urged him to refuse because a blackmailer will never be satisfied. Her demands will only increase. And so they have. When they did, I again urged my client to hold firm at five pounds, but he agreed to the amount without even making an attempt to bargain, which was very upsetting to me. The least he could have done was allow me to offer six so we could settle in the middle at seven and a half. A hundred percent increase is exorbitant and a terrible harbinger, for next time she will want twenty pounds and then forty. I know it is pin money to Lord Condon now, but the figure will be significant soon enough and by then it will be too late. The pattern will be set."

Bea detected more than a hint of regret in the solicitor's tone and wondered if the lovely creamware vase had been a piece by Josiah Wedgwood. If Ellis had only had the impudence to negotiate on his client's behalf without his approval, then he might have saved his lordship thirty pounds per annum *and* a valuable family heirloom.

Offering her sympathy, she contemplated how to ask about the source of the extortion. Despite the solicitor's candor, she knew he would take umbrage at any attempt to discover damaging information about his client and could not decide which approach would ultimately prove more successful: broaching the subject gently by implication or stating it forthrightly. As she was sure to be rebuked either way, she decided to follow the straightforward route. The sooner she gave offense, the sooner she could begin to overcome it and convince him that his telling them everything was in Condon's best interest.

Kesgrave, his thoughts seeming to align with hers, asked without preamble what leverage Miss Wraithe had over his client. "What does Lord Condon fear people discovering that he was willing to pay Miss Wraithe without protest or negotiation?"

As expected, the solicitor responded with indignation, his expression hardening to granite as he raised himself in his seat. Hotly, his tone boiling with insult, he said, "I would never reveal his lordship's secrets. Let me repeat myself so that we are clear: I would never reveal his lordship's secrets. There is nothing you could offer me that would induce me to betray my client's confidence or expose him to ridicule and further blackmail. You could offer me the entire Matlock estate to represent, its vast holdings and its innumerable legal tangles, and I would still refuse."

And yet beneath this ardent and vehement defense of his integrity was a faint undercurrent of uncertainty, as if he was open to discovering what would happen if Kesgrave laid the duchy at his feet.

Before informing him of Miss Wraithe's murder and applying the coercive pressure of her investigation, Bea allowed Ellis a minute to gather himself. He was breathing heavily, and his color was high.

But he did not require a minute.

After several seconds of silence, he said, "Having made

that clear, I must confess that Miss Wraithe does not in fact know any secret information that could harm Lord Condon. The articles in the *London Daily Gazette* that secured his downfall revealed the worst to all and sundry, and there is nothing left to hide. That was the reason I urged him in the strongest possible terms not to submit to her blackmail attempts. Let her run to *The Times* with the same old story about ill-treating children and betraying the trust bestowed on him by society. Nobody would care!"

It was there again in his voice, his genuine outrage at Condon's easy capitulation, and Bea imagined it was a struggle for him to restrain it when he discussed the matter with his lordship. Or were these exchanges conducted via the post?

The answer depended on how frequently Condon visited London.

"His lordship sees the matter in a different light," Ellis continued. "He is comfortable in Ireland, where few people know of the scandal. He is able to enjoy his estate and the privileges of his position without suffering the mortification of his disgrace. He knows he is fortunate, for other men who have found themselves similarly undone by the *Gazette*'s reportage do not have this option. In this frame of mind, he does not begrudge Miss Wraithe the payments. She was helpful to him during his tenure as patron of Fortescue's, a period that saw his wealth increase significantly, and he believes she earned the money. He considers it an annuity, and that is why he told me to leave it be. As I have said previously, I do not share his outlook on the matter, but my opinion is neither here nor there. It is Lord Condon's money and thus his decision. But perhaps he will reconsider his attitude when Miss Wraithe raises the fee again in a year or two."

Although Bea knew the amount demanded by Miss Wraithe was minor in comparison to the wealth of a great estate, she found it difficult to believe a man who exploited the helpless children consigned to his care for financial gain would be cavalier about any denomination. At the same time, Ellis's point was well taken, and if his lordship truly resented the expenditure, he would have made an attempt to push back against the original amount and the new sum. Even Miss Wraithe agreed. By all reports, she would have been more satisfied with a hard-won seven and a half pounds than the readily given ten.

It seemed like madness to Bea to agree to the larger amount only to slaughter the blackmailer a few days later to avoid paying the increase. Surely, there was some mitigating step Condon could have taken before arriving at murder as the best option.

Well, yes, of course, and that was negotiating.

Feeling as though she were thinking in circles, Bea decided to assume Ellis's central premise was wide of the mark: Miss Wraithe did possess extremely damaging information about Condon. It would not be extraordinary, given how closely they had worked together on their infamous scheme. That proximity would have given her an opportunity to discover things about him that nobody else knew.

Engaged in the worst of activities, he would reveal the worst of himself.

In that context, his refusal to haggle would make sense. Terrified of the truth coming out, he feared any response that might anger his tormentor was not worth the risk.

The question was, then, how involved in these atrocities was his lawyer?

There were, Bea thought, only two possible answers: Either Ellis knew everything or he knew nothing. If it was the latter, then Condon would have had to commit the murder on his own or assign it to someone he trusted. Given that he was arranging the homicide to rid himself of one blackmailer, Bea thought it would be foolhardy to expose himself to another in the same stroke. In that case, Condon would have had to have been in London as recently as two days ago. Proving his presence in the capital would not be difficult, as a man of his habits was accustomed to a certain level of comfort. Even if he chose to stay in a seedy inn on the fringe of town, the quality of his clothes and luggage would stand out as unusually fine.

And that was before he ordered a bath to be prepared to his exact specifications.

Alternatively, Ellis handled the matter on behalf of his client.

Lawyers were frequently called upon to perform unsavory tasks in exchange for generous compensation. Jordan, Lord Myles's solicitor, eagerly did the bidding of the worst crime lord in the city, and although those acts fell short of murder, they included theft and chicanery.

That was true, but Ellis had a sterling reputation. She would never have induced Kesgrave to hire him on the spot if the duke had not testified previously to his fine character. Risking utter ruin to further a client's agenda when his straits were not dire was more than foolish; it was idiotic.

Edmund Ellis did not strike Bea as an idiot.

Moving him toward the bottom of her list, Bea decided to continue with the straightforward approach that had served them well during the conversation and said, "Miss Wraithe is dead. She was murdered two days ago in her home, shot in the back of her head at about eleven o'clock in the morning. What evidence can you provide to prove your client did not do it?"

Intending to unnerve the solicitor, she succeeded only in amusing him, and as his lips curved in a faint smile, he returned the parry by asking what information she had in her possession that indicated that he did. "As his representative in all English affairs, I must insist on examining it."

"I have nothing yet, but it is only a matter of time," she replied darkly. "If his lordship is in London, I will find him, which I think you know. His lordship is not capable of stealth. If he is not traveling with a retinue of servants, he will have his valet at the very least. A few inquiries at some London hotels and a word in Mrs. Ralston's ear—you know Mrs. Ralston, I trust, for she is the greatest gossip among the *ton*—and I will have his location by dinner tomorrow. Or you can save me all that bother and tell me where he is now. If you refuse, I shall have to inform the magistrate that you had a hand in Miss Wraithe's murder, and as we both know how devious Lord Condon is, it is not hard for either of us to imagine him slithering off the hook to allow you take sole responsibility for his crime."

Ellis likewise found this prospect unworrying. "You are welcome to embark on all the wild-goose chases you wish, your grace, but none will alter the immutable truth and that truth is his lordship is in Ireland. He has not set foot in England since leaving in the wake of the scandal and he has no intention of returning at present. Furthermore, I am in fact intimately acquainted with his devilry and know that it stops short of murder. He would sell Miss Wraithe into indentured servitude a dozen times over if it would solve his problem *and* earn him another few pounds, but he would never have her killed or kill her himself. It is simply not the way he operates. I am sorry, of course, to hear of the old girl's passing. Any loss of life is a tragedy. It is something of a surprise to me because she seemed so indestructible," he added with a thoughtful frown, as if contemplating his own mortality. Then he lifted his chin and tilted it toward the duke. "Now, then, regarding our business, your grace, shall I send a letter to Mr. Grundy and Mr. Furst informing them of my new position as your solicitor?"

Kesgrave, advising Ellis to do nothing until he heard from the duke's steward in the next couple of days, rose to his feet and walked over to the solicitor's desk. He picked up a quill, which he dipped in ink, and found a slip of paper. As he began to write, the other man leaped to his feet and scurried over to offer his assistance.

"I am an excellent scribe and enjoy taking dictation," he said eagerly.

The duke assured him he was capable of jotting a brief note. Then he folded the paper, sealed it with wax, and handed it to the lawyer. "In the meantime, here is your first task. Please see that this is delivered promptly."

Ellis, his eyes practically glowing with delight, said, "The first of many, I hope."

Kesgrave's reply was noncommittal.

Bea, who watched this byplay with interest, also gave a reserved response, insisting that the Matlock affairs could not be overseen by a murderer.

Regarding her as something of a simpleton, the solicitor said, "Obviously not, your grace. Obviously not!"

Although deeply curious about the contents of the missive as well as its recipient, Bea waited until they had left the building before asking to whom it was addressed.

"Lord Colson," Kesgrave said. "I told him that Ellis swears his client is in Ireland and added confirming Condon's whereabouts to his list of tasks. I trust he will let us know as soon as he discovers something. Regardless, I am inclined to believe Ellis is innocent of wrongdoing. As I said, his reputation is pristine and he would have no incentive to get involved with anything so sordid and potentially disastrous to his career."

Hailing Jenkins, who was across the road, Bea admitted that she held the same general opinion. "But the fact that he was willing to provide information about a client, even if it was a limited amount, in return for a financial reward reveals that his scruples are somewhat flexible and that there is a price for which his morality may be purchased. I do apologize, by the way, for playing fast and loose with estate business. I hope my assumption regarding an insignificant assignment was accurate."

"Stephens will know just the thing," he said confidently as his groom opened the conveyance's door. "And I am not averse to giving him more work should he prove able. One cannot have too many competent people in one's employ."

Although Bea agreed in theory with this benign statement, it inevitably called to mind the colossal estate in Cambridgeshire, with its hundreds of rooms and thousands of acres of parkland and an army of servants awaiting her pleasure.

Clearly, it *was* possible to employ too many competent people.

She endeavored to smother these thoughts as she climbed into the carriage, for they served no purpose other than to undermine her focus. Miss Lark deserved better than to have the murder duchess distracted by her pinery, she thought in disgust.

Chapter Eleven

Kesgrave gave Jenkins the address of their next suspect: Charles Wigsworth. Like Mrs. Beveridge, he lived in a commodious townhouse on a fashionable quarter, and unlike her he was too busy conducting scientific experiments to see them.

His wife, however, begged to differ.

Overhearing the butler's attempt to turn them away, Mrs. Wigsworth instructed him to open the door wider so she could see who was calling, for Wigsworth senior was expected within the hour and she would not allow him to be turned away for the third time that month.

"I am sorry if his experiment is at a very important stage," she said briskly. "He will put aside his work and entertain his father like an obedient son. I am obliged to observe the proprieties with my own sire, which is a great deal more uncomfortable because he tells the same five tedious stories every time he visits and I am compelled to act as though I am fascinated."

The servant, abiding by her request, opened the door fully to reveal the Duke and Duchess of Kesgrave. Disconcerted by the sight, she frowned in confusion as she invited them inside. Then she apologized for the ramshackle reception. "My husband does not get many callers these days, mostly because he refuses to leave his laboratory to see them."

Bea followed the other woman down the hallway, which was painted a dark blue color that made the walls feel closer. "Ah, yes, I understand your husband is a man of science," she said, recalling Mrs. Beveridge's description. "What is his field?"

"Chemistry," Mrs. Wigsworth replied with a tight smile over her shoulder. "He claims to be on the verge of a discovery that will change the practice of medicine forever, but I fear he is only on the verge of doing himself grievous harm. The substances he uses are volatile and dangerous. Last month, he almost lost an eye in an explosion. He is recovered now, and his eyesight has been restored. I had hoped the accident would chasten him and he would decide to take up something benign such as fox hunting like his brother, but he is stubborn. I have tried to be patient. It was different when he worked in a cellar in Lambeth because then I did not know what was happening. But now I am compelled to worry because he is right here! He tells me all the time to steel my spine because he is working for the betterment of mankind, which is unfair. Of course I want mankind to be bettered—I am as public-spirited as the next woman—but not at the expense of myself or my children or my home."

Intrigued by the boldness of the claim, Bea asked what Wigsworth was working on.

"He is determined to discover a way to make surgical operations painless for patients via the employment of laughing gas," she replied impatiently. "It is a noble goal and I do hope he succeeds, but I cannot fathom what the unholy rush is. Charles could spend a few less hours in the laboratory and still better mankind. Having tea with one's wife would not set science back ten years."

Bea, recognizing the reference from a treatise she had read several years ago, asked if Wigsworth was trying to fulfill Humphrey Davy's optimistic claim about nitrous oxide. "He is certain it can be used to improve the surgical experience."

Again, Mrs. Wigsworth's cheerful expression tensed as she paused at the bottom of the staircase. "Humphrey! That devil! He has so much to answer for! No other wives are forced to attend card parties alone because their husbands have locked themselves in the attic to conduct experiments. It is all his fault, going on about the ideal combination of gases. If Humphrey is so certain it exists, then why does he not find it himself? I am sorry you have to visit the attic, but Charles adamantly refuses to come downstairs to entertain visitors. His father is due to arrive at four, and if I somehow get him to come down now, he will barricade himself upstairs, complaining that he has already lost too much time to social niceties. I cannot sit with his father alone for another hour. The man is beastly."

As they proceeded up the steps Mrs. Wigsworth added that her father-in-law blamed her for his son's fascination with chemistry, as it was she who introduced him to Sir Humphrey's work. "I convinced him to go to one of his lectures at the Surrey Institution because he kept waking the baby from his nap with all his hammering. Building a toy house for an infant—have you ever heard of anything so ridiculous! I thought the lecture would be an interesting distraction. I never imagined he would chuck all his responsibilities and become an ardent practitioner."

Mrs. Wigsworth sighed as she began the ascent to the third floor but did not ask Bea or the duke the purpose of their visit. If she thought it was odd or unnerving to have the murder duchess in her house, she was too well mannered to reveal it.

And yet not so well mannered that she would hold her criticism of the elder Mr. Wigsworth, whose odoriferousness made the ordeal especially painful.

"It is his hair—the pomade. It grows rancid if not washed out after a reasonable period and he refuses to clean his hair regularly because he is convinced shampooing too frequently makes you ill. If I have told Charles once I have told him a thousand times that if he really wants to do something to benefit mankind, he should invent a formulation for pomade that does not become fetid after a week. And here we are," she said, stopping in front of a door on the top floor, her breathing slightly labored from the exertion of climbing so high. Grasping the handle, she warned them that her husband would be impatient and rude. "Unless you can discuss all twenty-one principles of galvanism in detail. In that case, he will be impatient and slightly less rude."

Kesgrave noted that there were in fact only five tenets, as the science of electricity was still in its infancy. Mrs. Wigsworth, admitting that her previous comment had been flippant, looked at the duke with concern and advised him not to reveal any familiarity.

"My husband has been looking for a new patron ever since Lord Condon returned to Ireland and can be relentless in his pursuit if he believes he has a chance of succeeding. He will bore your ears off with his theories and pester you for an introduction to Joseph Bank. He is determined to publish his findings in the Royal Society's journal. It is all he cares about."

The duke said he did not know the famous naturalist.

"Any member of the Committee of Papers, then," Mrs. Wigsworth amended. "He is not selective. As soon as you enter, you must insist you are here to talk about something completely unrelated to science."

"We *are* here to talk about something completely unrelated to science," Bea stated.

"Yes, just like that," Mrs. Wigsworth said with an approving nod as she opened the door and called out to her husband, who was standing at a high table in the middle of the floor. He was wearing a leather apron over a linen shirt and loose-fitting trousers, his hands encased in gloves as they grasped a glass jar of a clear liquid. He wore spectacles that had slipped partway down his nose, and when he looked up to glare irritably at his wife, Bea noticed that most of his left eyebrow was gone.

Before he could complain about the interruption, Mrs. Wigsworth stepped away. "Visitors, Charles. The Duke and Duchess of Kesgrave. Do not forget your father will be here before the hour is out. I would suggest you clean up before coming to the drawing room, but you are a grown man who can make his own decisions. Do what you will."

With that, she closed the door with a firm snap.

Bea, drawing further into the room, noted that it was a capacious space that felt small due to a preponderous amount of furniture, stacks of books, and mounds of clutter. To one side there was a wash basin with variously sized bowls, a stove, and a device that looked similar to an onion-pot distillery. The other half of the room was crowded with three square tables, all piled high with papers and paraphernalia. A scale teetered on top of a partially opened box with a sherry-colored tube hanging out one side and appeared ready to fall if she exhaled too sharply.

Her concern proved overblown, however, for the occupant in the center of the room let out a hefty puff and the tenuous balance held. Only the pages of his journal fluttered. Testily, he told her that whatever they wished to discuss would have to wait. His work was in a delicate phase and could not be interrupted. "Make an appointment with my secretary. Good day," he said, returning the glass to the table with a meaningful thump. Then he opened a jar of white crystals and scooped up a few with a small spoon.

Although a window was open to ensure ventilation, Bea detected an unpleasant odor. It was a sweet, metallic scent mixed with sweat, and her stomach roiled in response. Ignoring the squeamishness, she said, "I am afraid our business cannot wait. We are investigating the murder of Agnes Wraithe and have reason to believe you are a suspect based on the fact that you were satisfying her blackmail demand of five pounds a month, which was soon to be ten."

Wigsworth's expression did not change, and if he already knew the former headmistress had been killed, he did not find her death as interesting as the crystals he was adding to the clear liquid. "As the woman is dead, I cannot see how the matter is pressing. She will be no less dead in a week. Make an appointment with my secretary and we will discuss it then. Good day!"

"As you are a man of science, I know you can readily identify the fault in your logic," she replied, drawing closer to his table and stopping when she could read the notations in his journal. They were primarily numbers measuring volume and time. "Speed befits an investigation because the sooner we can eliminate suspects, the quicker we can focus on the right one. Answers beget more questions. Now do tell us why Miss Wraithe was blackmailing you, and do not keep bidding us good day with increasing urgency. We have no intention of leaving without the information we expressly seek."

While Bea made these assertions, Kesgrave wandered the room, examining the items on the assorted tables, and Wigsworth's scowl darkened as the duke picked up a journal. Striding over to him, he snatched the book out of his hands.

"That is confidential information!" Wigsworth said hotly. "How do I know this supposed investigation is not a ruse to steal my work? I can name at least three men off the top of my head who would lie and cheat to gain access to my findings. I am farthest along in the race to create the first surgical pain ameliorator, and they all know it. I am very close to figuring out the best gas for introducing the vaporized nitrous oxide to the body."

Amused by the charge, Bea asked why the Duke of Kesgrave would deign to spy for a rival chemist just as his grace selected another journal, dated spring 1809. He perused the opening pages with interest until Wigsworth grabbed that book as well.

"It is more plausible than the Duke of Kesgrave taking interest in the murder of Agnes Wraithe, who I am not even sure *is* dead. She is too mean to die. If you wanted to trick me, you should have come up with a more credible tale. Now I bid you good day, your graces—if that is indeed who you really are," he added, his eyes narrowing in distrust as he clutched the journal to his chest. Then he swayed side to side as if to block more of the duke's view.

On one hand, Bea readily understood his suspicion, for the notion of a duchess who continually pressed her nose against murdered corpses was patently absurd, which was why Mr. Twaddle-Thum delighted in chronicling her exploits. But Mr. Twaddle-Thum *had* chronicled her exploits, and it was frustrating to encounter the one person in all of England who did not follow the gossip's reports with ardent interest.

Entertained to find herself regretting the limits of Twaddle's popularity, Bea urged him to summon a member of his household to confirm her credentials. "And it can be anyone at all: your wife, your valet, the scullion. They will all tell you that the Duchess of Kesgrave has a mortifying habit of identifying murderers. There have been several by now. It will take an extra few minutes, I am sure, but the duke and I are happy to wait. We are not on the verge of discovering the first surgical pain ameliorator, nor is our father about to arrive for a time-consuming visit."

He glared at her with intense dislike at the reminder of the unavoidable obligation and huffing angrily, he said, "Oh, very well, fine! But you must step away from my work. You may stand in the middle of the floor where you cannot read any of the data I have collected. I still cannot believe you genuinely care who murdered that harridan. Good riddance, I say!"

"Yes, I am sure you do," Bea murmured, taking several steps back from the table so that she was aligned with the stove. "She has been soaking you for five pounds a month for years, and when she increased the fee to ten starting in July, you realized it would never stop. She would just keep asking for more and more, so you decided to take action."

Returning the journal to the pile, Wigsworth smiled stiffly and said he had no idea what she was talking about. "Miss Wraithe was not blackmailing me. I do not know where you got that ridiculous idea. I barely knew the woman. As a supervisor of Fortescue's, I was not obliged to visit the asylum more than twice a year. My responsibilities were limited to raising funds to help feed the poor children and reviewing the financial ledger to make sure there was enough money to pay for their care and upkeep."

"Mr. Wigsworth, if you insist on wasting my time with all these lies, then I will have no choice but to waste yours," Bea replied kindly. "We found Miss Wraithe's records, which shows a monthly contribution from you in the amount of five pounds. Furthermore, your wife said you previously had a laboratory in a cellar in Lambeth. I can only assume she meant Fortescue's. You were there far more frequently than twice a year and knew the victim quite well."

He tried.

For several seconds, he stared at her with an intense look of concentration on his face as he struggled to come up with a reasonable-sounding explanation. Then he gave up with a petulant snort and said it did not matter. "Whether she was blackmailing me or not is irrelevant because I did not harm that woman."

"As you are a man of science, I am sure you understand why I cannot simply take your word for it. You have presented me with a theory and now I beg you to prove it," she said logically. "Otherwise, I am fairly certain the extortion is highly relevant because it gives you a motive for murdering Miss Wraithe, especially since she had doubled her fee going forward."

Wigsworth, cut to the quick by this uncharitable observation, said he did not have to prove anything. "My word is sufficient."

Bea tsk-tsked at the notion of a man of science defaulting to faith. "You know I must have evidence. Every theory must be substantiated. So again, Mr. Wigsworth, I ask you why Miss Wraithe was blackmailing you."

His expression grew fiercely obdurate, and she realized he cared more about keeping his secret than returning to his work. Now he was happy to waste time, and reminding him of his father's imminent visit was unlikely to yield results. She contemplated Mrs. Wigsworth's comment and wondered if Kesgrave had a connection at *Philosophical Transactions* whom she could exploit to gain the man's cooperation. Promising to arrange an introduction to one of the members of the journal's editorial board might induce him to speak. With his wide acquaintance, the duke must know someone at the Royal Society who had influence. Failing that, he would know somebody who knew somebody who would be happy to do him a service. He would not resent the commitment, would he, for it was considerably less significant than committing a portion of his legal business and he had accepted that arrangement with equanimity.

Resolved, she opened her mouth to make the offer, but Kesgrave forestalled her by saying, "You experimented on the children. That is why your calculations in these ledgers are based on subjects who are on average sixty pounds. That is the leverage Miss Wraithe had over you. If that information was known, you would never be published in the Royal Society's journal, let alone be allowed to join the ranks of its members."

Wigsworth shook his head at the accusation but made no attempt to deny it, instead lowering slowly onto the leather chair with a self-pitying sigh.

Aghast, Bea gaped at him, her jaw slack with shock as she realized the inadequacy of her fears. All those wild imaginings, all those unsettling nightmares filled with dark rooms and cold hunger, and she had never once conceived the horror of being subjected to scientific experiments by a monstrously ambitious chemist with dreams of glory.

Of course it happened, she thought. The children consigned to an orphanage were utterly without power. They were at the mercy of the people charged with ensuring their welfare and those caretakers were constrained only by their consciences—which meant nothing if they did not possess consciences.

Discomfited by her gaze, by the unwavering steadfastness of her revulsion, Wigsworth jumped to his feet in a jittery leap and exclaimed, "They were compensated! Each child was given a crown as well as the sense of satisfaction in knowing they had advanced the cause of science. And they were grateful for it! I swear, boys were lining up to volunteer. I had to turn them away. You must not imagine we were pulling them out of their beds in the dead of night and bringing them to a gloomy dungeon. It was all aboveboard and nobody was harmed!"

But Kesgrave scoffed at this claim, disgusted by Wigsworth's feeble attempt to rationalize what was clearly an appalling abuse of his position. "It was not aboveboard. Nothing about the sickening business was open and honest. Miss Wraithe would never have been able to blackmail you had you sought and gained the approval of the board of supervisors for your experimentation."

Wigsworth's posture grew pugnacious as his right hand curled into a fist and he took a step toward the duke as if to strike him for daring to make the allegation. But he held his place, growling with fury. "You know nothing! I had Lord Condon's sanction, and it was all going swimmingly. I gathered invaluable data. And then one of the boys had an unexpected reaction to the vaporous mixture. He fell unconscious and could not be roused. I am sure it was only a temporary condition, but out of an excess of caution, I summoned a doctor."

Here, he paused for several seconds, and Bea wondered if he required a moment to gather his thoughts before revealing upsetting information or if he believed she or the duke would laud him for his high-minded decision to seek help when it was not strictly necessary.

"That is how Miss Wraithe learned about my experiments," he continued. "The doctor presented Fortescue's with his bill despite my explicitly telling him to send it to my London address. The boy was fine! His recovery took longer than anticipated, and he was awarded an extra crown for his trouble. All was well. But Miss Wraithe would not let it end there. She kept insisting that his mental acuity had been dulled by the experience, which I know was nonsense. The boy had limited faculties before the accident, and I very much disbelieve he had been able to read the Bible. Even so, I could not allow anyone to find out because I knew how it would look. Mean-spirited men would think the worst and perhaps try to impede my progress. Corbyn and Webb would take the opportunity to malign me or invalidate my research. I agreed to the payments because the advancement of science is more important than my own principles. It would be only a short while anyway. As soon as I figured out the right formulation and published my results, Miss Wraithe's threats would lose all sway."

But they would not, Bea thought.

If anything, her threats would grow more powerful because something greater than the advancement of science would be at stake: his reputation. He could not allow his crowning achievement to be tainted by scandal. Miss Wraithe, recognizing the increasing value of her leverage, would raise the price of her silence even more.

By the time she was done, Wigsworth would have bought her a manor house in Surrey.

He knew that. Completely lacking in morality, he nevertheless possessed a fair amount of intelligence and would realize the situation required a more permanent solution.

With that in mind, she asked him where he was on Thursday morning at eleven.

He wrinkled his forehead in confusion, as though the question did not make sense, and then answered with a hint of contempt. "I was here, in my laboratory, where I spend all my time trying to solve one of the greatest mysteries of modern science."

"I see, yes," Bea said. "And who among the household can confirm that?"

"Everyone," he replied succinctly.

Surprised by the sweeping thoroughness of his claim, she said, "Every member of the staff as well as your wife can confirm you were in your laboratory on Thursday morning at eleven?"

"No, obviously not!" he sneered. "Every member of the staff as well as my wife can confirm my commitment to solving one of the greatest mysteries of modern science. None of them can confirm I was in my laboratory because none would have the disrespect to bother me when I am working."

"So you have no proof you were here during the time of the murder?" she asked.

"No proof!" he replied with derision. "All of science is proof. I can show you the results of tests I took on Thursday, which will have the date and time."

Although Bea would not consider such evidence to be conclusive, she allowed that it was a reasonable place to start. As he had arranged for Miss Lark to be arrested for the murder, he would have no reason to fabricate notes to protect himself against suspicion that would not fall on him.

It was as Kesgrave had said: Every murderer in London was not taking a rear-guard action against the Duchess of Kesgrave. Only the most diabolical killer would think of employing the precaution in the unlikely event an investigator sought his alibi.

Wigsworth stomped over to the table behind Kesgrave, sifted through the stack of books, and pulled out one with a green cloth cover. He flipped aggressively through the tome, snapping each page as he turned it, until he arrived at the desired date. His brow furrowing, he read for almost a minute before returning the volume to the heap and selecting another one. Again, he perused several pages, then dropped it onto the table with an annoyed thump. He made a third attempt with a leather-bound red book.

Finally, he said, "I did not perform any experiments on June eighteenth. I remember now that I spent the first half of the day cleaning my laboratory. It had been weeks since it had a proper scrubbing. Per my wife's request, I allowed the upstairs maid to clean every second Monday, but the clumsy girl spilled a jar all over my ledgers, rendering the numbers illegible, and I put my foot down. That was two months ago, and the work surfaces had gotten grimy. So I set aside the morning to clean everything. That is why I do not have notes to show you. But you will see that my laboratory is spotless. I believe that in itself is persuasive, but you may also speak to my wife. She will verify everything I have said."

"Except your whereabouts at the time of the murder," Bea pointed out with meaningful emphasis. "That your wife cannot verify because she is not allowed to enter your laboratory. When is the earliest your presence in the home can be corroborated?"

Protesting the insulting nature of her query, he admitted that he could not remember interacting with anyone before two in the afternoon, when he emerged from his workroom to call for more coals and a tray of crumpets and cheese. "Mary delivered the food and James carried up the coal. They will both testify to that fact," he added in a more conciliatory tone, seemingly aware that his belligerence had done little to further his cause. "I understand the information does not extend to the time period in question, but combined with my habits it should be convincing."

It was not, no, and Bea moved the chemist to the top of her list.

Kesgrave asked Wigsworth about his collection of pistols, which drew a blank look as the man insisted he did not have a collection of pistols.

Or any pistols, for that matter.

"As a man of science, I restrict my pursuits to only those that are relevant to my field of study," he explained, noting that since he had discovered his scientific proficiency several years ago, he had renounced all interest in the brutal sport of hunting. "I detest all guns, which you may verify with my wife. You can also ask my father, who taught me how to use a rifle and is disgusted by my renunciation. I understand he will be joining us soon for tea. He will be pleased to hear that I am a suspect in the murder, for he thinks it is very manly to shoot things. But maybe do not tell Emily, for it would distress her. And do not say a word about the blackmail. She is unaware of it."

Bea promised not to provide his wife with information she did not expressly seek, a half measure that elicited a frown. It was replaced almost immediately with a grimace, however, when a more dismaying thought occurred to him, and he inhaled sharply. "You won't tell anyone about the children, will you, your graces? Please do not!" he pleaded, a wheedling note entering his voice as he offered to acknowledge their contribution to science in his Bakerian lecture.

That he had already begun to compose his address to the Royal Society in acceptance of its highest honor was a sign of the utter confidence he had in the ultimate success of his endeavor. Although he had yet to arrive at the ideal formulation for delivering painless surgery via nitrous oxide despite so many years of trying, he perceived himself as triumphant.

It was, she suspected, an image he would kill to preserve.

Chapter Twelve

Although Marlow revealed no interest in his employers' progress as he greeted them in the entry hall at Kesgrave House, Bea felt compelled to provide him with a general overview of their investigation thus far. His willingness to not only accompany her to Newgate Prison without a word of protest but also to ensure that the visit succeeded in its aim meant that he was already involved. His sense of propriety would preclude his asking any questions, and allowing him to stew in his curiosity struck her as a poor way to repay his kindness.

He received her display of gratitude blankly, his expression altering briefly when she explained Mrs. Wraithe's fondness for blackmail.

The flicker on his face—it was horror.

Most definitely, yes, Marlow was appalled.

Unable to discern what precisely had earned his contempt, Bea chose to believe it was the victim's extortive habit, not her recounting of it, which left out many of the most egregious details.

She did not mention, for example, that Wigsworth had

used children under his protection as subjects in his chemistry experiments.

Bea wanted to mention it.

She wanted to scream it.

In the half hour since they had left the scientist in his laboratory pleading for their discretion, her revulsion had only intensified, and she had passed the return drive deep in reverie as she contemplated the best moment to expose his perfidy.

The presentation of his Bakerian medal obviously.

With everyone he wanted to impress gathered in one room—members of the Royal Society, his rivals, passionate dilettantes, reporters—the revelation would cause the most damage.

There he would be, at the podium, at the height of his powers, preening with false humility as he accepted the adulation of his peers.

And then splosh!

Like a fly swatted against a wall, Wigsworth would be reduced to a black speck.

It was a heady picture.

And yet unlikely to come to pass.

After years of pursuing his goal with single-mindedness, he had yet to achieve a significant advancement. Even with access to an unlimited pool of test subjects and a wanton disregard for decency, he had not identified the correct combination of gases.

As his failure was inevitable, Bea could not fathom why she had held her tongue. Marlow was a void, a dark chasm into which things fell and never emerged. Telling him about Wigsworth's depravity would be tantamount to telling no one, and still she had hesitated as though she owed Wigsworth something. In truth, she owed him nothing.

No, she owed him exactly what he had deemed the boys

at Fortescue's to be worthy of: one crown and sweeping indifference.

With this dark thought in mind, she concluded her explanation and requested tea be delivered to her office of rout cake enjoyment, where she intended to finally begin the Culpeper.

Here we go, she thought, settling into her favorite chair with the book.

But she only stared blankly at the page, not reading a word.

It was all very well to be sickened by Wigsworth's conduct, but was Mrs. Beveridge's behavior any better? In some respects, yes, of course, for she had not treated vulnerable orphans like specimens in a menagerie, but diverting funds meant to pay for food and clothes to one's pocket to purchase fripperies bore its own particular brand of degeneracy.

And that was *her* word, Bea thought somberly, inordinately annoyed that the hen-witted creature did not have the presence of mind to employ a weightier term such as *necessities* or *requirements.*

As if that would have lessened her repugnance.

It would not.

The situation was irredeemable, she thought, unbearably sad for all the children who had not been saved from deprivation and despair by Vera and Horace Hyde-Clare.

'Twas a topsy-turvy world indeed when she could look to her petty-hearted and small-minded relatives as the heroes of the piece.

Clearly, the only remedy was to shovel more money at Mrs. Caffrey. Having identified the one decent human being to oversee a children's asylum, she could ensure the administrator had the resources to do the work properly.

Ah, yes, so there was one bright spark amid the misery.

If only they could make copies of Mrs. Caffrey, like leaflets on a printing press.

Thoroughly disheartened, she wrenched her attention back to the Culpeper, determined to read at least one page before retiring upstairs to change for dinner.

Alas, she did not finish the first paragraph before she wondered what wretched thing they would discover tomorrow about Mrs. Knowles and Mr. Dibdin. Hearteningly, she told herself it could not get much worse than performing experiments on orphans.

Famous last words, your grace.

Catching sight of a movement in the doorway, she swiveled her head to the right and saw Kesgrave standing on the threshold. In his grasp he had the tea tray and she watched with interest as he placed it on the pedestal table in the center of the room.

"Are the staff in full rebellion, then?" she asked curiously, laying the book to the side as she rose from her comfortable chair to join him at the table. "Was it my apprising Marlow on the progress of our investigation? Did that finally give them such a disgust of me that they will no longer do my bidding? I must admit I am surprised that Joseph would turn against me. Of all the servants, he seemed the most impressed by my abilities. I do not think it is inaccurate to say that he hopes one day to be a lady Runner himself."

A smile teased at his lips as he said she had no cause to doubt the footman's enduring esteem. "I actually took the tray from his grasp, and you may be assured he let go of it with the utmost reluctance. I do not think he believes I am capable of successfully executing the duty, and if you peer into the hallway, I am convinced you will find him hovering outside the door."

In fact, she did not have to peer.

Joseph stepped into the entrance as though he had been

summoned and asked if there was anything else she needed. She assured him she did not.

"Very good," he said with an approving nod, then left the room.

"Joseph is satisfied with your performance," Bea said with undue sobriety. "Perhaps if you keep up the good work, you will finally get that promotion to second footman. One can only hope."

"Yes, brat," the duke said, sliding a teacup toward himself as he lifted the pot.

And then she saw it, next to the plate of rout cakes.

As she stiffened, Kesgrave said, "I thought since your spirits are already low, the chart could not ruin your mood. We can review it together. I promise it is not as bad as you think."

Finding this reasoning specious, she gestured to the cushioned chair next to the hearth and said she was already engaged in an activity. "I am learning about herbal remedies. It is fascinating."

"What is fascinating is that you can learn anything without looking at the page," he replied, pouring the tea. "You were staring vacantly into space for a good five minutes."

Startled to discover she could be oblivious to his presence for any length of time, she accepted the cup and said she understood now why Joseph had been so worried about his ability to deliver a tray. "A well-trained servant discharges his responsibilities promptly. You shall never make second footman if you continue to be so cavalier in your execution."

"Another dream dashed," he said soberly.

He imbued the statement with just enough disappointment that Bea wondered when he had last been deprived of something he wanted. It cannot have been recent, she decided, for it was his singular privilege to be blessed with not only the means to do whatever he wished but also the sort of disposition that allowed it. And now he wanted to discuss his inconceivably grand home in Cambridgeshire on the premise that it was not as bad as she thought.

No, it was worse.

As he unfolded the sheet, she narrowed her eyes and asked if he had rifled through her escritoire himself or asked her maid Lily to do it for him.

Displaying no alarm at the accusation, he calmly replied, "Neither. Stephens made multiple copies, as he realized the document would be helpful to him as well."

Of course he did!

All those lovely rows and columns—so much helpful information to be ascertained at a glance.

Kesgrave, pulling his chair closer to hers, placed a pastry next to her teacup. "It is not a panacea, but I have been told on multiple occasions that a rout cake instantly improves any situation."

A smile flitted across her features as she clarified that it improved any situation involving a Hyde-Clare. "Specifically, a Vera Hyde-Clare. But your argument is correct, your grace."

Lifting the teapot to fill his own cup, he said that he had frequently wished she would stop investigating dead bodies out of concern for her physical well-being. "This is the first time I am concerned about your emotional well-being. I do not like seeing you so sad."

With a meaningful look at the chart, she murmured, "I am not so sure that is true."

Ignoring the taunt, he announced that Lord Colson had struck him as capable. "He would take the information we have discovered and follow it to its logical conclusion. He would find the killer, I am certain, and you are allowed to step back from the things that cause you pain."

It was a radical notion, to be sure, for Beatrice Hyde-

Clare had often hidden from the things that caused her pain, but stepping back—blatantly, honestly, in full view of everyone?

No, she had never dared.

Her goal had always been to draw as little attention to herself as possible, to create the opposite of a commotion, and outwardly refusing to do something was among the worst ways to evade notice. The freedom to decline was yet another privilege of rank and wealth.

Granted it now, she could not avail herself of the option.

What Kesgrave said about Lord Colson was on the mark—he *was* competent—and although she knew her proficiency in identifying murderers was uncommon, she was not so egotistical as to believe it was unprecedented. There was more at stake this time because of the duke's personal connection to the accused, and that made ceding control to someone else even harder.

But it was not concern for Verity Lark that kept Bea steady.

It was the children.

The feckless cruelty of the supervisors caused her tremendous pain, yes, but stepping back would solve nothing.

It would hurt either way.

Even so, she cited her agreement with Miss Lark as the reason she would continue. "It is the shooting lessons, you see. If left to Prosser's devices, I will never acquire the skill to win a duel."

If the thought of his wife keeping a dawn appointment unsettled him, he did not reveal it as he asked whom she intended to call out. Blithely, she assured him it was merely a precautionary measure.

"I am relieved to hear it," he said, scooting his chair even closer and gently brushing his fingers against her cheek. "It is a damnable world, Bea, and I am sorry for it—for all of it."

She leaned against him, grateful for the warmth and solidity, and observed with wry amusement that he could have done a better job with his creation. "I hope you are making detailed notes for your next universe."

Taking no offense in the implied hubris, he assured her he was keeping a diligent record. "Item number one on the list: no venality. Item two: more rout cakes."

"On that head, at least, you have done an admirable job," she said graciously.

"There will be rout cakes at Haverill Hall, you know," he offered with soothing comfort, which he promptly undermined by adding, "And a dozen rooms you may choose as your office."

Although she did not appreciate the reminder of the home's crushing size, Bea bravely straightened her shoulders and leaned forward to examine the chart. There was some validity in the duke's logic, for in truth she would rather think of the large manor house than a shambling cluster of maltreated boys holding out their hands to collect a meager crown. The other half of the bargain did not matter—Wigsworth could have lopped off a pinkie for all they cared—because something was better than nothing, especially for those who had none. Money was coercive, and to argue that the orphans had volunteered was the height of disingenuousness.

Wigsworth knew that.

It simply did not interest him.

Kesgrave, perceiving the change in her attitude, began by explaining how Stephens had organized the information, denoting what the colors meant and how each category pertained to the running of the estate. He provided brief lectures on each portion of the house as it became relevant to the discussion—the numerous kitchen fires were detailed when mentioning the cooking staff (demarcated in purple ink)—and he pulled up short when he realized the steward had used blue to indicate the workers who took care of the parkland. Green was clearly more suitable.

"Perhaps Stephens thought to match the sky," he said solemnly, almost to himself.

Bea, watching his brows tighten with bewilderment, felt affection swarm through her, and she found herself genuinely baffled by how to proceed: make an impish comment poking fun at his earnestness, remain silent to see how deep his confusion would go, or launch herself into his arms.

The last, yes, obviously that, she thought, carefully sliding the teacups toward the center of the table to make sure nothing spilled before pitching forward and pressing her lips against him. On a startled laugh, Kesgrave tugged her onto his lap, then rose to his feet and carried her back to the overstuffed armchair where she usually spent a fair amount of time reading. Settling them comfortably, he proceeded to demonstrate how he felt about the untimely interruption.

A good while later, as she was straightening the hemline of her gown, Bea accused him of deliberately distracting her with his pedantry. "You know I cannot listen to you detail meaningless distinctions without feeling overcome with desire."

He conceded the accuracy of the allegation but nevertheless insisted the information would prove useful to her as mistress of Haverill Hall. "There is a book on its history in the library that I think you will find edifying. But, yes, I did use a previously identified weakness to my benefit, and if you are still looking for an imperfection in me, that is one: I will not hesitate to exploit an advantage to lighten your sorrow."

Bea's heart thudded softly in her chest, the expression on his face gentle and gorgeous, and rather than stare at him dumbly, which she could do for hours—happily!—she rallied for something to say. "That is a boast disguised as a flaw, your grace."

He grinned and suggested she should also count false humility among his faults.

The clock struck five, sparing her dignity, for she was very close to responding with an insipid sigh, and she pointed out there was no time left to review the chart. "We must go upstairs to change for dinner."

"Well, step one was to convince you to look at the chart," he replied with smug affability. "All in all, I would say it was a good first day's work."

Unable to decide if she was charmed or peeved by the complacency in his tone—most likely both, in equal measure—she asked how many steps comprised his plan. "One dozen or two?"

"A half," he said as he led her to the hallway. "There are only six steps."

As Kesgrave had invited his grandmother to dinner to apologize for having to cancel the night before, Bea did not have time to get into a protracted debate about the quality and content of each step. Consequently, she contented herself with repeating the word *only* with wry emphasis.

Arriving well before the appointed hour, the dowager was waiting impatiently in the drawing room when her hosts appeared and demanded to know everything that had transpired since she had left Beatrice in Berkeley Square the day before. With a glance at the closed door, Bea obliged, sparing no detail, and the dowager was alternately outraged, annoyed, shocked, and disgusted. She had never held a good opinion of Mrs. Beveridge because she had pushed in front of her at the refreshment table at the Kittersons' ball a dozen years ago, but Wigsworth had struck her as a benign if habitually inattentive figure. Horrified by his abuses, she settled on the same solution as Bea and pledged to have Spivey make additional funds available to the capable Mrs. Caffrey in the morning.

"I wish I could do more," she said as Kesgrave offered his arm to escort her to the dining room.

As it had been more than a fortnight since the duke and his grandmother had been on anything but coolly polite terms, the dowager had much news to impart, starting with her useless physicians' most recent prescriptions and ending with a complaint about her cousins plaguing her with their concerns about her frailty.

"If only they had seen you wielding your cane against Miss Lark's assailant," Bea said rousingly. "Perhaps if you sent a missive detailing your exploits to Mr. Twaddle-Thum, he could write an admiring item that you could distribute to all relevant parties."

Although she had said it facetiously, Bea was not surprised to see a pensive look enter the dowager's eye before she shook her head and said that Miss Lark would not like for her heroics to be broadcast to a large audience. "She relies on her anonymity for her work."

Amused, Bea said, "And I do not?"

The dowager swore the murder duchess—oh, yes, she liked that new epithet—was aided by her notoriety, then added that even a London reputation had its limits. "We shall have to think of some way to establish you in the country, my dear. We want to make an impression."

"No, we do not!" said Bea, wincing at the authority in the dowager's assertion and promptly changing the subject to Hartlepool's filly. "Did he manage to make it out to Watford today or did he spend his time at home with his nephew?"

"Both," Kesgrave said. "He made Netherby accompany him to Stratten's."

As Bea had been teasing, she found this reply remarkably

funny. "So that is to be his solution? To keep his nephew in his line of sight at all times?"

The dowager's inelegant snort revealed what she thought of this plan.

They finished eating a short time later, and although Kesgrave encouraged his grandmother to linger over port, she refused. "Bea has one of her lessons in the morning and needs all the rest she can get in her condition. And I am weary myself. Maria called for tea, and you know how exhausting she is, Damien, with her bad hip and refusal to get an ear trumpet despite being quite deaf."

Indeed, Kesgrave did, for he had heard this charge many times before, but he held his tongue and allowed her to grumble at length as he escorted her to the door.

Chapter Thirteen

Alerted to the murder duchess's interest in Miss Wraithe's premature death by Alicia Beveridge, Mrs. Knowles welcomed Bea and Kesgrave into her home with gracious enthusiasm, lamenting the wretchedness of the circumstance while pledging to make the experience as pleasant as possible. She would answer their questions without equivocating, volunteer all the information she could, and keep her temper on an even keel regardless of how discomfited she was by their invasiveness.

"And rout cakes!" she added with a peal of delighted laughter as she pointed to a plate displaying Her Outrageousness's favorite pastry. "You see how determined I am to make this interview painless? They were freshly baked this morning. I had my cook prepare another batch yesterday afternoon in case you came to see me then. I am nothing if not prepared."

The room was lovely, with deep rose-colored walls, vibrant flowers, and moody still lifes, and Mrs. Knowles gestured to a pair of chauffeuses beneath a painting of a table laid with oysters, lemons, and beer. "Sit, please sit," she said, lowering herself onto a third chair, her elegant figure swathed in a velvet-trimmed silk gown that was far too beautiful for a quiet day at home. She had also dressed in expectation of their company. "I hope you are not churlish with Alicia for warning me of your visit."

In fact, Bea was, yes, quite, for the notice had given the suspect all the time she needed to arrange things to her liking, as demonstrated by the lovely dress and rout cakes. Presumably, she had applied the same level of care to her alibi.

"She knows I had a contentious relationship with Agnes and would be interested in her murder, especially if I am a suspect," Mrs. Knowles continued as she poured the brew into light blue teacups that contrasted nicely with the room's pink cast. "To be perfectly candid, I must confess that I believe Alicia is worried that I might have had something to do with it all. She is a dear, so I am resolved not to take offense, but it is a little troubling to find out one of your friends thinks you could be a coldblooded killer. I would not be so disheartened by her concern if Agnes had been slain in a moment of passionate fury, for it is acceptable to be overwhelmed by one's emotions. Calmly shooting someone, however, is abhorrent. I am sure that is not how I would do it. I rather think I would have run Miss Wraithe through with my foil, preferably after a protracted duel wherein I leap from the table to the staircase to the chandelier. I saw that in a play once and thought it looked like great fun."

Caroline Knowles did not resemble a swordsman with her narrow wrists and delicate frame. She had an interesting face, a slightly crooked nose and a bottom lip that was out of proportion to her top one. Not yet thirty, she had been a widow for eight years, her husband dying tragically young only a few months after their wedding in an ill-advised carriage race. A neck-or-nothing hothead who did not perceive the advantages of sobriety when engaging in a contest of speed, he had driven his horses into a ditch and snapped his neck when the conveyance overturned. After an extended period of mourning, she reemerged into society and had just accepted an offer from a widower with young children when the Fortescue's scandal broke. Gallantly, she ended the betrothal rather than allow his august name to be tarnished alongside hers.

At least that was the story that had made the rounds. It was always possible that the jilting went in the other direction and Mrs. Knowles's former beau kindly permitted her to take the nobler part.

Contemplating the timing of the widow's downfall, Bea wondered if she resented Mr. Lark for dashing her romantic prospects. Nurturing a deep bitterness, she might have seized the opportunity to revenge herself on the reporter while dispensing with a troublesome blackmailer. She would have learned Mr. Lark's true identity from Mrs. Beveridge, who had already demonstrated an eagerness to pass on information as soon as she got it.

With this in mind, Bea accepted the tea with a grateful murmur, then asked Mrs. Knowles about her relationship with the victim. "You said it was contentious?"

"It was, yes, for all my sins," Mrs. Knowles admitted with a knowing smile. "The old girl was stubborn and prickly, which I realized quickly enough. I joined the board of supervisors at Alicia's urging, as she knew I needed something to occupy my time after my husband died, and it was true. I threw myself into my new responsibilities with an enthusiasm that was perhaps not equal to the assignment. I saw right away that Agnes was brusque and impatient with her charges, and I made lots of little suggestions to try to nudge her toward being kinder to them. She had a combative attitude, as though the children in her care were an enemy army trying to trick her into ceding territory, which was so silly. They were dear and adorable urchins who wanted only a gentle word. I tried to provide as many as possible, but I could visit only so often and Agnes was there all the time. If only she could temper her stance just a little. She refused. But I never stopped trying to be a softening influence in her life."

Bea found this reply fascinating.

Here was Mrs. Knowles, who was fully complicit in the abuses at Fortescue's, speaking earnestly of kindness and consideration. Miss Lark's revelations had spared none of the supervisors. Her hostess not only knew of Condon's malfeasance but also gave it her tacit approval by not protesting or making a fuss. To turn around now and claim to have always had the children's best interests at heart required a dizzying amount of temerity.

Seemingly aware of her guest's thoughts, Mrs. Knowles acknowledged the contradiction and attempted to reconcile the competing notions by attributing one to the other. "Knowing the harsh reality awaiting the little dears when they left the safe haven of Fortescue's made me determined to ensure their stay there was as happy as possible. I believe a happy upbringing gives a child the resilience he needs to flourish as an adult regardless of the difficulties they may encounter. I am the first to admit I failed in many respects. I should have been more forthright with Agnes instead of gently hinting her in the right direction. Condon told me I was wasting my time, and I have a habit of deferring to masterful men. My husband was quite strongminded, which one would have to be to race the London Road on a moonless night."

It was a feeble defense, and Bea wondered if Mrs. Knowles actually believed it or if it was something she had made up on the spot to justify her actions. A willingness to submit to a domineering man could excuse all sorts of behavior.

But that inclination had little to do with Mrs. Knowles's relationship with the former headmistress, and Bea found it strange that her hostess could describe their relationship without mentioning the extortion. Curious as to the transgression, she asked forthrightly.

Mrs. Knowles showed no alarm at the query and even nodded smoothly. "Alicia said you would want to know. You found Agnes's little book with my name in it, I understand. Well, I am determined to tell it to you straight without dressing it up in fine linens. I made a horrible mistake, and Agnes knew about it."

Despite her resolve to speak frankly, she was reluctant to continue and paused to fiddle with her tea, dropping a clump of sugar into the brew, mixing it thoroughly, and taking a cautious sip. As it was now too sweet, she added more bohea and stirred again. Then she drank deeply.

With a deprecating smile, she apologized. "It seems the prospect of unrestricted honesty makes me thirsty. It is the fear, I suspect, as I have never said these words out loud. I hope, your graces"—and here she looked at Kesgrave as well—"will keep my confession between the three of us. But I understand if necessity compels you to share it with others. I would only ask in that circumstance you limit the number of people. Do not, I beg you, tell that rapacious reporter Mr. Lark. He does seem to take a particular interest in orphanages, does he not? It is as though it is a personal mission for him. I do not blame him, for they are rife with abuse and that is what he is meant to do: kick up dust to sell newspapers. Everything is a nine days' wonder to journalists, who are always running toward the next exciting story. They never stay in place for long. It is an interesting profession and I think—"

But she did not share her thought. Instead, she abruptly stopped speaking and closed her eyes tightly. Then she took a deep, measured breath. "I am sorry. This is more difficult than I had anticipated. And I am trying so hard to be brave. I swear this is me marshaling my courage. I knocked down one of the orphans with my phaeton."

If she had expected to feel a sense of release once the words were out of her mouth, then she had gravely misjudged her own response. Instead of relief, her grim expression tightened, and she fidgeted with the sugar spoon for a few seconds before pushing the cup away and splashing tea onto the table. Despite these signs of agitation, her tone was cool when she announced it was a lie. She did not knock down one of the orphans with her phaeton. "My phaeton ran her over."

Then she paused again, her hand swatting air as she reached for the teacup, which she had moved beyond her grasp. Now she leaned forward, clutched it by its rim, and drew it back to her. Gripping the handle as if to take a sip, she continued. "*I* ran her over in my phaeton. She died from her injuries the next day. I killed her. It was an accident. I killed her. She is dead and it is my fault. Agnes was so kind about it. I was distraught and she treated me kindly and my only thought was: She knows what it is like. She had some horrible accident in her past and that is why she could empathize. She told me it was not my fault. She said the children run everywhere, even into the drive, without any thought of anyone else. That might be true. It probably is true. But it was my fault. The horses were out of control. I had no business driving a high-perch phaeton, but I cut such a dashing figure with the reins in my hands and my best bonnet tipped at a jaunty angle. Barty would have been so impressed."

Her voice lost some of its aloofness as tears began to well in her eyes, and she had to stop to swallow past the lump in her throat. "She was such a sweet child, six years old, with blond hair and a slip of a nose. Her eyes were light brown, and she was missing her two front teeth and had the most adorable lisp. I summoned my own physician to attend to her, but it made no difference, for her injuries were too severe. The doctor kept her sedated with laudanum because he said she would be in terrible pain as soon as she woke up. Her body was so broken and all she had been doing was chasing a ball on the lawn. A harmless child playing a sad game of catch by herself and my beast of a team ran her down. Something in the road scared them and they careened out of control. I sat with her all afternoon and pleaded with her to get better. I told her she had so much to live for. I would adopt her myself and she would have a room fit for a princess and she would wear silk gowns and everything she wanted. And through it all Agnes comforted me," she said with a harsh laugh. "I thought she was being kind, but she was really just keeping a running tally so that she could figure out the correct sum to demand as payment."

Blotches of red stained her cheeks as the crying intensified, and she ruthlessly brushed away the tears. "She was so vile, then, not even allowing me a short respite to reconcile what I had done. Susie was not cold in the ground before Agnes lamented how awful it would be if people knew I had killed a child in my care. She would do her best not to mention it, but word had a way of slipping out if she was not constantly vigilant, and for that she would require an inducement of five pounds per month. She was sly and artful until she was not. I was so shocked by her turn I could not understand what she was saying, which forced her to repeat it in plain language without any cunning. I agreed to pay without arguing because I just wanted it to go away. I directed my steward to send her the money on the first of every month and tried not to think about it again. Then the *Gazette* articles came out detailing her and Condon's scheme, and everyone was horrified by my greed because they assumed I was making money on the backs of those poor children too. I did not bother to defend myself because what I had done was indefensible, and so I broke off my engagement to a lovely man because I knew then I did not deserve happiness. I believe that brings us to now."

Mrs. Knowles, tears streaming down her cheeks, sniffled indelicately, and Kesgrave held out a fine linen square. She accepted it with a sputter of amusement at her egregious oversight. "I knew this would happen. I cannot think of the incident without crying, and yet despite all my preparations, I forgot to slip a handkerchief into my pocket. But I did arrange a plate of rout cakes! That is something at least. Let us see, then, what is next? I have shared my opinion of Agnes and revealed the horrible truth that haunts me. I believe that leaves only my alibi. Where was I on Thursday at eleven in the morning?"

Despite her anguish, which was palpable, Mrs. Knowles spoke smoothly, easily, without any of the gasps or heaves that usually accompanied sobbing. Bea, recalling the other woman's boast about always being prepared, wondered if she and Kesgrave were being treated to a performance and braced for an oddly specific alibi that would be verified by an army of servants.

"That is correct, yes," Bea said. "Where were you at the time of the murder?"

"At the linen draper," she announced, adding that the clerk had very kindly given her all his attention as she wrung her hands indecisively between two shades of green despite the other customers waiting for his assistance. "Pea green or apple green? Pea green or apple green? I went back and forth a dozen times, which was tedious, I'm sure, but Mr. Novello's smile never wavered. And he did not bat an eye when I decided on celestial blue. He will remember me, I am certain."

Although it was not exactly the response Bea had anticipated, it was close enough to it to make her extremely vexed with Mrs. Beveridge for giving her friend enough time to devise an alibi that would be challenging to refute. Although Bea had no wish to impugn the honor of a shop clerk she had never met, she did not think securing his cooperation would be very difficult. A handful of coins could be very persuasive, especially when a significant majority of them were guineas. If he proved resistant to an outright bribe, then perhaps Mrs. Knowles could make a large purchase to impress his employers.

Just how many yards of celestial blue had she bought?

"Thank you, yes, that is helpful," Bea said, contemplating the trickiness of the situation. In an attempt to address it, she asked about the other customers.

Startled, Mrs. Knowles said, "Excuse me?"

"You mentioned other customers at Argyle Smith & Co. waiting for Mr. Novello's assistance," Bea reminded her. "I would like the name of one so I can confirm your story."

"You have Mr. Novello," she replied, her voice lilting with confusion and possibly a hint of apprehension. "He will confirm everything I told you, although I am sure he is too well versed in his profession to describe my indecisiveness as tedious. He will say I have a meticulous eye for detail."

"And we will talk to Mr. Novello," Bea assured her. "But we will need someone else to verify the story. The one witness is not sufficient to exonerate you."

Mrs. Knowles frowned and pressed the handkerchief to her eyes, which began to water again. "What about the footman who escorted me? I can call for Percival right now. You may interrogate him as long as you wish. And I will take myself off to another room so that you will not be able to accuse me of directing his answers. Let's do that, shall we? I think it is an excellent idea!"

Obviously, it was not.

Any manipulation that applied to a shop clerk applied doubly to a servant.

Patiently, Bea explained her objection, emphasizing the fact that the suspect had had plenty of time to establish a false alibi.

"You *are* churlish at Alicia for warning me," Mrs. Knowles said darkly. "It is not my fault that she is such a thoughtful friend, and you are horrible to use it against me."

Bea asked again for the name of a fellow shopper.

"You are being beastly, and you do not even know it!" Mrs. Knowles cried, crossing her arms in front of her chest. "Fine! Have it your way, then. Mrs. Ralston was there. The greatest gossip in all of London was at Argyle Smith helping her daughter select drapery, and it will be the utter ruin of me when you call on her at home to ask specifically if she saw me there yesterday. You might as well take out an ad in the dailies announcing I am a murder suspect."

Grimly amused by the tantrum, Bea was no more eager to interview the infamous prattler about Mrs. Knowles than Mrs. Knowles was to be the subject of the interview. Mrs. Ralston was coarse and brash, and after six seasons of ignoring Beatrice Hyde-Clare, she had spent three months pursuing the Duchess of Kesgrave. The society matron recognized the value of information and gathered gossipy tidbits like banknotes to be traded for goods. Made aware of Bea's interest in Mrs. Knowles, she would poke around until she discovered Miss Wraithe's murder and its chief suspect.

It was a daunting prospect, to be sure, but Bea's reputation as a lady Runner would insulate Verity Lark against Mrs. Ralston's vulgar curiosity. And if it did not, what recourse did Mrs. Ralston actually have? Even her curiosity was not rapacious enough to compel her to call on Newgate and demand to see an inmate.

Nevertheless, Bea was happy to be reasonable about it and said they would start with Mr. Novello and consider the matter from there. If he provided the names of other customers, then they would not require Mrs. Ralston's confirmation.

Mrs. Knowles hailed this solution as more than fair. "I appreciate your willingness to work with me to arrive at a compromise. I realize the circumstance is not ideal."

Having ascertained all the information they required, Bea and Kesgrave rose from their seats, startling their host, who pointed to the plate of rout cakes. "Oh, do stay! Now that we have dispensed with all the ugly business, we can have a proper visit. I would love to hear your thoughts on Mrs. Bemetzrieder's performance in *Eccentricities, or Mistakes at Madrid.* Or Gunter's new raspberry ices."

Bea declined, insisting they had more interviews to conduct, and Mrs. Knowles made a second bid at convincing them to linger by asking whom else they were considering for the murder.

"Do say Charles Wigsworth," she said, answering her own query. "I know nothing to his discredit, but Agnes called him a ghoul, which is meaningful, as she was rather ghoulish herself. I always assumed she knew something awful about him. Lord Condon, of course. I cannot see him taking the trouble to hire someone to do it for him and he would have to hire someone because he is still hiding in Ireland. Plus, he and Agnes always got on like a house on fire. Two peas in a pod, they were, despite the disparity in wealth, breeding, and rank. And what about this Lark fellow who caused all the trouble in the first place? He was scathing to all of us but appeared to nurture a particular hatred for Agnes. You might think I am being fanciful when I say it seemed personal, but that is how it struck me. I wondered if he might have been a former resident of Fortescue's."

An astute observation, it exposed the limits of Mrs. Beveridge's confidences. Although she had warned her friend about Bea's investigation and imminent arrival, she had said nothing about Robert Lark's true identity. She shared that revelation only with Mrs. Featherstone-Haughton, doubtlessly because the other woman already knew about her cozy relationship with Miss Wraithe. In contrast, Mrs. Knowles appeared to have no idea.

In light of Miss Wraithe's habit of extorting former supervisors, it made sense that Mrs. Beveridge would want to keep their friendship quiet. Revealing it would invite speculation as to her own transgression, and she did not want that.

It was bad enough that Miss Wraithe knew about her affair with the gardener.

Bea assured her host that Robert Lark was on her list of people to interview, then asked her if she had any thoughts about Dibdin.

"Dibdin," she repeated with a hint of confusion, as though she did not recognize the name of her fellow supervisor. "You mean Arthur?"

"Yes, Arthur Dibdin," Bea affirmed.

Amused, Mrs. Knowles asked what he could possibly have to do with the murder. "He was old and frail and feeble-minded long before the *Gazette* published its articles on Fortescue's. Is he even still alive? What motive would he have? Not blackmail! Agnes called him a doddering buffoon, and I do not think she was wrong. If he is capable of anything more than drooling into his porridge, I would be shocked. Condon only had him on the board because he was a crony. He approved of everything his lordship wanted—as did I. As did we all! But Dibdin was the only one who truly did not know what was happening under his nose because he rarely knew what was happening under his nose. And that *is* the oblique reference to nasal mucous you suspect it is. Never have I known any human so disposed to runny noses and so undisposed to handkerchiefs."

Tightening her fingers as she spoke, Mrs. Knowles belatedly realized she still held the duke's linen square in her grasp and blushed lightly. Gently folding the cream-colored swath of fabric, she promised to have it returned to Kesgrave House after it was laundered. "Perhaps I should be more careful whom I describe as feeble-minded," she added with a self-conscious titter.

Gently, the duke told her she may keep it, which embarrassed her further, and seeming to grapple for something to say that was unrelated to the handkerchief, Mrs. Knowles repeated her assertion that Dibdin must be long dead by now. As his name had a check next to it in Miss Wraithe's daybook, Bea was reasonably sure he had been alive as recently as June first, but she allowed that anything was possible. Perhaps a descendent had continued to pay the levy to protect the family now. In that case, the old and feeble-minded man had gotten into quite a bit of trouble if it mortified the next generation as well.

Leaving their host to wring her hands over the full plate of rout cakes, Bea directed Jenkins to take them to the fashionable emporium in St. James, which he did with only a modicum of grumbling over the snarl of traffic he would inevitably encounter en route. Even with the crush of vehicles, he maneuvered the horses smoothly and arrived in excellent time. Entering the building, she discovered it was crowded with the afternoon set, and their efforts to locate Mr. Novello amid the throng were hampered by shoppers delighted to greet the Duke of Kesgrave as he selected his linens.

Luckily, the customer most determined to enjoy a quiet

tête-à-tête with his grace amid the bustle was none other than Mrs. Ralston herself. An intimate of Bea's aunt, she felt entitled to the duke's attention and boldly threading her arm through his, pulled him to the side where she could not only give her opinion on color schemes but also lament his unfortunate situation.

Dragooned into such dreary domesticity on a pleasant spring afternoon! He should be riding in Hyde Park or boxing at Gentleman Jackson's or even fishing on the heath.

Men of action should be active!

Although couched as concern for Kesgrave, it was actually a criticism of Bea, whose good fortune in nabbing a duke still struck Mrs. Ralston as the height of insolence.

Amused by the reproach, which would have withered Aunt Vera, Bea drew her brows fretfully and expressed sympathy for the poor woman—forced to visit Argyle Smith twice in one week. "You were just here on Thursday, were you not?"

Mrs. Ralston did not find it strange that her movements were known to Bea. An inveterate gossip, she equated attention with importance and assumed people were as interested in her as she was in herself. Consequently, she confirmed that she and her daughter had called earlier in the week to pick out curtains for the latter's dining room, a simple process that was made more difficult by a tiresome patron who monopolized her favorite clerk's attention for almost an hour choosing between two identical shades of green.

"It was that wretched woman Mrs. Knowles," she added with a tart snap of her tongue. "You know, the one who sold those defenseless waifs into slavery to line her pockets. Shameful! And now she is using that blood money to decorate her house. As I said to Lady Stirling last night, I cannot think of anything more immoral or depraved."

Genuinely appreciative of the information, the attainment of which had been the sole purpose of the visit, Bea thanked her for her help and darted a look at Kesgrave, who extricated his arm from the matron's grasp. Then they left the building without pausing to speak to another soul, and Mrs. Ralston, relaying the exchange to Mrs. Drummond-Burrell later that evening at the theater, said it was as though the Duke and Duchess of Kesgrave had visited the emporium expressly to see her.

Chapter Fourteen

Arthur Dibdin was not dead.

Spry and energetic at seventy-eight years old, he appeared fully in control of his bodily fluids and he neither drooled from the mouth nor drizzled from the nose.

He was, to be sure, confounded by Bea's and the duke's appearance on his doorstep, but that was more a function of ignorance than senility. Unaware that Agnes Wraithe had been shot in the head, he could not conceive of himself as a murder suspect. Once he discovered her fate, however, it made perfect sense to him.

"You are here to ask about the blackmail," he announced, his pale green eyes dull from age and yet still able to sparkle with amusement. "Well, well, well, do come in and let us talk about it. You will tell me how it was done, won't you? Shot in the head, you say. But from the back or the front? Did she know it was coming? Did she see who shot her? I hope she did. I hope she looked her killer dead in the eye and felt terror. And surprise—surprise that someone had the spine to end her petty little life."

Dibdin led them through a dimly lit hallway with stucco

walls to a drawing room with dark-stained ceiling beams and a porcelain tile floor. Tudor in style, it was at once cool and cozy, with a cluster of low-slung furniture in one corner that made the space feel larger than it was. Contributing to the effect were the walls, which were bare and streaked with dirt where paintings once hung. Showing them to a settee whose embroidered array of flowers had seen better days, he invited them to sit down. "Why don't we start with your telling me how you learned of the blackmail. Wraithe promised she would never say a word about it to anyone as long as I paid in a timely fashion."

His demeanor was disconcerting—the gleeful twinkle, the sense that their visit was somehow anticipated despite being thoroughly unexpected—and Bea provided the simplest answer to the question. "We found the book she used to record her transactions."

"A book!" he said, his delight over this seemingly mundane aspect of household budget management readily apparent. "She did not mention a book, but she would have to maintain a ledger of her expenses, would she not? It is the only way to know how much money one has for the butcher and the collier. To be fair, I never asked if she would record my information somewhere, so I suppose the fault is mine for not considering the possibility. Tell me, how many of us are there? I know she had Wigsworth on the hook because it is he who told me about her inclination in the first place. The blighter is doggedly closemouthed. I had to give him four glasses of my best wine before he would admit to her enthusiasm for extortion."

It was, Bea thought, a lot of information haphazardly given, and she focused on what she believed he was saying. "You plied Wigsworth with wine to find out if he was being blackmailed by Miss Wraithe?"

"I had no choice," he said, his expression turning earnest.

"The money end of things did not follow a logical course, and it suddenly occurred to me one day that something havey-cavey was going on. The conditions at Fortescue's were always just this side of deplorable. Like the blankets—they were threadbare despite the fact that money had been set aside to buy new ones. I had made the provision myself. Where, then, did the money go? I asked Wigsworth because he was in charge of auditing the accounts. I expected him to provide a reasonable answer or to be as confused as I, but he responded angrily and told me to stop bothering him with stupid questions. His inexplicably aggressive response made it clear he was hiding something, and that is why I plied him with the wine. He told me that Wraithe took money from the coffers every month and he could not report her to anyone because she had him over the barrel. I could not get him to tell me what he had done to put himself at her mercy, but it was enough to know that he was at her mercy. With that information, I was able to get a general sense of her scheme. I was the only one who cared to figure out what she was doing. The others were on the board because it burnished their reputations to appear charitable."

Although he spoke mildly, Bea could feel his contempt for his former fellow supervisors. He thought they were callous and selfish. And yet for all his moral superiority, he had wound up in Miss Wraithe's daybook alongside them.

Perhaps he had been done in by overconfidence.

Convinced he knew where the traps were laid, he failed to notice them underfoot.

Where she saw carelessness, however, Kesgrave noted calculation.

Leaning slightly forward, the duke asked Dibdin if he had deliberately allowed Miss Wraithe to discover him in a compromising position.

The other man chuckled and said he would never allow

something as unreliable as "discovery" to undermine his scheme. "I made certain she would find me by placing my compromising position directly in her path. I feared I was being too blatant about it, but for all her cunning and guile, she did not find it suspicious."

Piecing together his motive, Bea said, "To earn her trust, you had to show yourself as just as untrustworthy."

"It was the only way I could think of to get close to her," he explained with agreeable candor. "She was a prickly fiend, suspicious of everyone, and I had to prove that I was no better than she. If I had no moral authority, then I could not judge her. And it worked. After a while, she stopped being so guarded with me and let small things slip. She liked to show off, I think. Having Wigsworth under her thumb made diverting the funds to her own account easy, and she wanted me to admire how cleverly she arranged it. But as candid as she was about her embezzlement, she was hush-hush about what she and Condon were doing. I knew it was something nefarious because Condon is not an honorable man. That is how I came to join the board of supervisors, as a favor to Condon's father, who was one of my oldest friends. He had hoped that the weight of responsibility would give his wayward son purpose, and he asked me to be an older, wiser influence. I agreed because I knew he was right. Condon needed a steady hand."

If Dibdin's hand was steady, it was also weak, for his presence had done nothing to guide his lordship toward the path of the righteous. "Did you know about the illicit trade? Did you figure that out?"

Frustratingly, he said yes, then no. "After two months of spying, I could make only an educated guess. Among the duties of a supervisor was to use our social connections to help provide the children with the means of supporting themselves after they leave Fortescue's. For the girls that typically meant finding them employment as a maid in a respectable household, and while many of the boys were sent north to work in manufactories or the mines, the ones who showed the most promise were given the opportunity to learn a trade and perhaps establish their own business. I was the only one among the board who took that responsibility seriously. Every so often they would assist. Beveridge once found employment for a girl as a seamstress in Fleet Street. But by and large, I did most of the work with the help of my steward and one of the wardens at the asylum. That is how I noticed that children were leaving without placements, some who were too young for a profession. When I asked where they had gone, I was told they had been adopted. I knew that to be untrue because nobody wanted them."

Realizing what he was saying, Bea felt swamped again by anger and despair. She knew horrible people existed in the world—her parents had been killed by their dearest friend—and yet she was continually amazed by the venality the supervisors displayed. "You knew enough to be horrified and troubled. You *cared* enough to harm your reputation to find out what Miss Wraithe was doing and then you let her carry on doing it."

Unruffled by her accusation, Dibdin smiled and asked musingly, "Oh, but did I? You may recall a series of damning articles that were published in the *London Daily Gazette* that detailed the many atrocities at Fortescue's."

No, Bea thought, her eyes darting to Kesgrave to see if he was as outraged as she by the astounding impertinence of Dibdin daring to claim credit for Verity Lark's work. His expression was blank, and she endeavored to ape his bland neutrality as she turned back to her host.

"That was my doing," he announced.

Again, she was struck by the audacity of the falsehood, and all but decided in that moment that Dibdin must be the killer. Finding himself a suspect in the murder for which he had failed to secure an alibi, he was making up one outlandish lie after another to create an elaborate fiction that he assumed would be too unwieldy to disprove.

It was a last resort, a panicked response, one that would inevitably collapse under its own weight, and yet he spoke with surety and conviction.

The secret to a believable lie was confidence.

Assertive men who spoke with authority ran the world.

Everyone knew that, especially Dibdin, and Bea allowed that he might actually be clever enough to concoct a tale that would hold together under close inspection. An agile mind that could account for several factors at once was capable of many difficult or seemingly impossible things. With the right assortment of truths and half-truths, he might have sent her scurrying in circles for days, successfully evading detection and getting away with murder. That Kesgrave happened to be related to Robert Lark was an improbable stroke of bad luck.

Curious to see how far he would take his fabrication, Bea owned herself surprised by the information and asked if he had been a reporter in an earlier phase of his life.

Dibdin, tsking reproachfully, told her not to be so literal. "I did not write the articles. I initiated them. The editor of the *London Daily Gazette* is a former resident of Fortescue."

Well, yes, that much was true, Bea thought cautiously.

"As I said before, helping to settle former charges into respectable professions was among our responsibilities as supervisors, and when Somerset Reade was fourteen or fifteen, I arranged an apprenticeship for him with a printer. I followed his progress and knew he had established his own newspaper, the *London Daily Gazette.* Given his history at the asylum and need for sensational stories to scandalize the public, I assumed he would take an interest in the corruption at Fortescue's. I was correct," he added smugly.

Prepared for a display of confidence, Bea did not know what to make of his complacency. He seemed truly pleased with himself for what he had managed to accomplish, which made her wonder if he had actually accomplished something.

He could not be telling the truth, could he?

"But first I needed to draw his attention to the problem," Dibdin continued. "And please keep in mind that at this point in time I did not know what the problem was. I had only my suspicions. So I sent an anonymous letter to Somerset Reade explaining that there were children for whom I could not account and advising him to send someone to investigate. He did immediately. A few days later, a reporter was poking around the grounds asking questions about the management of Fortescue's and about the provisions in the pantry and who had access to the accounts. I was greatly disappointed because the boy was a terrible reporter. He said he was a gardener but could barely hold shears without dropping them, and I caught him peering through the windows. I had to take him in hand and all but lead him to Wraithe's door. Truly, I had expected better of Somerset Reade."

Bea felt her uncertainty increase at the description of the reporter, who was clearly one of Miss Lark's characters. During their interview at Newgate, she had mentioned the Turnip, an incompetent fledgling who manipulated people into doing the hard work for him out of irritation, exasperation, or disgust.

"He realized his mistake soon enough and sent a seasoned reporter to poke around," Dibdin said, noting that Robert Lark was indeed a shrewd customer. "He took the information I had given the nincompoop and used it to uncover the Waithe and Condon's scheme and their secret network of thieves, scoundrels, procurers, brothel owners, night watchmen, and estate agents. He located several of the victims and told their stories. He even convinced some members of the network to speak to him, and they are quoted in the articles. They all claimed to have been coerced into participating in the sale of children, which I am sure is a lie, but every allegation was another nail in the coffin. Condon and Wraithe were ruined, just as I had intended."

"Not just Condon and Wraithe," Bea pointed out.

"No, not just Condon and Wraithe," he agreed with an air of resignation. "My plan worked a little too well, and I was swept out of the stable with the rest of the muck. I did not anticipate that Lark would paint such a damning picture of the whole board. I assumed he would focus his energies on Condon and Wraithe and allow the rest of us to go about our business. But that is not what happened."

As nothing in this account exonerated Dibdin of murder, Bea decided to take it as fact. She would confirm the details at a later date with Miss Lark or Mr. Somerset Reade, but for the purposes of the interview, she would accept his version of events. In doing so, she wondered why he continued to pay the monthly blackmail.

"If it was not real, as you said," she said.

"The trouble is, it *was* real," he replied with gloomy earnestness. "That is, for all intents and purposes. It was staged. The girl was never in danger from me, I swear. But Wraithe caught us in a position that would be ruinous to my reputation if word of it spread. I could *say* it was a performance for her benefit alone, but isn't that what I would insist in any event? To anyone's ears but my own, it would ring false and hollow, and I am too old to weather a second scandal. It is enough that half of London thinks I condone the sale of children into misery. The outrage is particularly keen on behalf of the thirteen-year-old girls sold to elderly husbands, and considering the method by which I earned my way into Wraithe's damning book, it was better that I pay than risk exposure. I have three children whose respect I wish to keep.

And then there are the eight grandchildren. Five pounds per month is a small price to pay for my dignity."

But is it, Bea wondered, glancing around the bare room, which was in need of several improvements. The walls, for example, could use a good scrubbing to remove the dirt streaks that outlined where paintings used to hang.

She assumed they had been sold to pay the bills.

Likewise, the staff was sparse.

Dibdin had not only answered the door himself but also refrained from offering them refreshments. If he employed a cook or a butler, they were too busy with other tasks to attend to basic responsibilities.

In that circumstance, five pounds per month was a considerable sum.

His penury was strange, Bea thought, contemplating the largest stain, which was over the sideboard on the wall opposite. Although Dibdin identified helping to place children in respectable professions as the chief duty of a supervisor, their main contribution was in fact financial. Affluence was frequently a prerequisite, as they were called upon to donate their own funds to ensure the maintenance and prosperity of the institution. Additionally, they were obliged to flatter and charm their wealthier connections who typically held more exalted positions in society into donating generously to the cause.

That was how charities worked.

At one time, Dibdin met those conditions.

"And yet it seems as though you could put those five pounds per month to much better use," she noted softly.

Her host smiled wryly and asked if she meant he could restore the paintings. "As odd as it will sound, I must confess that I have grown fond of the marks. It is as though the lines of discoloration are their own works of art. But your point is well taken, and it is correct. I have come down in the world in recent years. I want to say I made a few bad investments, but it is much worse than that. I just made one. It was a hoax from the very beginning, and I was an easy target to swindle because I believed I was too astute to be tricked. During the negotiation, I was convinced I had the upper hand and that the representatives of the mining company would be mortified when they realized I had taken shameless advantage of their ignorance."

Dibdin paused, his eyes focused on the tarnished wall across the room, and as he exhaled, he seemed to shrivel. Suddenly, he looked like the frail and feeble-minded man of Mrs. Knowles's description. "My children know nothing of it. They have no idea. I am fortunate in that none of them have had reason to visit London in the past year. It cannot last. I had a message from my daughter on Tuesday suggesting they might come for the little season. I live in dread of the moment they find out because then they will know that I am a senile old fool. I would happily pay *ten* pounds a month to put off that eventuality indefinitely."

A lofty goal, Bea thought.

Dibdin realized it, too, and grimaced at the grandeur of his aspiration. "Even that meager amount is beyond my means, especially on top of my payment to Wraithe."

"A payment that was to double on the first of the month," Kesgrave added.

Startled by the pronouncement, Dibdin lowered his head with shame and acknowledged it was true. The price of Wraithe's silence had gone up sharply, and he could ill afford to cover the increase. "It is a relief to be spared that expense going forward."

If he had any sense of admitting to an excellent motive, he did not reveal it with a sudden start or an effort to modify his statement. Aunt Vera, hearing herself utter something vaguely incriminating, would blather incoherently for several minutes before falling into an awkward silence.

Dibdin was unperturbed, his gaze lingering on the wall as he imagined the inevitable confrontation with his children. Bea, watching him silently, pondered the timing of the murder, for his penury had recently become a pressing concern. Fleeced within the past year, he did not immediately feel the consequences of his poor decision, as his financial difficulties would have mounted slowly, month by month. The burden of satisfying Miss Wraithe's blackmail demand might have only just become onerous.

A blackmail demand, she reminded herself, that he had assumed voluntarily to root out corruption at Fortescue's and save the impoverished orphans from the diabolical schemes of its overseers.

It was decidedly unfair, having to pay a blackhearted extortionist when he could barely afford his servants.

She was a villain through and through.

And yet he was the one who suffered.

It would be such an easy thing to kill her. She was mean and miserly. Nobody would miss her. Nobody would lament her passing. And he had already revealed how he would do it, looking her dead in the eyes, delighting in her terror, preening over her surprise that someone had the spine to end her petty little life, before spinning her around and releasing the bullet into the back of her skull.

An expensive pistol would number among his possessions, provided he had not sold it yet to pay his bills.

But leaving it behind—that did not align with his current situation.

A man who was forced to sell the canvases on his walls to cover basic amenities would be disinclined to leave something as valuable as a Bernard Michael pistol behind.

The fact that the gun was abandoned at the scene argued in favor of his innocence.

Perhaps, she thought.

Or maybe he was a seventy-eight-year-old man who discovered after shooting Miss Wraithe in the head that cold-blooded murder was an anxiety-inducing proposition. Overcome with horror at his actions, he might have lost his grip on the gun. It might have slipped out of his trembling hands, and seeing it lying on the floor, he realized it was better to leave it where it lay than spend another minute in that wretched house trying to pick it up with trembling fingers. At that point he had one goal and one goal only: to leave the grisly scene as quickly as possible.

The theory had merit, which meant the next step was finding out if Dibdin had an opportunity to kill Miss Wraithe or if he had been under the watchful gaze of his servants during the time of the murder. To a large part, the answer depended on how threadbare his staff actually was.

"I have been patient and forthright in answering every question put to me," Dibdin announced suddenly. "But you have not addressed a single one that I raised. How *did* Wraithe die? Did she see her killer? I hope so. I hope she had time to realize she was getting everything she deserved for decades of wickedness. If you would please tell me, then I will know how to picture her in her final moments. It is mean-spirited of me, but I do not care. She was a blight upon the world, and I am glad she is gone."

Bea, finding his enthusiasm distasteful, could not decide if it argued for or against his guilt. A murderer who feared apprehension would make an effort to appear subdued by the circumstance itself or sad at the thought of death itself, and his failure to adopt a more decorous pose indicated he felt no need for pretense.

Did that confidence stem from not being the murderer or not fearing apprehension?

Whereas previously he had displayed no self-consciousness, now Dibdin heard the callousness of his words and immediately sought to rectify the damage by claiming the news had unsettled him. He had imagined the moment of her death for so long, he could not believe it had finally come. Alas, this explanation was no better, which he readily acknowledged, and rather than make a third attempt at a suitable response, he shrugged in acceptance. He was glad and there was no point in feigning otherwise.

"And now you are wondering if I am the killer," he said with a disapproving frown. "It is understandable, I suppose, but I would hope that if I did slaughter that unholy termagant, I would have the sense not to cackle about it to company. You have not yet told me how she was shot. If it was from behind, then you may be certain it was not I. I would never refuse the opportunity to gloat in the face of her pending death."

It was not distastefulness, Bea realized as his expression lightened again, for that was merely a matter of style or aesthetics. Although Dibdin's glee was unsettling as a singular response to an act of violence, her discomfort with it arose from its commonality. Most victims were loathed by one or two of the suspects she interviewed, which was only to be expected, as few people were universally liked.

Dugmore, for example, had been resented by much of his family, but his daughter and granddaughter felt genuine affection for him.

But it was rare to have a victim who was universally disliked.

It required a particular type of person to make everyone detest them, and Bea found it lowering to her spirits to encounter so much hatred. That their hatred had the power to demoralize her when murder itself served as an inspiration was utterly confounding.

You are a strange and perverse creature, she thought, as she acknowledged the accuracy of Dibdin's statement. She *was* wondering if he was the killer. To that end, she asked him where he was on the eighteenth at eleven in the morning.

"Here," he replied smoothly, waving his hand in front of him as though presenting a lavish gift. "I was in this precise spot: this room, this chair, this fire. Only the book is different. Today, I am reading *Soldier of Fortune.* On Thursday I was still reading *Glenarvon,* which is not my usual style, but I wanted to see what all of the fuss is about. Even if I do not go out in society much anymore, I like to stay current. I must say that Lady Caroline is far braver than I could ever be. Imagine having the gall to satirize Lady Jersey. She is fearless."

"Can anyone attest to your presence here at the time of the murder?" Bea asked.

Dibdin furrowed his brow uncertainly. "Yes, definitely. Well, possibly. The truth is, I do not know. I made a genuine effort to find the book interesting, but it is not to my taste. Melodramas are so monotonous. I nodded off for a couple of hours, and I cannot say if any of my servants looked in on me during that time. I hope at least one opened the door and saw me sleeping. If not, then I am afraid I am without an alibi. You will have to take my word for it that I did not kill Wraithe."

Obviously, no, she would not.

For the duration of the investigation, the only suspect's word she would take was Verity Lark's. Everyone else was presumed guilty.

When asked who among his staff was working on the morning in question, Dibdin listed three positions—footman, cook, maid of all work—then apologized to the duke for having to let his valet go in February. "I was able to hold on to the butler until May, but then practical concerns had to supersede. I rarely entertain anymore, and the wine cellar is decimated."

While Dibdin issued these laments, Bea summoned the servants and asked them to relay what they were doing at around eleven o'clock on the morning in question. All three cited time-consuming activities that engrossed them for more than an hour. Only the footman could recall seeing Dibdin in the drawing room at all, and that was at eight o'clock.

"He was drinking coffee while reading *The Black Dwarf*," the footman added to his employer's consternation. "I remember the title because when I first saw it, I thought it was called 'The Black Dawn.'"

Coloring slightly, Dibdin realized he had in fact not been reading *Glenarvon* on the day in question. "I finished it the week before—and it was hard work, too. You are right, Samson, it was *The Black Dwarf*. I fell asleep right after Hobbie invited Earnscliff to spend the night at his farm. There was a lot of description then, which I found boring. All the Waverly novels bore me. I do not know why I keep reading them."

As Bea had yet to read the book herself, she could not speak to the significance of the plot point, but she appreciated his attempt at specificity. Narrative details did not, however, comprise an alibi, which Dibdin realized. Although he winced in apparent distress, he gamely insisted it did not matter if his servants could not confirm his whereabouts. "I did not murder Wraithe, so you won't find anything that supports it. It will all come out all right in the end, and when you do find the culprit who murdered her, your grace, I hope you will convey my gratitude."

But his laugh was stiff and awkward, indicating he was not quite as sanguine as he endeavored to appear, and as Bea and Kesgrave settled into the carriage to return to Berkeley

Square, she sighed with relief at having two excellent suspects. At the same stage in their previous investigation, they had ruled out all the likely contenders and had started to look farther afield. Although that eventuality might yet occur, it felt good to be on such solid footing.

"Whom do you prefer?" Kesgrave asked, adjusting his position so that her shoulder rested gently in the crook of his arm.

Without pause, she said Wigsworth, for he was monstrous and would do anything to advance his agenda. "At the same time, I am not sure I believe Dibdin is the hero he makes himself out to be. Perhaps he arranged the indecent clutch for Miss Wraithe to discover or perhaps he was just caught in an indecent clutch. But we can confirm other aspects of his story, which I think he knows. Even if Miss Lark were not in danger, Mr. Somerset Reade would answer queries from Her Outrageousness."

Revealing that he had also contemplated the identity of Mr. Twaddle-Thum in the wake of his restraint, the duke posited his own theory—namely, that the editor himself was the famous gossip. "In aggregate, that is. Every reporter for the *Gazette* gathers the information and he composes the article. It would explain how he has been able to create the sense that he is everywhere at once."

Intrigued by the theory, Bea allowed it was not without its logic. Somerset Reade's financial stake in the newspaper's success was unquestionable, he was an experienced reporter, and having a team at his disposal provided him ready access to information on a wide range of topics. Furthermore, he had remained in London for the duration of the war—unlike Lord Colson, whose responsibilities as the spy known as Typhoeus required him to dash off to the Continent from time to time—and would know to leave off tormenting Miss Lark's brother's wife without her saying a word.

Amused by the prospect of Twaddle becoming embroiled in the investigation, she wondered if he would invent an infuriating nickname for himself to bandy about liberally in his report.

Kesgrave, perhaps giving the absurd proposition more consideration than it deserved, suggested the editor would make the effort only if he became a recurring character in his own column. "How many murder investigations do you imagine the editor of the *Gazette* being embroiled in?"

A fair question, she thought, and yet impossible to know. "As I could not imagine the Duke of Kesgrave being embroiled in one, let alone more than a dozen, I shall refrain from speculating on the general premise that there are more things in heaven and earth than are dreamt of in my philosophy."

Kesgrave, allowing a dramatic shudder, chastised her for playing fast and loose with the truth, and to prove the number of investigations did not exceed twelve, began to list victims in chronological order, as though they were ships in the Battle of the Nile.

It was a deliberate provocation, and although Bea rebuked herself for succumbing readily to the obvious ploy, she nevertheless turned sinuously in his arms to press her lips against his. They had all evening to discuss ways to prove which of their suspects murdered Miss Wraithe, including interviewing the neighbors and ... and ...

But the idea slipped from her mind as the duke's fingers skimmed the bodice of her gown and, shifting more comfortably in his lap, she decided whatever thought she had could wait.

Chapter Fifteen

Although Bea frequently observed Aunt Vera scowling with frosty dislike at Lady Abercrombie in the drawing room of Kesgrave House, it was highly unusual to see her glaring at the countess *and* the Marquess of Ware's second son. It required some effort, as the targets of her dissatisfaction sat on opposite ends of the low table and she had to twist her head back and forth between them, as if watching a game of tennis.

Despite the challenges it presented, she kept her eyes on each caller in succession, her eyes narrowing with suspicion when the beautiful widow laughed throatily, then with confusion at the ne'er-do-well's polite response to this determined flirting. A brief, panic-stricken expression crossed Aunt Vera's features when she realized she would have to look away from both visitors to greet her niece, but her countenance cleared as she darted to her feet and scurried to the other side of the settee.

The new position broadened her view.

Now she could see everyone at once.

Amused by these antics, Bea wondered if her aunt was

offended by what she perceived as Lord Colson's receptiveness to the countess's coquetry or affronted by his history of immoderate drinking and excessive gambling.

"Well, thank goodness you have finally returned," her aunt said with an air of aggrieved impatience, as though the interval she had been made to wait—which, Bea knew from Marlow's report, was only twenty-four minutes—had been an interminable age. "I still have so many more important things to do today and cannot be made to cool my heels here indefinitely."

Well, no, that was not right, Vera realized, her face paling at the implication, which was highly insulting to Kesgrave. Obviously, she meant to say that she had additional things to do that were important, not that she had things to do that exceeded this visit in importance. "You must be aware, your grace, that I hold you in the highest esteem and as a consequence consider you the *most* important thing."

Oh, but that was wrong as well, for she would never dare to presume to tell him what he *must* know. "You are free to know or not know as much or as little as you like. Indeed, you may choose complete ignorance if that suits you."

Lady Abercrombie, her own patience worn thin, owned herself unsurprised that the other woman would proselytize for nescience. "Knowing nothing has served you well."

As Aunt Vera glared at the hateful peeress, Bea turned to Lord Colson to apologize for the chaotic reception and beg him to give her a moment to settle other matters. Before she could speak, the countess added that she had not called to render judgment on Mrs. Hyde-Clare's mental acuity or lack thereof. "We have more pressing business to address."

"She is here for your mother's manuscript, which we decided I would take in hand," Aunt Vera said with admirable calm, for the notion of allowing her sister-in-law's radical treatise to be published horrified her to the tips of her toes.

Nevertheless, it was a sacrifice she was resolved to make as an act of repentance.

Bea, who had yet to decide if she wanted her mother's work to be widely distributed, informed her aunt that she had mistaken the situation. "Lady Abercrombie is here for the plans for the nursery at Haverill Hall."

With an airy wave, Lady Abercrombie said she had gotten the drawing a week ago from Stephens. "He is remarkably efficient. I must warn you, Damien, that I intend to lure him away, for I am in desperate need of a reliable steward."

Untroubled by the threat, Kesgrave wished her the best of luck in that endeavor while Vera gasped at the impudence of trying to pinch a ducal servant.

Bea looked again at Lord Colson to offer an apology.

"I am here to discuss the house party at Haverill Hall," her ladyship continued. "I thought we could draw up a provisional guest list and begin to think about dates."

Although Bea could imagine few things more horrifying than hosting the beau monde at the excessively vast estate, she chose to be entertained by the countess's tack. "You may compile all the lists you wish, but it will not compel me to agree to something I find utterly objectionable."

Seemingly baffled, Lady Abercrombie asked why she would compel something that had already been achieved. "You agreed to the house party days ago."

Bea knew it was nonsense and yet still felt a chill shiver down her spine. "I did not."

"I wrote to you about it," the countess said. "Twice, in fact."

Oh, yes, all those letters lying unopened in the bottom drawer of her escritoire. She imagined they contained all sorts of outrageous proposals. "I have not yet replied to those letters."

"But you did! Your lack of reply *was* the reply. Silence is approval. Everyone knows that. Do they not, Lord Colson?" Lady Abercrombie said, batting her liquid brown eyes at him provocatively before returning her gaze to Bea. "You see? He did not answer. That is plainly a yes."

Aunt Vera, whose missives had also been consigned to the bottom drawer, endorsed this sentiment, and Bea wondered to what else she had given tacit approval.

Her curiosity was immediately satisfied by her relative, who announced that she and Uncle Horace looked forward to seeing her at Red Oaks.

Having resolved to ignore her aunt's reply, Bea found herself too bewildered by the unfamiliar name to comply. Before she could stop herself, she sputtered, "Where?"

"Mr. Holcroft's ancestral home," her relative explained. "He has invited the family to visit over the summer, and you must come with us because you are a duchess. Your elevated status is a credit to our family, even if it does not make any sense, and Flora needs our support. She has little to recommend her."

Before Aunt Vera could amend her statement to include her daughter's many—er, *several*—accomplishments or her ladyship could make a sneering comment about the little cousin, Bea said with sweeping dismissal that their concerns were neither here nor there. "As Kesgrave and I have important business to discuss with Lord Colson, I must bid you goodbye. We shall resume this discussion at a more convenient time."

While Aunt Vera cited the inviolateness of agreements arrived at by tacit approval, Lady Abercrombie narrowed her eyes dubiously and asked the identity of the victim.

Appalled by the notion of her ramshackle niece dragging the august duke into yet another unseemly investigation, Vera inhaled sharply and wondered how it was possible for one person to encounter so many cadavers. "I swear, we were not constantly tripping over dead bodies prior to our stay in the Lake District. Our entire lives—lived without a single murdered corpse, and now, since meeting you, your grace, they are everywhere we turn," she exclaimed, her voice rising plaintively at the seeming injustice. She held her peace for a count of three, then started violently when she realized she had unintentionally implied that the preponderance of bodies was somehow the duke's fault. "Obviously, it is something Bea is doing, although I cannot put my finger on what exactly."

Equally mystified by the strange ubiquity of carcasses, Bea took no offense at her aunt's remarks. Instead, she agreed with the observation, then assured her aunt and the countess that the victim was nobody of note in an attempt to shuffle them out of the room. "It is the villain in a scandal at an asylum for orphans."

"Oh, well, that is all right, then," Lady Abercrombie said, happy to leave Beatrice and Kesgrave to their detecting, which she found excessively dreary. "As the only interesting malefactor in an orphanage scandal has already taken himself off—a gun, was it?—I shall leave you and Damien to your little intrigue. I am not even the least bit curious as to what this has to do with the charming Lord Colson, with whom it has been a pleasure to pass the last half hour. I hope to see you again soon, my lord, perhaps at the Red Lantern. As for you, duchess, we shall reconvene at a later date to discuss the guest list. There is no rush, for we have plenty of time, and it is merely a formality, as I have it more or less settled on my own."

Although confident Kesgrave was no more inclined to consent to the lovely widow's plan than she, Bea nevertheless felt a frisson of alarm at these words. She had been just as determined not to submit to the peeress's murder mystery dinner party play, and yet a week later she was sitting in her ladyship's drawing room reading a detailed description of the character she was to assume for the duration of the evening.

The Countess of Abercrombie had a way of manipulating events and people to get exactly what she wanted. The two situations, however, could not be compared. Hosting an intimate gathering in one's own home was categorically different from arranging a bucolic sojourn at a duke's family seat.

Patently, Bea had nothing to worry about.

Relaxing her posture, she watched her ladyship take her leave of Kesgrave, regaling him with tales of her lion cub's latest exploits and urging him to visit Grosvenor Square to see Henry for himself. "He is growing so big," the countess said, drawing closer to the entrance, an expression of relief on Aunt Vera's face as she watched the other woman leave. Now that her bête noire was departing, she could have a proper conversation with her niece.

No, she could not, for Bea knew Lord Colson's patience had to be wearing thin by now because her own had stretched to a sliver. Contemplating how to encourage her relative to run along, she decided describing Miss Wraithe's corpse would do the trick. Horrified by the indecorousness of mentioning a dead body in polite company, Aunt Vera would quit the drawing room with an air of injured disgust and report back to her husband that their niece's degeneracy showed no signs of relenting.

Vera Hyde-Clare had no more use for murder investigations than Lady Abercrombie, although she could not help but stare with dismay when a victim of high social standing undermined his consequence by allowing himself to be murdered in a fashion so unseemly it drew Bea's attention.

Plainly, the current case did not meet that qualification. Miss Wraithe was beneath the *ton*'s notice, and the only interesting malefactor in an orphanage scandal had arranged his own exit.

Oh, but wait, Bea thought as she realized she had no idea to what event the countess's remark referred. It had nothing to do with Fortescue's, which meant there was a second orphanage scandal.

That in itself was unremarkable.

Orphan asylums were hellish pits where children were routinely mistreated by the people whose purpose was to protect and nurture them. Nobody doubted that they were all awful and corrupt.

But for the corruption to be exposed—that was highly usual.

"Who was the malefactor?" Bea called, halting the widow's progress as she strode to the door. "A few minutes ago, you described someone as the only interesting malefactor of an orphanage scandal. Who was that?"

Agog at the display of ignorance, her ladyship asked if Beatrice had spent a significant portion of her life under a rock. "Or were you ill for several months? Otherwise, I cannot conceive how you managed to avoid all word of it. It was a few years ago now, but for a while it was the only thing on anyone's lips, and I am sure nobody has forgotten a single detail. Upon consideration, I realize Hottenroth's downfall occurred in October, when you would have been rusticating. Word of it might not have reached your obscure little corner of the country."

It was clear, however, from Aunt Vera's shudder of revulsion that some aspect of the scandal made it all the way to Bexhill Downs. "That man's name should not be uttered by any decent human. What he did to those children is an abomination."

"For once your aunt and I are in agreement," Lady Abercrombie said with a wry smile. "Hottenroth's depravity is shocking even to me, and I once played Venus in a pantomime at the Hellfire Club."

Aunt Vera shivered dramatically again as Lord Colson explained that Giles Hottenroth had donated generously to an orphanage near the market in Spital Square and was given the run of the place. "They called him their patron saint, and he repaid their trust by molesting the children, boys and girls alike."

"He treated it like his own personal harem, doling out access in small doses to men whom he deemed worthy of the experience," the countess added with a moue of distaste. "Brownell told me all about it years ago in an inexpert bid to woo me to his bed. His father, you see, was among the aging roués with whom Hottenroth shared his munificence, and Brownell thought I would find the secret information titillating. He imagines himself a dangerous rakehell like his father when in fact he is a lecherous puppy with no charm who refuses to relent. All these decades later and he continues his pursuit! Notwithstanding Brownell's own titillation, the *haute ton* knew enough to appear appalled and expunged Hottenroth from its ranks. White's and the Four Horse club revoked his membership, Almack's barred his entry, and his wife was so desperate to distance herself, she moved in with her sister, with whom she had publicly quarreled a few years before. He tried to brazen it out, but when his brother gave him the cut direct in Bond Street, he realized it was futile and marshaled the only bit of honor he had left."

But even this was not enough for Aunt Vera, who called his final act a selfish indulgence, for the supposedly noble deed left his family in dire financial straits. "The estates were mortgaged to the hilt and his wife, who had no personal fortune of her own, was forced to survive on crumbs from her sister. There were two children, a son and a daughter if I am remembering it correctly."

Lady Abercrombie confirmed her recollection, adding that the son was a hothead. "He came down from Oxford after Hottenroth shot himself and bounded around London looking for someone to shoot. I believe at one point, he tried to call out his uncle. It was all very sordid, and I am sure he would have gotten himself killed sooner or later had his sister not stepped in and taken him in hand. Unlike him, she remained calm, coolly assessed her marriage prospects, and nabbed a parvenue. The brother returned to Oxford, and the mother moved in with her daughter."

Bea, digesting this information, realized there had been references to similar scandals during their interviews. Condon's solicitor had intimated it, had he not, with his comment regarding his lordship's comfortable situation: *He knows he is fortunate, for the other men who have found themselves similarly undone by the* Gazette's *reportage do not have this option.* And Mrs. Knowles had noted Robert Lark's predilection for writing stories about orphanages: *It is as though it is a personal mission for him. I do not blame him, for they are rife with abuse and that is what he is meant to do: kick up dust to sell newspapers.*

As there could not be two reporters in London who cared enough about orphans to uncover their abuse, she assumed Miss Lark had written multiple exposés, a supposition Lord Colson confirmed.

Intrigued, Lady Abercrombie asked who Miss Lark was, then abruptly shook her head and instructed Bea not to answer. "I do not wish to be drawn into one of your wretched investigations. I shall take my leave before you say another word. If you require further information, then you must apply to Derrick Hottenroth directly or even Mrs. Featherstone-Haughton," she said, swiveling on her heel and striding again toward the door.

But it resonated with Bea immediately—that long, lumbering behemoth of a name—and she called after the countess, stopping her yet again as she was about to step into the corridor. "Featherstone-Haughton. You said Featherstone-Haughton."

Placidly, the widow confirmed that she had indeed said the name Featherstone-Haughton. "As well as several others, I might add. Names were, in fact, the primary purpose for my visit—to decide which ones to include among the list of guests we invite to your inaugural house party. The importance of the event cannot be overstated. Having established you in town with elegance and verve, I can do no less for the country. Clara would expect it of me. If I could host the gathering in my own home, I would, for nothing unsettles me more than having to rely on the judgment and servants of others, but my estate is in the Derbyshire Dales, which is too far from Cambridgeshire to be of use."

Aunt Vera, realizing either she had been remiss in her duty to her niece or she would not merit an invitation to the party if the Countess of Abercrombie was in charge of issuing them, stepped forward to announce that she would oversee Bea's country debut.

It was the least *she* could do for the dear girl's dead mother.

Her ladyship trilled with mirth and noted that *least* would describe Mrs. Hyde-Clare's efforts to a tee, as Bea reminded Kesgrave that Mrs. Featherstone-Haughton was Mrs. Beveridge's friend whom she called Feathers. "Her brother is a hothead who likes to shoot things, and he has access to the information Miss Wraithe discovered through his sister. Feathers is Mrs. Beveridge's closest friend, her kindred spirit and sworn confidant. She tells her everything."

"Then we must go," Lord Colson said.

"Go where?" Lady Abercrombie asked, perplexed by the sudden change in conversation.

Kesgrave answered with a look at Bea. "Mrs. Beveridge's, I

think. Let us start by finding out how much Feathers knows and the likelihood of her passing information to her brother."

"Yes, that is exactly right," Bea replied.

While the countess asked what Alicia Beveridge had to do with anything, the duke summoned Marlow and told him to have Jenkins bring the carriage around again. "And please ask Mrs. Wallace to prepare a snack for the duchess, something that is easy to transport."

"Cheddar and a nice piece of crusty bread," Bea suggested.

Aunt Vera pressed her lips together in a display of ardent disapproval and insisted that all of Bea's running around could not be good for the babe. "You need plenty of rest and to eat properly—at a table, for one thing! Cheese and bread are not sufficient, and a moving carriage is terrible for your digestion. Your physician cannot condone such behavior, dashing around London after murderers, and would advise you to temper your activities. All those years of your shirking your duty to your family to read novels in secret nooks and corners and now when you should be spending your time resting quietly, you refuse to sit still. If the doctor you hired to oversee your care does not recommend these basic precautions, then I must not only question his credentials but also impugn your good sense in retaining his services."

As it was Lady Abercrombie who had recommended the physician, Aunt Vera was in fact impugning the countess's good sense, something she did at regular intervals but only in the privacy of her own home. Discovering she had delivered the cutting critique in person, she turned a bright shade of pink and remained silent as her ladyship asked her to list the qualifications she deemed necessary in a doctor. The query was facetious, and as Bea left the drawing room, she heard the widow propose a series of increasingly absurd answers. "Grow onions in his kitchen garden? Execute the Mail

Coach? Walk across ice in the winter without falling through?"

In the entry hall, Bea found Mrs. Wallace waiting with a dainty hamper, which she offered with an apology for not having cheddar on hand, only Cheshire and Wensleydale. Bea assured the housekeeper these substitutions were more than acceptable and carried the basket out to the drive, where Jenkins helped her climb into the carriage.

As soon as the door swung shut, Lord Colson revealed his impatience to address the business at hand by immediately launching into his discoveries for the day. "Lord Condon remains in Ireland as his solicitor said. His London house is still shut up tight. A layer of dust covers every surface, and a family of rats have taken up residence in the drawing room fireplace. His solicitor dispatched a letter to him this afternoon—it specifically discussed your visit—and it was addressed to him in Ballygiblin. Finally, I spoke with Lionel Boyle, who returned from Dublin yesterday. He saw Condon on Wednesday at an event for the Royal Dublin Society at Leinster House."

An impressive display of thoroughness from a man whose most famous accomplishment was accruing a mountain of debt so large he had no recourse but to steal from his family, it was a rudimentary day's work for London's favorite gossip and England's most accomplished spy.

"Regarding the solicitor, Edmund Ellis, I can find no evidence to support his involvement in the Wraithe's murder," his lordship added. "Condon makes up only about fifteen percent of the Ellis's monthly receipts, which is too little to persuade him to risk the noose himself. He has no identifiable ties to the underworld to make hiring a killer easy, so he would have to trust a cut-throat he met in an alley or a tavern. That would expose him to all sorts of ugliness with little advantage for him. Condon might have paid him a large sum of money for the service, but again, I do not think Ellis is reckless enough to take the risk. Perhaps if Condon's account made up a significant portion of his business, but he has a thriving concern and plenty of other clients. He would continue to prosper if Condon took a pet and decamped to another firm."

Bea, who was delighted to remove the Irish lord from contention, listened silently as Lord Colson exonerated the parents of the six children whom Miss Wraithe had plagued. With the help of an associate, he had verified their whereabouts during the time of the murder. "Lastly, I confirmed the report regarding the brooch. It is as described and in the rotation office."

"We likewise eliminated Mrs. Knowles by confirming her alibi," she said, tearing off a piece of bread and pairing it with a slice of Cheshire. "We were unable to do the same for Dibdin, who, like Wigsworth, claims to have been tucked up safely in his home. Neither man can produce a witness who can attest to that."

His lordship nodded and noted that Bea's letter from the evening before said that Wigsworth used the children at Fortescue's as subjects in his experiments but did not include the nature of those experiments. She shared it now and felt his fury when she mentioned the boy who required medical care and whose mental faculties had been permanently diminished by the procedure. Then she related the account they had gotten from Arthur Dibdin, and although Lord Colson did not dismiss the suspect's claim that he had worked with Mr. Somerset Reade to reveal the truth, he saw Miss Lark's steady hand behind it.

"If Dibdin did in fact compromise himself to earn the Wraithe's trust so he could discover her nefarious schemes, then it was only because Verity had given him the idea," Lord

Colson said. "She found the perfect disguise to prod his conscience, I am certain of it."

Bea, wiping crumbs from her fingers on the linen serviette Mrs. Wallace provided, paused suddenly as she realized Lord Colson's feelings for Miss Lark were far more profound than she had originally supposed. That he was thoroughly besotted, she had observed from the first.

But the faith he displayed in her abilities, his determination to credit her with almost superhuman qualities, pointed to an affection far greater than mere infatuation.

He loved her ridiculously.

Kesgrave, appearing to find nothing inordinate in his lordship's faith in Miss Lark, allowed that a manipulation was possible, as a man with Dibdin's high self-regard could easily fall prey to an outside influence. "In the past year, he lost a significant portion of his fortune to swindlers by assuming he had the upper hand."

"His recent penury makes him an excellent suspect," Bea added, returning the cloth to the basket before tearing off another piece of bread. "All those years paying what he considered to be a voluntary fee and then all at once it was a hardship. He despised her, of course. They all did. And into this mix we add Mrs. Featherstone-Haughton's hothead brother, Derrick Hottenroth, who has no reason to detest Agnes Wraithe. He did not know her. I cannot make sense of his motive to kill her, and yet I am willing to bet he knows of the link between Miss Lark and the victim, thanks to his sister. Perhaps they were working together and had a falling out. When we talked in prison, Miss Lark hypothesized that the shadowy figure wanted Miss Wraithe to do something with the information about Robert Lark other than blackmail and she refused—and *that* is why he killed her. If Hottenroth enlisted Miss Wraithe in his revenge and they quarreled over how to proceed, he might have soured on their partnership and decided to eliminate her as a complication. Then, knowing Thimble was about to arrive to bully Miss Lark, he dropped the gun to the floor, arranged Miss Wraithe in the position he thought most damning, and ran out."

"Because his plan all along was to do some sort of grievous harm to Miss Lark," Kesgrave said.

"And her plan all along was to soak her for money to pay for her school," she replied. "Two fundamentally different approaches to revenge. Miss Wraithe was ornery and possessive of her blackmail schemes, according to Mrs. Beveridge. She realized too late that he intended to kill her golden goose, she objected, they argued, and he shot her."

"Or maybe she took one look at the gun in his hand and realized he was a fatter goose," Kesgrave countered. "If she recognized its value, she might have turned her rapacious gaze on him."

"True," Bea murmured, selecting another square of cheese as the carriage drew to a stop in front of Mrs. Beveridge's home. "After all that we've learned, I would expect nothing less from her. She was an opportunist to the core."

Lord Colson said the appeal of these theories was they drew all the elements together at the right time and place. "In the absence of a shadowy figure controlling the action, I have struggled to understand how the timing could have worked out so thoroughly to Verity's disadvantage. It seemed like more than mere horrible luck."

Although Bea did not share his predominantly sanguine outlook on the nature of fortune, she liked the theory as well and opened the carriage door to begin proving it.

Chapter Sixteen

Mrs. Beveridge, who believed she had handled the previous encounter with the murder duchess with something approaching aplomb, categorically refused to allow another. Folding her arms across her chest, she shook her head and issued a vehement no. "Absolutely not. I managed to squeak by yesterday by the skin of my teeth and only did so by coming up with an ingenious lie to explain your presence. By the way, your grace, you are organizing a new club to rival Bentham's now defunct Henley Sporting Club, and are considering my husband as a founding member," she said to the duke. "Your plan is in its earliest stages and rather than propose it directly to William, you thought it would be prudent to assess his interest by asking me first. Although you may be able to point to several flaws in this story, my husband lacks the ability to use critical thinking skills when his ego is flattered. It is his most endearing quality. Indeed, it is his *only* endearing quality! But I can do nothing with *this*."

Here, she pointed to Lord Colson as her top lip curled in a sneer. "There is no yarn I can spin that would explain this man's presence in our house. He is a disgrace to his name *and* his country. Oh, yes, my lord, I saw the item in the paper earlier this week about your attempts to claim credit for someone else's heroism! Thank God we have patriots like the brave Mark Kingsley."

Although Bea had little patience for this nonsense, she knew they would never get satisfying answers if Mrs. Beveridge was in a state of nervous excitement and calmly suggested they take a turn around the square. The neighbors might see them, but the servants would not.

Despite her lady maid's garrulousness, Mrs. Beveridge refused the option and led them to the drawing room. She asked them to remain standing in case her husband returned from his appointment at his club. "It will look less cozy, and I can tell him you were on your way out. Now explain to me why you are here again to plague me and do be quick about it!"

Bea, complying with her request despite the quartet of lovely green velvet bergères next to them, promised not to take up much of her time. "We just have a few more questions."

"How is that possible?" Mrs. Beveridge grumbled. "I told you everything I knew yesterday. It is just like Agnes to be more vexing to me in death than in life!"

"They are in regard to Mrs. Featherstone-Haughton," Bea said.

Startled, Mrs. Beveridge repeated the name as if she had heard it incorrectly, and Bea confirmed their interest. Specifically, they wanted to know how much information she had shared with her friend. But this notion further puzzled their host and she stared blankly for several long seconds. Then, seeming to recall her anxiety about her husband's imminent appearance, she said, "I tell Feathers everything. We have no secrets between us. There! Are we done? Lovely! Do leave without saying a proper goodbye. You do not have to stand on ceremony with me."

Darting a look at Kesgrave, Bea said, "So you *did* tell her Robert Lark's true identity."

Disgruntled by the need for further discussion, Mrs. Beveridge glared at the relentless murder duchess and said she had not. "Feathers is among my dearest friends, and I would trust her with my life and, more importantly, to tell me if the color of my new bonnet makes my cheeks look sallow. But put my financial well-being in her delicate hands? Never! If I told Feathers the name of the reporter and she blabbed it about, then Agnes would know it was I who scuttled her blackmail scheme. She would consider it the greatest betrayal and renew her efforts to extort me."

Disconcerted by the unexpected answer, Bea sought to clarify what precisely Mrs. Beveridge had told her friend, which earned her another angry glower. "Dear God, how many times do I have to repeat myself! I told Feathers everything but the reporter's true name. She is my closest friend and confidant. I withhold nothing!"

It was still possible, then, that Mrs. Featherstone-Haughton passed on enough information to the hothead brother for him to discover the name on his own. Frequently, the most challenging part of solving a mystery was knowing there was a mystery to solve. Or rather than waste time doing his own possibly time-consuming research, he might have approached Miss Wraithe directly and suggested they work together to enact revenge on the despicable reporter.

It was a link, tenuous, to be sure, but a link nonetheless.

"Could Mrs. Featherstone-Haughton have mentioned your conversation about Robert Lark to her brother?" Bea asked.

A thoughtful expression softened Mrs. Beveridge's features as she allowed it was possible. "She has him over for tea once a week, and they do have to talk about something. Derry is no help, the beast. He just sits in her drawing room in sulky silence like a petulant child. She is a saint to put up with his nonsense. I would have washed my hands of him years ago. But I suppose she knows how much he detests the weekly meeting and enjoys turning the screw. You see, that is why it never does to make sacrifices for people. They do not appreciate it!"

Recalling Lady Abercrombie's description of Mr. Featherstone-Haughton as a parvenue, Bea assumed this was a reference to her husband. She had married him only to save her family from penury. One would expect her brother to be grateful. "Why does Hottenroth resent her?"

Mrs. Beveridge, her expression darkening in response to the query, swore she would not allow herself to be turned into the meanest prattler to satisfy the murder duchess's prurient interest. "If you want to gossip, then I suggest you call on Mrs. Ralston or Lady Jersey. They will be delighted to tell you all sorts of salacious details about people you do not know. But I will not discuss my dear friend's personal tribulations for your titillation. She has been through enough already, what with her father's cowardly behavior and that vulgar husband of hers, whom she would never have wed if not for the mountain of debt the estate was saddled with and having the care of her mother and brother. That they are both too selfish to appreciate her sacrifice attests to the fact that they were not worth saving in the first place."

It was, Bea thought, a surprisingly edifying answer for a refusal, and rather than respond defensively to the accusation of prurience, she pressed for further information about what had been revealed. "Her family objects to her husband? Mrs. Hottenroth would have preferred to remain with her sister?"

"The murder duchess is already so well informed," Mrs. Beveridge murmured with a disapproving twist of her lips before replying that the situation was more complicated than a simple matter of preferences. "Mrs. Hottenroth is relieved to be free of her sister's charity but wishes it could have been arranged in a more dignified manner. She forgets how limited her daughter's options were. Suitors were not clamoring to align themselves with the family of a man who had foisted his attentions on dozens of small children before shooting himself in the head. Featherstone-Haughton was the best she could do, and I understand her mother's objections. I myself find it difficult to be in his presence for more than twenty minutes without feeling as though I want to crawl out of my skin. He has an oily way about him, slithery like a snake, and he looks at you as though there is a tear in your bodice that you have not noticed yet. It is quite unpleasant."

"And does Mr. Hottenroth resent his sister for the same reason?" Bea asked.

Now Mrs. Beveridge smiled. "If only his bitterness were so reasonable! No, the puppy is still sulking because he was not allowed to run off to India to make his fortune. A friend's uncle had arranged a position for him with the East India Company, and Feathers made him return to Oxford as their father wanted. He has been a perfect brute ever since."

"He bears a grudge, then?" Lord Colson asked.

Although she did not relish having to acknowledge the Coal Son in her own drawing room, Mrs. Beveridge glanced at him out of the corner of her eye and said yes. "Hottenroth is like a dog with a bone. He never lets anything go. As I said, Feathers is a saint for putting up with him after everything she has been through. That said, she does have a remarkably generous husband. Featherstone-Haughton is obscenely wealthy and has never asked her how much a new fichu costs. He could not care less about the price of things. He actually wants his wife to be well turned out because he knows it is a credit to him to have an elegant spouse who is admired by the beau monde and supports all her mad starts. When she decided to have a signature feather embroidered on every item she owns, including her chemises, he did not say a word. Whereas my husband!"

As Mrs. Beveridge described the apoplectic fit William would have if she had dared to insist on such an unnecessary extravagance, Bea looked at Kesgrave and his lordship, both of whom appeared to have the same thought as she: They must interview Hottenroth at once. He was the only suspect who had a connection to the victim and the accused. He had a motive and the means to purchase an ivory-handled flintlock if he did not already own one, and the violent temperament.

"Even so, it is a charming affectation," Mrs. Beveridge continued, noting that not everyone could wear a vanity motif with grace and élan. "Poor Lady Rosehurst, the dear girl is trying hard with her roses but failing so dreadfully even the prince regent has been moved to snideness, observing at the Larkwell ball that he could barely see her for all the bramble bushes. And he would know, would he not, because he has his own insignia with all those ostrich feathers. They're not as elegant as Feathers' feathers, but they clearly served as inspiration."

The juxtaposition of Feathers and feathers gave Bea pause, and she immediately recalled the brooch at the center of the scrap around the corner from Clement Lane. Thimble did not say the design was the Prince of Wales's emblem; he said it was *similar* to it.

A lovely and expensive piece of jewelry bearing feathers suddenly appeared on a stretch of pavement in a derelict district just in time to delay the arrival of the Runner Miss Wraithe had recruited to intimidate her blackmail victim—it was too much of a coincidence, was it not?

It was, yes, far too much, Bea thought, and she closed her

eyes to focus on the other piece of evidence in the magistrate's possession: the gun.

How had Miss Lark described its pattern?

As feathery!

A silver-mounted, single-trigger, over-under pocket flintlock bearing an intricately carved feathery design on the ivory handle that bore a vague resemblance to the fleur-de-lis and the maker's mark of Bernard Michaels.

Mounting evidence or misdirection?

Surely, the latter, Bea thought. The ubiquity of Mrs. Featherstone-Haughton's signature motif was proof of her innocence, for nobody would be so bacon-brained as to leave an item bearing her personal insignia at the scene of a murder. If anything, it underscored the brother's complicity: Needing something to cause a ruckus in the street, he had borrowed the brooch from his sister—at which time he had most likely not even noticed its design.

If this explanation was plausible, it failed to account for the feathery pattern on the pistol. Hottenroth, who had stomped around town in the wake of his father's suicide looking for someone to hold responsible with a bullet, did not need to steal a flintlock from his sister. The only reason to take it was to make her appear guilty.

Did he resent her that much?

If so, then he was playing a diabolically complicated game involving multiple layers of scheming and chance, and as Bea contemplated the dizzying complexity, she heard Kesgrave in her ear yet again: I do not think every murderer in London is taking a rear-guard action against the Duchess of Kesgrave.

The incrimination of Verity Lark had been so neatly arranged, Hottenroth could have no reasonable expectation of anyone looking twice at the brooch or the gun.

It was too many layers, Bea thought. The game was too deep.

Remove the brother from contention and focus on Feathers.

She, too, would have no reason to expect anyone to connect the brooch to the gun. They were discrete entities discovered in separate locations. The only thing they had in common was Thimble: He held them both in his grasp and barely looked at either.

Incapable of comprehending the utter inanity of Feathers using feathers in her crime, Bea asked Mrs. Beveridge how long her friend had been sporting her signature style. As this was the topic of conversation as far as their host was aware, she did not find the question strange and replied that it had been more than two years.

Kesgrave, however, looked at Bea sharply.

"And they decorate everything she owns?" she said.

"Everything!" Mrs. Beveridge replied, her own amazement at the accomplishment readily available in her tone. "Night rails, gloves, bonnets, reticules, walking gowns, even booties. I do not think she has missed a thing. Featherstone-Haughton indulges her so! As he should. He married well above his station, and even if the scandal still keeps them on the fringes of society, he has risen higher than he deserves."

Two years, Bea thought, wondering if that was enough time to allow the wearer to forget the presence of an identifying mark. If pervasiveness had rendered it invisible, then Feathers could have dropped her feathers without even realizing she was leaving damning evidence behind.

"And when did you share Miss Wraithe's plan to blackmail the reporter with Mrs. Featherstone-Haughton?" she asked.

Mrs. Beveridge pressed her lips together as she reviewed the previous week. "Tuesday, I believe," she replied uncertainly before repeating it more firmly. "Yes, it was Tuesday. William was cross with me because I was away from home when his sister called and he was forced to sit with her and the children for a full hour. He relies on me to make sure everyone behaves and to keep the conversation flowing. She is *his* sister but he does not know the first thing to say to her, which is absurd, for all one has to do is ask about their mother and Cecily will issue an endless stream of complaints for an hour. Regardless, she had sent a letter saying she would call on Wednesday but got her dates mixed up and came on Tuesday. And I was with Feathers."

"And you mentioned that she has her brother over for tea once a week," Bea said. "Does that occur on a regular day?"

If this query struck Mrs. Beveridge as irrelevant, she gave no indication as she replied, "Thursday, around three, I believe."

If that was accurate, then Hottenroth could not be the killer, Bea thought, turning the full weight of her attention to Feathers. She was no tearaway. According to Lady Abercrombie's account, she had kept a cool head in the wake of her father's demise, dispassionately assessing the damage to herself and her family and identifying the most beneficial course of action.

Would a woman with such a resolutely practical approach risk committing murder to avenge a grievance that was almost three years old?

She would not, no, Bea decided, especially not if she had teetered on the brink of ruin once before and knew from painful experience the precarity of respectability. Mrs. Featherstone-Haughton would not endanger everything she held dear for the fleeting gratification of revenge.

It was inconceivable.

And yet the feathers!

If the evidence was irrefutable, then it was Bea's reasoning that had to be faulty. She refused to doubt her understanding of Mrs. Featherstone-Haughton's character. The woman was too logical and cautious to court disaster, which meant she had not courted disaster. From Mrs. Featherstone-Haughton's perspective, shooting Miss Wraithe to incriminate Miss Lark was as safe an undertaking as visiting Rundell and Bridge to purchase a necklace. The prospect of being apprehended for murder had not struck her as a viable outcome.

Mrs. Featherstone-Haughton believed she had executed a flawless crime.

And with good cause.

There was nothing to connect her to the victim. Only their mutual friend, Mrs. Beveridge, linked them together, and the association was flimsy at best. Her scheme was planned down to the minute. She knew where everyone would be and when, and the players in her little drama accommodated her by appearing precisely when expected.

But how had she known?

Addressing her host again, she asked another seeming non sequitur. "When Miss Wraithe told you about her plan to blackmail Miss Lark, did she say how she would deliver the threat or when?"

Mrs. Beveridge professed not to comprehend the question. "Do you mean did she tell me what words she was going to say and on what day of the week? She was an irksome bore whose company grated on one's nerves, but she had a few social graces. She did not give me the particulars, but I assumed she would waste no time in delivering her ultimatum. Agnes was always so fast to act on her ideas, sometimes to her detriment."

"Would Mrs. Featherstone-Haughton know that?" Bea asked.

"Know what?" Mrs. Beveridge snapped with waspish displeasure.

"That Miss Wraithe was likely to act quickly on the information regarding Robert Lark," she explained calmly. "Was her propensity to act swiftly something you had mentioned during one of your many plaintive tête-à-têtes with Feathers?"

Although Mrs. Beveridge protested the trivializing nature of the description, she allowed that it was possible that she had revealed enough about Miss Wraithe's habits that her friend would surmise an immediate response. "But I did not specifically say that Agnes would have the reporter in her cheese press by the end of the week because I did not know that."

Nodding, Bea considered the chronology again: Tuesday to Thursday. Mrs. Featherstone-Haughton had forty-eight hours to discover Miss Wraithe's plan and figure out how to exploit it to her benefit. The former headmistress was too cynical to trust someone she had just met. The killer knew that, so she would not have approached the victim directly to propose they work together. Feathers was too astute to waste time on a futile effort and she would not want to establish a link. In the same way, adopting a persona à la Miss Lark and earning Miss Wraithe's trust would not have been feasible in the available amount of time.

How, then, did Mrs. Featherstone-Haughton find out information that Verity Lark herself had learned only the night before from a letter delivered to—

The letter!

Bea pictured the table in the front room, its surface littered with papers, some of which were earlier versions of the message Miss Wraithe ultimately sent to her target.

Feathers read those earlier drafts, Bea was certain. She broke into the house and searched for all the information she could find. As careful as she was, she had been sloppy because Miss Wraithe had noticed. She had complained to Thimble that the Cox boy had broken into her home but could not identify a single thing that had been stolen, not even toys from the mantelpiece.

Even as the evidence mounted, Bea remained baffled.

Why murder Agnes Wraithe, with whom Mrs. Featherstone-Haughton shared a common enemy?

Or was Bea assuming too much?

She had no idea if Feathers loathed the reporter for destroying her family. Per Mrs. Beveridge's description of the marriage, the union had turned out well for her friend on the whole. Hoping to find out, she asked if Feathers held Robert Lark responsible for the tragedy that befell her family.

Having answered half a dozen questions about her friend without pause, Mrs. Beveridge now displayed concern and narrowed her eyes. "What is going on? Why are you so interested in Feathers?"

Lord Colson, who seemed to perceive the direction of Bea's thoughts even if he had not made the connection between the murder weapon and Feathers' distinctive motif, pressed the question. "Does Mrs. Featherstone-Haughton resent Robert Lark?"

An ornery look entered Mrs. Beveridge's eyes as she folded her arms across her chest and announced that she did not have to answer. "It is still my home."

His lordship responded by sitting down.

Mrs. Beveridge gasped and glanced at the clock.

The minutes to her husband's inevitable return were ticking away, but she held her ground.

Kesgrave took the bergère across from Lord Colson.

Their host tightened her arms mulishly, determined to withstand their cruel obduracy with an unflinching implacability of her own. Then, just as Bea took a step toward a chair, she gritted her teeth and said, "Feathers nurtures no affection for the man ... woman ... *reporter* who brought about her father's destruction and she was fascinated when I mentioned Agnes's discovery. That is why I did not tell her Robert Lark's true identity. She seemed a little too interested. But I understood! Robert Lark drove her father to suicide. But for you to think she had anything to do with Agnes's murder is madness. She did not know her. She never met her. Whatever thought you have in mind is preposterous, and I must insist that you expunge it at once!"

"I am sure you are right," Bea said with a placating softness. "We are no doubt grasping at straws and appreciate your patience in indulging us for so long. If you would provide us with Mrs. Featherstone-Haughton's direction, we shall get out of your way before your husband returns. He will have no idea we were here."

These words had a terrible effect on Mrs. Beveridge, who wanted them simultaneously to leave immediately and remain indefinitely so that she could defy their request. Her indecision lasted only as long as it took Lord Colson to lean back comfortably in the chair and cross his legs. On a squeal of frustration, she rattled off a Mayfair address and begged them to leave.

"Delighted to," his lordship said amiably as he unfolded his tall frame from the chair.

Mrs. Beveridge darted another look at the clock as they proceeded to the door, and they had just turned into the corridor when her husband strode up the hallway. Panicked, she looked at her guests—well, no, not guests, intruders—and raised her hands as if to shove them back into the room. She controlled herself, however, and pasted an eager smile on her face. "Thank goodness, William. You almost missed your callers! The Duke of Kesgrave returned to issue a personal invitation to his driving club, but Lord Colson is also a founding member, which I told his grace is an insurmountable problem because you would never countenance driving a team next to a man of questionable morality. Why, think of the horses! They are leaving now. They have another appointment, and it cannot wait. I am glad you are here to greet them, however fleetingly."

By *fleetingly,* she meant a nod in passing as she swept the visitors out of the house, and Beveridge did not have time for more than a confused wave.

As soon as they climbed into the carriage, Bea launched into her theory regarding Mrs. Featherstone-Haughton, but Lord Colson and Kesgrave, alerted to her thoughts by her questions, had already figured out the details for themselves. Consequently, she turned their attention to motive, for she remained confounded why the killer had chosen Miss Wraithe.

His lordship suggested the victim's main appeal was her expedience. "Feathers needed a victim to incriminate Verity and the Wraithe was right there and had conveniently already arranged a meeting. All she had to do was twist it to her advantage."

"But she did know her to an extent," Kesgrave observed, noting that Mrs. Beveridge had subjected her friend to years of plaintive conversation about the victim. "Based on that alone, Mrs. Featherstone-Haughton might have developed an intense dislike. If Miss Wraithe had any redeeming qualities —and I understand that it is highly unlikely *if*—they were not included in Mrs. Beveridge's stories. Perhaps Feathers chose her simply to end the complaining."

Both explanations made sense to Bea, who found it oddly fitting that a woman who had used so many people to satisfy her own goals had been used in the end to satisfy someone else's.

"She is not expecting us," she said as the carriage stopped in front of 100 Mount Street. "That is, she is not expecting anyone to suspect her in Miss Wraithe's murder. She believes she has committed the ideal crime and will not say anything revealing. She will keep her silence."

"The brooch will trace back to her," Lord Colson said confidently. "Her husband or mother or brother or even Mrs.

Beveridge will recall seeing her wear it. If not, the jeweler from whom it was commissioned will remember the order. The same applies to the gun. As it bears her signature design, someone at the firm will remember her. It might take some time to gather the evidence, but it will be done. I am sure of it. No crime is without its flaws."

Indeed, it was not, Bea thought, striking the door knocker against the brass plate. Her entire career as a lady Runner had been predicated on that basic truth.

Although it took longer than expected, their call was answered by the butler, who informed them with a regretful shake of the head that they had the wrong direction. The residence belonged to Viscount Whaplode, his wife, and their three children, all of whom were in Bournemouth visiting relatives.

"I suppose we should not be surprised that she lied," Bea said with sanguine acceptance as they returned to the carriage. "She did send her friend Mrs. Knowles a missive warning her of our interest. She seems determined to interfere with our investigation. Where to now?"

"Tilly will know the address," Kesgrave offered cautiously.

She would, yes, Bea thought, feeling some of her equanimity drain away at the prospect of the interview. Her ladyship, recognizing the opportunity, would inevitably withhold the information until Bea agreed to her house party scheme.

Something of the moment's urgency, however, must have transmitted itself to the countess, for Lady Abercrombie gave them the information without quibbling, and twenty minutes later, their carriage stopped in front of the correct home to find Mrs. Beveridge standing by the door with a satisfied grin. Delighted with herself, she watched Bea descend from the conveyance and called out, "She is gone! Feathers has flown and you won't find her. She will disappear into the crowded streets of London and you will never see her again. She is a phantom!"

It was a galling turn, to be sure, allowing herself to be duped by the facile ruse. It was so rudimentary, Russell and Flora had used it when they were children to escape elocution lessons with the governess. They would leave a note saying they were in the grove when they were in fact in the garden.

Sighing with exasperation, Bea contemplated their next step. Obviously, Mrs. Beveridge would not give them a credible description of her friend's appearance, which they would need to find her, but presumably the servants would be willing to cooperate in exchange for compensation.

Or would their time be better spent looking for the culprit without delay? The detour to Mount Street, then Grosvenor Square, had cost them only a half hour, and Feathers had to spend some amount of minutes gathering her belongings. She could not simply dash out of her home with the clothes on her back. At the very least, she had to find enough cash to tide her over until she found a place to hide.

Deciding each of them should search in a different direction, Bea spun on her heels to propose the plan to Kesgrave and Lord Colson when a flash of red caught her eye.

There, halfway down the road, her thrice-plumed bonnet bobbing from side to side as she struggled to hoist the heavy valise that was almost half her size, was Harriet Featherstone-Haughton.

Chapter Seventeen

Mrs. Beveridge watched Bea watching her friend stagger with considerable difficulty along the pavement, her progression hampered by the overly large case. For a moment, they both stood there, seemingly transfixed by their respective sights, then Bea shook off the strange immobility to chase after the murderer. Mrs. Beveridge, lunging forward with a mutter of "Goddamn it," threw herself onto Bea's back, her fingers struggling frantically to gain traction on the slippery silk of Bea's dress. She squealed with vexation as she slowly slid to the ground and, free of the restraint, Bea ran as fast as she could down the block, fully expecting the other woman to abandon her luggage and bolt in the other direction.

Feathers did not.

Instead, she stopped where she was and stood in the middle of the pavement, her body partially shielded by the voluminous valise, which Bea did not realize until it was almost too late to slow down. As it was, she had just enough time to calculate her distance from the bag and adjust her speed to grasp Feathers by the right arm without tackling—

Pain jolted through Bea as she felt her own arm being tugged mercilessly and she stumbled several steps to the left before finding herself pressed against Kesgrave's chest. Holding her tightly against the broadcloth of his coat, his voice a low rumble beneath her ear, he growled, "She has a gun, Bea. She has a gun."

He was furious but not angry, Bea thought, aware the description was nonsensical but unable to come up with another way to explain the clutch of his fingers on the back of her neck, gentle with suppressed fury.

Ah, but scared.

That was the other way to explain it.

Bea pulled back, and although the duke momentarily tightened his grip, he ultimately loosened his arms and allowed her to move away. Mrs. Beveridge's shriek tore through the air as Bea turned to look at Mrs. Featherstone-Haughton.

And there it was, yes, as plain as day, a flintlock pistol with an ivory handle, its twin barrels glinting in the late-afternoon sun.

It was aimed at Feathers' head.

That was to say, Feathers was holding the muzzle against her own temple and smiling with grim satisfaction. "I suppose this is how Papa felt, all noble and smug, knowing he was depriving the world of its righteous indignation. It is not fun feeling superior to a man who blew his brains out, is it? You want him to live a good long life in disgrace, inhaling your condemnation with every breath he draws. He escaped that. Papa was always smarter than everyone else. People thought they knew him, but they had no idea who he was. They do not know me either. I am sly and clever and generous and patient. I did it for you, Alicia."

Stunned, Mrs. Beveridge gasped and opened her mouth to speak, but no words came out.

"Now you are free of her," she added with a sweet smile. "You are no longer obligated to spend tedious afternoons listening to her complain about her horrible little life. Most of us have been egregiously abused by fate, and we do not go around bewailing our misfortune. Featherstone-Haughton is no prize, but you have never heard me say a word against him. It is mortifying to travel about everywhere, whining about the choices you have made."

Bea kept her eyes on the gun. It was pressed against the woman's temple at the moment, but that could change in a heartbeat.

And where was Kesgrave?

To her left and slightly behind.

She did not move her head but could see a hint of him on the periphery.

Lord Colson was to her right, on the other side of the valise that she had almost tripped over.

Tears formed in the corner of Mrs. Beveridge's eyes as she wrestled with how to respond to her friend's confession, and wiping her cheeks with trembling fingers she eked out a breathless, "Thank you." Then she bit her bottom lip as if to stop herself from saying more.

While Mrs. Beveridge struggled to contain her sobs, Feathers regarded her with peaceful munificence, as though she had known her friend would be moved to speechlessness by her generosity.

As if to testify to the pervasiveness of the murderer's calm, her hand did not shake at all. Feathers displayed no apprehension at her current predicament, and Bea wondered if the other woman considered shooting herself to be a practical solution to an otherwise intractable problem.

With an affable dip of her head, Feathers accepted Mrs. Beveridge's gratitude and said her actions were not entirely selfless. "I had to pick someone to shoot, and your Aggie was the perfect candidate. Even if she did not bedevil you with her incessant bleating, she was an unrepentant blackmailer. To be sure, I have no love for any of her victims—Wigsworth is vile and Knowles is heartless—but I object to her on moral grounds. A person should not go about sticking her nose into other people's business. Curiosity is a vice, and using knowledge for a wicked purpose is sinful."

Although Mrs. Beveridge paled further at this explanation, she grasped gratefully at the tiny morsel of normality it contained and validated this opinion of Wigsworth. "He *is* vile."

"He came to dinner once at Stone's prompting and discussed the size of my breasts. As a man of science, he claimed to take a scholarly interest in the female mammary gland. Stone thought it was hilarious and laughed his top off," Feathers continued mildly. "But then Wigsworth asked for money to support his scientifical experiments and Stone told him he did not make bad investments. Wigsworth left in a huff."

Uncertain how to reply, Mrs. Beveridge darted a glance at Bea before saying Featherstone-Haughton was correct to refuse. "His experiments will come to naught. He had been working on them for years with no results."

As the two women conducted this exchange, Lord Colson stepped closer to the valise, slinking ever so subtly to its right, to approach Mrs. Featherstone-Haughton from the left side. His gaze was steady as he stared over Mrs. Beveridge's head at Bea and Kesgrave.

He had a plan.

Having exhausted her conversation on Wiggy, Mrs. Beveridge fell silent, and the duke, seemingly eager to resume the chatter, asked Feathers why she had chosen to incriminate Miss Lark for murder rather than killing her outright.

Feathers, tilting her head slightly to the left to address him, asked with a mocking lilt, "What is the fun in that? I shoot her and she is dead. It is over, and she has not endured an infinitesimal fraction of my father's suffering. But the horror of Newgate and the terror of knowing what is to come, the long climb up the short ladder to the noose, and me, standing in the front row of the onlookers with a knowing grin—that is revenge good and proper. Agnes earned a quick and painless end for uncovering the truth about Robert Lark for me. I had tried to find him myself, you know, years ago when the articles first appeared. Every time I called on the newspaper office to meet him, he had either just left or was out of town, and as the months passed, I lost interest. But then Alicia told me that Robert was in fact a spiteful woman who had herself been raised in an orphanage, and her virulence against my father suddenly made sense. I realized she had targeted him specifically. She hates virile men."

Slowly, smoothly, almost as though he were not moving at all, Lord Colson drew nearer to Feathers, his gaze still intent as he looked at Bea and the duke.

Oh, but no, not her.

Just the duke.

His lordship's meaningful stare was directed solely at Kesgrave, who seemed to respond to some unspoken command as he asked Feathers how she had managed to time the arrival of the Runner so perfectly. "It is as though you were directing a play."

As Bea was the one who usually asked the murderer a series of questions to keep them distracted long enough to figure out a way to disarm them, she knew precisely what Kesgrave was doing. Most killers appreciated a little fawning. Mrs. Featherstone-Haughton was no exception.

"Thank you, yes," she replied graciously. "I was rather

impressed with how well it all worked out myself. The biggest challenge was discovering when she planned to meet with Lark. I had to sneak into her house for that, which was not easy, but luckily there was a letter detailing what I needed to know sitting on the table in the front room. After that, everything fell into place as though it were preordained. It was indeed a play and I was its director, and I moved the actors effortlessly around the stage. Agnes greeted me with civility and displayed no alarm when I explained that I was there to register my displeasure with the woman who had ruined my father. She welcomed my suggestion and agreed to place the chairs in front of the fire to make for a cozy discussion. She sat where I told her to sit and was grumbling about the Runner being late when I shot her."

Mrs. Beveridge shuddered at how plainly the other woman said it, at how placidly she described taking another human's life, and her friend acknowledged the dismay while assuring her it was unnecessary. Agnes died doing what she loved best: complaining.

"You are a saint for putting up with it for so many years," Feathers added in that same amiable tone, as if she were holding a spray of flowers against her temple, not a deadly weapon. It had been several minutes now and still her arm remained steady.

A cool head indeed, Bea thought, noting that Mrs. Featherstone-Haughton was giving her full attention to her friend. It was the perfect opportunity for her to lunge forward and tackle the murd—

Of all the reckless and stupid ideas, your grace!

Lord Colson was right there, only two feet from Feathers, a plan clearly in mind, and any attempt she made would ruin it.

"In all your descriptions, you never conveyed the pitch of her whine," Feathers continued in that same conversational tone. "It is like listening to a barn owl squawk, is it not?"

As tears streamed down her cheeks with renewed vigor, Mrs. Beveridge stared blankly in reply, her lips pressed tightly together, perhaps unwilling to speak ill of the dead. Feathers, seemingly annoyed by the lack of agreement, shifted her eyes toward her friend just as Lord Colson crept yet another inch closer. Whereas previously he had been on the far side of the valise, now he was abreast of her, a fact she seemed on the verge of realizing if her furrowed brow was an indication.

Desperate to help him, Bea foundered for a question, something, anything, to distract the other woman from his lordship's position, and sputtering incoherently, she called out, "The house!"

It worked, yes, drawing Feathers' attention.

But not just her attention.

The killer, twirling furiously to the right, glared at Bea with vehement dislike.

Taken aback by the heat of the vitriol, Bea struggled to cobble together a coherent question and remembered the scratches on the door. "Did you pick the lock? Is that how you got in?"

Feathers laughed, and although the sound was scathing, she appeared genuinely amused. She even pulled the gun away from her temple as she replied with sneering derision. "I wager that *is* what you want to know, your grace, for you have no respect for anyone's privacy. The sanctity of home is nothing but a joke to you, and you slither around respectable members of society like a snake, prying into matters that are none of your concern. You think you are so clever, taking ruthless advantage of an elderly man who could barely remember his own name."

It was a reference to the Stirling ball and the confession Wem had made there. The fact that Mrs. Featherstone-

Haughton was able to twist the heartrending scene into an injustice for her parents' killer was an indication of her deep loathing.

"You are the worst of the lot because you do it for the glory," Feathers continued. "You are vain and prideful. Why is that, your grace? Were you an uninteresting child whom nobody loved so you crave the adulation of complete strangers to make up for all that you missed in your youth? Even Verity Lark, an abhorrent reporter, is not as odious as you. She at least has the decency to create a phantom to soak up the fame and attention. You hoard it all," she said, her voice rising with fury.

Although Bea had not intended to incite her anger, she recognized its utility, for Mrs. Featherstone-Haughton was too enraged to notice Lord Colson's edging progress. He was now within arm's length of her, and with the gun no longer pressed against her temple, it was the perfect moment to strike.

And yet he did not.

His eyes were still focused intently on Kesgrave.

Messages were exchanged.

Lord Colson was waiting for the sign.

Despite the flash of anger, Feathers was nevertheless as composed as ever and her voice was genial as she explained that she had hired a pair of young ruffians to knock on Agnes's door and run away repeatedly. "I knew eventually she would storm out of her house to blame the children next door because that is what she always did. Isn't that right, Alicia? As anticipated, she did not have the presence of mind to close her door behind her, so I entered and looked around. As I said, the letter was right there on the table, waiting for me. I trust your voracious curiosity is appeased, your grace? Very good," she said pleasantly, inhaling deeply with a gratified air.

It was like a bud on a willow tree, the breath, soft and

gentle and smooth, the air around it barely moving, echoing the eerie calm in the instant before a clap of thunder, and Bea saw Feathers lift her arm. The hand raised, the finger pulled, and Lord Colson pounced, his left leg sweeping forward to knock Feathers backward so that the pistol discharged upward. Kesgrave, shoving Bea to the side, leaped over the valise to clamp Feathers' wrist in a tight grip before she could discharge the second ball. The weapon clattered to the pavement as Feathers' shoulders hit the ground and she shrieked with fury, her legs flailing wildly in futile rage. Mrs. Beveridge screamed at the top of her lungs, the bloodcurdling sound summoning the neighbors who had either missed or ignored the gunfire, and they stared in silence as the Duke of Kesgrave wrestled a screeching woman to her feet.

Another spectacle, Bea thought, regaining her balance.

And there was Twaddle himself, picking up the pistol and slipping it into his pocket.

Would he be able to resist writing about the scene?

But even as she enumerated all the ways the exhibition appealed to the gossip's sense of high drama, she knew he would not repay her kindness with further scorn. Whereas previously he had withheld his mockery out of deference to Miss Lark, now he would out of respect for Beatrice herself.

Mrs. Beveridge, beginning to whimper, her cheeks blotchy from tears, appeared no more able to comprehend what had transpired than the random gawkers peering from their doorways.

Kesgrave, adjusting his grip on the writhing Feathers, looked at Bea. "You are well?"

"I am, yes, naturally, for I was never in danger," she said.

And it was the truth, she thought. Kesgrave and Lord Colson had sorted out the entire matter between them with their meaningful glances. All she had to do was go where instructed and not gum up the works.

A ghost of a smile appeared on the duke's lips as he replied, "You do not have to sound so chagrined about it, brat."

She did not, no. Having raced down a staircase in slippers wet with a slick substance in near darkness and thrown herself into the air several feet to stop a murderer from escaping, she had had her fair share of daring feats. It was perfectly reasonable that Kesgrave and Lord Colson had deftly thwarted Mrs. Featherstone-Haughton without her assistance.

And yet she felt quite cut out of the discussion.

'Twas utterly irrational.

Feathers, still struggling to free herself by violently twisting her body, called to the stunned onlookers and begged them to intervene on her behalf. "You must save me. You must! You cannot stand by and allow this ... this *mad* duke and his addle-headed wife to maul me, an important member of this community. I am your neighbor. I live among you!"

Mrs. Beveridge, her dismay at her friend's conduct somehow deepened by this public appeal, muttered, "Good Lord, *she* is mad. I had no idea, your graces. You must believe that I saw no evidence of her crumbling mental faculties. During our visit on Tuesday, she seemed just as sympathetic and kind as always, but it is obvious now that she is deeply unwell. Has she always been like this, and I refused to see it, or is it a recent change?"

Incensed by these questions, Feathers whirled on her heels to glare at her friend and snarled, "You traitor! You turncoat! I *freed* you from that whining albatross. I saved you from that sniveling troll and you have the astounding audacity to insult my sanity. I will tell you who is mad. It is you, Alicia, if you do not think there will be grave consequences for your actions. I will avenge these insults. I will prevail and then you will see!"

Issued with an unsettling blast of rage, these threats did nothing to disquiet Mrs. Beveridge, who stepped away serenely and murmured with incredulity that she did not know Feathers at all. "She is a complete stranger to me, this woman. It is almost as though I have never seen her before."

Seeking to deliver a physical blow, Feathers wrenched her shoulder against Kesgrave's grip as she reared forward, an attempt to throw off his restraint that proved as ineffectual as her previous efforts, and Lord Colson withdrew a length of twine from his pocket. He bound it around her wrists, which did little to still her thrashing, and stuffed a handkerchief into her mouth to quiet her squalls.

"Thank you, Lord Colson," Mrs. Beveridge said, brushing back an imaginary strand of hair at her temple, as if the experience had been as physically discombobulating as it was mentally. "That is a vast improvement."

Spectators began to return to their homes as their interest waned, and his lordship said he would handle the matter from there. "I will bring her to the magistrate and arrange Miss Lark's release. You have both done more than enough. To be sure, I never doubted the accuracy of Mr. Twaddle-Thum's reports, for I have found him to be a reliable chronicler of my own life, but I did not expect to be so impressed with Her Outrageousness's deductive skills. I cannot thank you enough, your grace."

Bea did not consider it a taunt.

Twaddle citing himself to her in an effort to express his sincere gratitude—it felt almost like an apology, and perhaps even confirmation, as though he had been aware of her speculation.

Hearing his lordship reaffirm his faith in the Duchess of Kesgrave's much-vaunted abilities upset Mrs. Beveridge terribly, for she had demonstrated none. Twisting her fingers together as the color rose in her cheeks, she apologized for refusing to believe Feathers could be the villain. "I should not have warned her. I only came here because I would want someone to tell me if I was the main suspect in one of the murder duchess's investigations. Her innocence seemed as assured as my own. In making that decision, I put your and the duke's lives in danger and that is unacceptable. I am sorry."

Having made this simple explanation, however, she went on to reiterate just how wrongheaded Bea's conclusion had seemed to her. "Even when Feathers ran to her bedchamber and began tossing things into a valise, I thought she had decided that sequestering herself in the country was the only way to avoid the ridicule of being thought a murderess by an influential member of society. And then, when I began to suspect the truth, I assumed she acted with good cause, that she was another one of Agnes's blackmail victims. If she had killed her to save herself, then I wanted her to escape. I am ashamed of my own actions and how terribly I misjudged her."

Kindly, Bea told the chastened woman that she was not the first person in the world to inaccurately assess a friend's character. Furthermore, most assessments were accurate until they were not. "Perhaps the information about Robert Lark created the mental instability."

As Mrs. Beveridge had eagerly delivered the news about Miss Wraithe's discovery, she took little comfort in this comment. Tears welled again in the corners of her eyes.

Kesgrave, accepting Lord Colson's offer, instructed him to take their carriage. Hailing a hack with a squirming captive in tow would be difficult, and Mrs. Featherstone-Haughton, seemingly determined to affirm the observation, redoubled her efforts to free herself. She puffed her cheeks to dislodge the handkerchief, which remained decisively in place, and her face turned an alarming shade of red. Recognizing the futility, she exhaled through the nose and allowed her breathing to return to normal.

With a wave of his arm, the duke summoned Jenkins, who had watched the chase unfold from his perch in the carriage, and sought his assistance in transferring the murderer to the vehicle. Conceding the futility of her efforts, Feathers implemented a new strategy, wherein she ceased resisting altogether and allowed her muscles to grow slack. When she would have dropped to the ground, Lord Colson heaved her over his shoulder like a sack of potatoes, carried her to the conveyance, and deposited her on the bench. She grunted angrily as he secured her ankles with another piece of twine.

Satisfied with his handiwork, he climbed into the carriage himself and promised to send word as soon as Miss Lark was released from prison. Then he thanked them again.

Jenkins tugged at the reins and the horses trotted into the road.

Mrs. Beveridge watched silently as the vehicle disappeared around a corner, an expression of relief on her face even as her cheeks glistened from tears. "I hope she gets the medical attention she requires. It will be horrible if they just throw her into Newgate with all the filth and degenerates. But I suppose that is something for her husband to worry about now. Oh, dear, her husband!"

Reminded of Mr. Featherstone-Haughton, she wondered if it fell to her to inform him of his wife's homicidal turn or if she could rely on one of the neighbors to mention it. "Or the servants. They must have seen the whole horrible thing unfold. If they did not, they will hear of it by dinner. Or could I just send a note?" she asked softly before giving herself a firm shake. "No, Alicia, you must be brave! At least the information is so upsetting, he will forget to undress me with his eyes."

Her supposition that the staff had seen everything was

confirmed by the cluster of servants gathered near the doorway, and although the majority of them darted back inside as Bea drew closer, a footman ran forward to relieve Kesgrave of the valise. Mrs. Beveridge, heaving a great sigh, followed the servant inside.

As the door shut with a firm clap Kesgrave took Bea's arm and suggested they hail a hackney on the next road over, which had more traffic.

With a look of sly amusement, Bea assured him she was not so frail nor the cherub so large that running a few dozen yards had worn her out. "It was barely a half block, your grace, a distance so slight, even my flimsy footwear was sufficient. I think I can manage the walk home. It is not that far."

The duke, however, appeared unconvinced and pointed out that her forgoing the opportunity to advocate for sturdy boots in the wake of the foot chase indicated she was wearier than she realized. "Or are you merely saving your arguments for Nuneaton?"

"That plan has little hope of succeeding after your warning to him," she replied tartly, keenly aware she needed a new tack and wondered if she was focusing on the wrong thing. Her original goal had been sturdy boots by Hoby, yes, but perhaps she should devote her energies to the pair itself. There had to be dozens of skilled cobblers in London who would be delighted to take the Duchess of Kesgrave's money. All she had to do was find one.

Mrs. Palmer would have a few ideas.

Bea resolved to send her friend a missive asking for suggestions in the morning. The sooner she commissioned a pair, the more likely she would have it in hand before she left for the country.

Unsettled by the reminder of their imminent departure for Haverill Hall, she resolutely directed her thoughts to another subject and confidently asserted her theory. "Lord Colson is Twaddle."

"Is he?" the duke asked mildly. "Why do you think that?"

Although slightly disappointed by his underwhelming response to what she considered to be a shocking announcement, she calmly explained her reasoning, starting with his lordship's most recent assertion. "He claimed Mr. Twaddle-Thum is a reliable chronicler of his life, but we know that is false because Lord Colson is the daring spy, not Kingsley. Twaddle is too astute to allow himself to be led astray by his own prejudices, which means he knows very well that Kingsley is not Typhoeus. The only reason he would lie about it is to protect himself, and consider it: A successful spy would have all the skills necessary to be a successful gossip, and he is a second son, so he could have needed the money. Furthermore, it accounts for his relationship with Miss Lark and her friends. They have the sort of closeness that takes years to establish."

Hailing her logic as sound, Kesgrave asked when she would press him to confirm her hypothesis. "Tomorrow or the day after?"

"The weekend at least," she said, generously allowing him time to recover from their ordeal. "And I do not require him to confirm anything. I merely want him to know that I have figured out the truth and that I appreciate the respite. While we are on the topic, however, I will try to ascertain if he has plans to resume tormenting me."

"Or you can just enjoy the respite," he suggested.

Bea glanced at him wryly. "But *can* I?"

With a laugh, he agreed it was doubtful as he clasped her hand in his, and Bea knew the picture they presented, the Duke and Duchess of Kesgrave, strolling along a public road holding hands like a pair of besotted rustics. The display was worse than her most outrageous antic, and she knew society would prefer she returned to exposing killers in the middle of ballroom floors than corrupting its most illustrious member with her easy affection.

"As compelling as your evidence is, I am not convinced it is he," Kesgrave said.

"That is because you have a competing theory to promote," she noted slyly. "I am sure Mr. Somerset Reade has a lot to recommend him as a vile gossip, but he simply does not have the qualifications of his lordship."

"I find it curious that it is only after Twaddle ceased writing about you that we both began to speculate about his identity," he observed idly.

"That is because Verity Lark was our first clue," she replied. "Before it became apparent that she was the connection, we had nothing upon which to construct our theories."

Kesgrave ardently disagreed, asserting with confidence that England's most accomplished lady Runner required nothing so facile as clues to begin arriving at masterful deductions.

Somehow it still felt strange to hear it, the admiration in his voice, the utter confidence in her abilities, and although her instinct was to quibble over his word choices—perhaps *proficient* was more accurate than *accomplished* or the designation of *only* more appropriate—she accepted his praise without protest.

"And how long will you wait until beginning your shooting lessons with Miss Lark?" he asked.

Bea squeezed his hand as they turned right onto Dean Street, not at all surprised that he remembered the deal she had struck with his half sibling. "I am not sure. I would think she needs more time to recover from her ordeal than Lord Colson, and yet she does not strike me as the sort of person who allows herself to sit still. Her method of recovering might be to give pistol instruction."

"You must permit her to withdraw from the agreement," Kesgrave said.

"I must?" she murmured, her eyes darting sidelong to take note of his expression. His certainty startled her, the way it announced an unknowable truth as fact, and she could not decide if Miss Lark's withdrawal was what he wished would happen or what he expected to happen.

"It is up to Miss Lark to establish the parameters of the relationship," he explained, adding that the bargain she had made with the accused had been coerced. "Not by you in particular but by circumstance itself, and there is no telling what she would have agreed to if she had the freedom to consider the proposal without the specter of the gibbet or the discomfort of Newgate. Miss Lark must already feel in debt to me for intervening on her behalf with Sidmouth. This will compound it. As carrying a debt is a terrible burden, I believe the only kind thing to do is allow her to figure out how she wants to discharge it. If the notion of giving you lessons is acceptable to her, then by all means take the lessons. But if it is not, then we must permit her to withdraw from the agreement and decide how she wants to proceed in the way that does the least damage to her sense of self. I respect Miss Lark too much to mortify her."

Well, yes, of course, she was always trying to find his hideous flaw, she thought, as she listened to the excessive decency of this reply. It defied the laws of nature, his goodness, and if she sometimes feared he was the wistful invention of her own fevered brain, it was simply because a calm one could not conceive of him.

The Duke of Kesgrave should not exist.

And yet there he was, as plain as day, flouting the dictates of decorum by holding his wife's hand on Hill Street for any passerby to see.

Overcome by a surge of affection, she leaned closer, just a

little, only slightly, but enough to convey something of her yearning and delight because his hand tightened its grip on hers.

They were not far from Kesgrave House.

It was only fifteen minutes now, perhaps twenty if they strolled leisurely.

But it felt like an eternity to Bea, who was exquisitely aware of his presence beside her, of the heat emanating from the press of his fingers against hers, and knowing it would never do to succumb to impulse, she grappled yet again for a distraction.

No, not Hoby.

They had discussed the bootmaker to death.

And Feathers' remarkably cavalier approach to murder—too grim.

But the pursuit to apprehend her!

That was notable, for it was the second investigation to end in a chase on a public street, and as they crossed Wells, she wondered if they should add running to her roster of lessons.

"Running?" Kesgrave repeated with an amused lilt, his left eyebrow raised in a way that only increased his appeal. "You mean to be put through your paces like a prized Arabian?"

Obviously, she did not.

Eton and Harrow and the many other brutal institutions to which English gentlemen were sent to be put through *their* paces surely had training regimens of some sort to ensure the enduring physical stamina of the ruling class.

That was what she meant.

But she made no attempt to clarify her point because he asked if she had her eye on the Ascot gold cup, causing his lips to quiver in that irresistible way.

And in the middle of Mayfair, she succumbed just a little.

BEA AND THE DUKE RETURN WITH ANOTHER MYSTERY SOON!

In the meantime, look for Verity Lark's latest adventure:

A Lark's Release.

Available for preorder now.

My Gracious Thanks

Pen a letter to the editor!

Dearest Reader,

A writer's fortune has ever been wracked with peril - and wholly dependent on the benevolence of the reading public.

Reward an intrepid author's valiant toil!

Please let me know what you think of A Murderous Tryst on Amazon or Goodreads!

About the Author

Lynn Messina is the author of almost two dozen novels, including the Beatrice Hyde-Clare mysteries, a cozy series set in Regency-era England. Her first novel, *Fashionistas,* has been translated into sixteen languages and was briefly slated to be a movie starring Lindsay Lohan. Her essays have appeared in *Self, American Baby* and the *New York Times* Modern Love column, and she has been a regular contributor to the *Times* parenting blog. She lives in New York City with her sons.

facebook.com/AuthorLynnMessina
x.com/lynnmessina
instagram.com/authorlynnmessina

Also by Lynn Messina

Verity Lark Mysteries Series

A Lark's Tale

A Lark's Flight

A Lark's Conceit

A Lark's Release

Beatrice Hyde-Clare Mysteries Series

A Brazen Curiosity

A Scandalous Deception

An Infamous Betrayal

A Nefarious Engagement

A Treacherous Performance

A Sinister Establishment

A Ghastly Spectacle

A Malevolent Connection

An Ominous Explosion

An Extravagant Duplicity

A Murderous Tryst

A Vicious Machination

And Now a Spin-off from the BHC Mysteries Series:

A ~~Beatrice~~ Flora Hyde-Clare Novel

A Boldly Daring Scheme

Love Takes Root Series

Miss Fellingham's Rebellion (Prequel)

The Harlow Hoyden

The Other Harlow Girl

The Fellingham Minx

The Bolingbroke Chit

The Impertinent Miss Templeton

Stand Alones

Prejudice and Pride

The Girls' Guide to Dating Zombies

Savvy Girl

Winner Takes All

Little Vampire Women

Never on a Sundae

Troublemaker

Fashionista (Spanish Edition)

Violet Venom's Rules for Life

Henry and the Incredibly Incorrigible, Inconveniently Smart Human

Welcome to the Bea Hive

FUN STUFF FOR BEATRICE HYDE-CLARE FANS

The Bea Tee

Beatrice's favorite three warships not only in the wrong order but also from the wrong time period. (Take that, maritime tradition *and* historical accuracy!)

The Kesgrave Shirt

A tee bearing the Duke of Kesgrave's favorite warships in the order in which they appeared in the Battle of the Nile

Available in mugs too!

See all the options in Lynn's Store.

Printed in Great Britain
by Amazon